"WITH ALL DUE RESPECT, SIR," SAID RIKER, "WE'VE BEEN SITTING HERE ALL AFTERNOON, WAITING FOR YOUR REPORTS."

"We know it's incredible," said Geordi.

"What we'd like to know is what we can do about it!" Beverly chimed in.

"Admiral, please forgive my crew," said Captain Picard. "But you can understand their—our—impatience. Especially since you've taken the matter out of our hands."

"Captain Picard, I'll not mince words." Admiral Davies cleared his throat and assumed a deeper, stentorian tone. "By the power vested in me by the Federation I find the USS *Enterprise* a total loss. And as I have been advised by my science officers that its very presence here at Starbase 210 is a danger, I am ordering that it be towed by tractor beam out to a safe portion of space . . . where it shall be destroyed by photon torpedoes."

D0089670

Look for STAR TREK Fiction from Pocket Books

Star Trek: The Original Series

Star Trek: The Next Generation

Star Trek: Deep Space Nine

Most Pocket Books are available at special quantity discounts for bulk purchases for sales promotions, premiums or fund raising. Special books or book excerpts can also be created to fit specific needs.

For details write the office of the Vice President of Special Markets, Pocket Books, 1230 Avenue of the Americas, New York, New York 10020.

STAR TREK®
THE NEXT GENERATION™

'25

GROUNDED

DAVID BISCHOFF

POCKET BOOKS

New York   London   Toronto   Sydney   Tokyo   Singapore

The sale of this book without its cover is unauthorized. If you purchased this book without a cover, you should be aware that it was reported to the publisher as "unsold and destroyed." Neither the author nor the publisher has received payment for the sale of this "stripped book."

This book is a work of fiction. Names, characters, places and incidents are either products of the author's imagination or are used fictitiously. Any resemblance to actual events or locales or persons, living or dead, is entirely coincidental.

An *Original* Publication of POCKET BOOKS

POCKET BOOKS, a division of Simon & Schuster Inc.
1230 Avenue of the Americas, New York, NY 10020

Copyright © 1993 by Paramount Pictures. All Rights Reserved.

STAR TREK is a Registered Trademark of
Paramount Pictures.

This book is published by Pocket Books, a division of Simon & Schuster Inc., under exclusive license from Paramount Pictures.

All rights reserved, including the right to reproduce this book or portions thereof in any form whatsoever. For information address Pocket Books, 1230 Avenue of the Americas, New York, NY 10020

ISBN: 0-671-79747-6

First Pocket Books printing March 1993

10 9 8 7 6 5 4 3 2 1

POCKET and colophon are registered trademarks of Simon & Schuster Inc.

Printed in the U.S.A.

For Michael Cassutt

Tennis on Stardock sometime, Mike?

Acknowledgments

I'd like to thank a few people for their help and support while I worked on this book:

Donald Maass, Kevin Ryan, Karen Erickson, Dennis Bailey. The staff and actors, past and present, of STAR TREK: THE NEXT GENERATION, for constant electronic stimulation and inspiration. And a special thank you to that great hard SF writer, Charles Sheffield.

GROUNDED

Prologue

Stardate 45229.6

CAPTAIN JEAN-LUC PICARD started to tug at his uniform, but stopped himself. The habit—that firm grasp of the resilient red-blue fabric, that steady and knowledgeable reorientation of the synthetic fibers around his slim, muscular torso—was something he used as an almost subconscious signal of authority. Now, though, he was no longer on the *Enterprise,* nor was he in authority.

Nor was he in uniform.

He was wearing dull black mufti. Coveralls. They felt odd and unusual. The lack of his familiar rank pins on his collar and his comm unit upon his breast made him feel almost naked.

They were keeping him waiting, and he didn't like it.

Not one bit.

Sitting beside him in uncomfortable, tense silence were three others from the USS *Enterprise* crew, waiting as well. Commander William Riker looked as though he would much prefer pacing the office in which they sat. His eyes started about and he scratched at his dark beard. If anything, thought Picard, his Number One was taking the situation far less calmly than he was. Riker was a take-action-now sort, and the frustration of the past days was plainly etched on his face. He, too, wore the same black coveralls on his big-framed body, and seemed to like it about as much.

Sitting beside him, looking calm and poised as usual, was Dr. Beverly Crusher. Her legs were crossed, her arms folded. She was frowning, and her usually smooth forehead was furrowed. She was showing some uncharacteristic age lines around her eyes. The tension, no doubt . . . Still, she looked lovelier than ever, her red hair somehow even more vibrant and alive against the black of the bulky, ill-fitting coverall that had been issued to her. Her smooth face seemed calm, but those blue eyes were filled with worry. She smiled a flicker of encouragement at him, and uncomfortable that he'd been caught looking at her, he only nodded back curtly.

She said, "Look, we've got some of the best scientists, technicians, and engineers in the Federation here, Jean-Luc. I'm sure they'll solve the problem. That's why we've come here, isn't it?"

"We're here," said Picard, ruefully, "quite simply because our other options were exhausted."

"Yeah, right, the best technicians, the best scientists, the best engineers," said Lieutenant Commander Geordi La Forge. "And they won't let me do what I do, dammit."

"Geordi, these are unusual circumstances." Beverly Crusher placed a comforting hand on the engineer's shoulder. The handsome black man leaned forward, clasping his hands and shaking his head. Picard looked at him, still not used to the way Geordi looked.

His pupils, dull milky white, stood out naked against his corneas. On either side of his head, the red lights of his implants blinked. Geordi was truly blind now, his VISOR gone.

"Unusual? Seems like the usual to me," said Riker, impatience straining his voice. "The usual bureaucratic nonsense. I just hope it wasn't a mistake coming here."

"We didn't have a choice, Number One," said Picard, moving uncomfortably in his temporary outfit.

"We should just be grateful we *got* here," said Beverly, snapping a significant look at Riker.

"I guess so," said Geordi. "I guess so. . . . I mean, I *hope* so."

Unable to sit any longer, Jean-Luc Picard rose and walked to the viewport. The usual wild havoc of stars, bright and dim, spread across the velvet of the universe, holding their awe and mystery into pinpoints of light, but Picard did not stare at them with his usual appreciation and wonder. The viewport of the office had an excellent view of some of the docking ports of the starbase, as well as a wonderful vista of the huge vessel's spinning hub. Wires, catwalks, gondolas, protruded against the vast gray of the hull. Usually Picard enjoyed looking at starbases. Such marvels of space engineering, they were . . . monuments to the ingenuity of sentient life . . . marvels of architectural achievement for the Federation. . . .

Now, though, it was all just an insignificant interplay of light and shadow.

At other times, he might also have appreciated just how large and elegant an office this was, filled not only with certificates concerning the rank and achievements of its occupant, but a fine aquarium filled with dozens of varieties of rare aquatic life. To say nothing of the tasteful array of holographic art upon the far wall, the cutting edge in computer and desk design, and the very finest in sleek furniture. The temperature was a little cool for Picard, but he had to admit that it, along with the muted lights and the bubbles in the aquarium, gave the room a sense of peace and serenity. The odors, too . . . sandalwood? A touch of myrrh and Cassiopeian jasmine? Masculine odors . . . stern and authoritarian smells, for certain, that was supposed to boost one's sense of security under the command of this individual as one consulted with him in the office. Unfortunately, all this calmed Picard not one jot. Certainly he wore his usual facade of stern dignity. But inside . . .

No, he told himself. Come, Picard. Where is your mettle . . . ? He ground his teeth a moment, concentrated and . . . Ah! there it was. Deep, deep within him. Bedrock. Firm and strong. His sworn obligation to duty, to preserve the tenets of justice and discipline that embodied the noble cause of the Federation. Ideals were not just gauzy nothings. They were the anchors of the spirit, and Jean-Luc Picard had his commitment to truth and loyalty to his service and to his cause, and nothing could ever sway him.

He must always remind himself of that. . . . He was a man of ideals, nothing more and nothing less. Other matters were hardly as significant. . . .

Even this . . .

"What's keeping the guy?" Riker said, bounding out of his chair and going to the desk, certainly headed for the communicator to demand an explanation for the tardiness.

Beverly reached by her side as though for her PADD, but of course, found nothing there. She could not hide her chagrin. Instead she craned her neck, finding a digital time-display device angled on the contours of the desk before them. "The meeting was called for fourteen hundred hours, and it's a quarter past."

"I just don't like the feel of it." Geordi's frustration was obvious. "I wish they'd at least give me a cane and a Seeing Eye dog. Then I wouldn't feel so damned helpless."

"I'm sure they'll find a replacement for your VISOR soon, Geordi," Beverly said, comfortingly.

Riker shook his head in frustration. "They've just no conception of the importance of time."

"It is not something we've got a lot of!" said Geordi.

"People, please calm yourselves," said Picard, modulating his voice to both reassure and command. "The crew of the ship is safe. We have reached safety. That is what matters. . . . All else is insignificant in comparison."

"What about Data?" said Geordi.

"I have promised you, just as I promised Data—he will be provided for, whatever the outcome." Picard straightened his shoulders and rubbed a hand over his smooth, bare pate. If he couldn't tug on his uniform, at least he still had that.

"But, Jean-Luc," said Riker. "The *Enterprise*. We're talking about our ship. . . ."

"Our home . . ." said Beverly.

Picard stiffened and turned away. "I repeat, our crew is safe. We will do what we can about the ship, to the utmost of our abilities. But we should not let sentiment mar our sense of place or duty."

They said nothing, but he could feel them staring at him.

He sat back down and folded his arms, waiting.

Less than a minute later, two men walked in. One was Admiral Davies, a jowly, slope-browed man with penetrating night-black eyes and a streak of gray though his dark, bushy hair. He had long, apelike arms that were joined together thoughtfully now over his large belly. Weight control was easy in the twenty-fourth century, but many of the upper echelon of the Federation chose to remain husky as an odd symbol of the gravity and seniority of their office. For Davies, his girth made him look older than he really was, a plus in a universe where men were still mortal and time clocked in duty still made a difference.

Admiral Davies was commander of this sector of the Federation and the high-ranked man on this, Starbase 210. He had held the position only two years, but already had won wide acclaim for the wisdom of his decisions and the accomplishments of the sector in achieving both the philosophical and practical goals of the Federation.

Unfortunately, if Captain Jean-Luc Picard had his druthers, he would have gone to another starbase. He and Admiral Davies had crossed paths before, initially in Starfleet Academy, when Picard had been a freshman and Davies a senior. Those crossings had not always occasioned sparks, but neither had they always been without friction.

. And now it was Admiral Davies's decision as to what was to happen.

The other man was taller, slender, younger, but with tired blue eyes. He was too thin, as though he spent all his time on work and far too little in recreation or nutrition. He held a PADD and immediately went to the computer console and started punching up numbers.

"This is the starbase's chief science officer, perhaps the finest in Starfleet," said the admiral without any preliminary niceties. "Dr. Rolf Chavez."

Pictures of the *Enterprise* began to pop up on a viewscreen. Layouts, superimposed with the way the vessel looked now. The graphics, Picard noted, were top-notch, with even greater detail than the *Enterprise*'s computer afforded. Dr. Chavez studied the busy screen for a moment and then turned around, a sober look on his sour face. "Incredible. Quite incredible."

"With all due respect, sir," said Riker. "We've been sitting here all afternoon, waiting for your report."

"We *know* it's incredible," said Geordi.

"What we'd *like* to know is what we can *do* about it!" Beverly chimed in.

"Admiral, please forgive my crew," said Captain Picard. "But you can understand their . . . *our* impatience. Especially since you've taken the matter out of our hands."

"You came here for help, following procedure, regulations, and direct subspace communication quite splendidly as usual. We can't fault you for that." The admiral stroked his double chin. He looked as though he'd like to sit down, but he remained standing as though in deference to the *Enterprise* crew here looking quite troubled and out of place in their ill-fitting black jumpsuits. He gave a quick *you or me?* look to Dr. Chavez, nodded to himself, and then continued addressing himself formally to the highest-ranked amongst them:

"Captain Picard. Dr. Chavez is here to give you the total report, but I'll not mince words. This is the upshot." He cleared his voice and assumed a deeper, stentorian tone. "By the power vested in me by the Federation, I find the USS *Enterprise* a total loss. And as I have been advised by my science officers that its very presence here at Starbase 210 is a danger, I am ordering that it be towed by tractor beam out to a safe portion of space, where it shall be destroyed by photon torpedoes."

Silence descended on the room.

Picard found himself at a loss for words. He looked at Will Riker and Beverly Crusher, who were registering a similar stunned look.

And Geordi La Forge . . .

Geordi just stared into space, blind.

Chapter One

One Week Before

Captain's Log, Stardate 45223.4:

The *Enterprise* has received a distress call from a remote scientific station upon the planet Phaedra in the Xerxes system. The message was from Mikal Tillstrom, son of Dr. Adrienne Tillstrom, a xenogeologist of note. The distress call was patchy and disrupted by some electromagnetic phenomenon, which is not surprising. Xerxes is known for its odd electromagnetic fields. Enough of the message came through, however, to establish that some sort of disaster has overtaken Science Station 146, and emergency aid is sought. Then the message was disrupted and ended.

I have ordered the *Enterprise* on a course and heading that will take us to Xerxes in a day and a half. Rescue operations are being prepared.

I know Dr. Adrienne Tillstrom, though I have not seen her in many years. She is a fine person as well as a brilliant scientist. I only hope that we can save her and her son from whatever catastrophe has occurred.

9

THE SUN SHONE DOWN from a clear blue sky, pleasant and warm on Will Riker's back. In the near distance, breakers crashed on the shore, spume filling the air with a fine, salty tang. Sea gulls hovered above the sea, occasionally darting down for fish, and the breeze was just right to cool the players and not compromise the game.

"Here you go, Will," said Geordi, grinning in bathing suit and bare feet. He tossed his friend the white inflated ball, and Riker caught it easily. Geordi pointed at the net above the sand held up by two aluminum poles. "The idea is to boink the ball over that black mesh thing over there, but not past the tennis shoe markers."

Riker glared at the engineer. The last two times he'd served, he'd fouled out by hitting the ball too hard. As he was a fine-caliber sportsman of many games, the two foul-outs had been particularly galling.

"Yes, Will," said Deanna Troi, a laugh in her voice. "Just get the ball over and we'll cover for you the rest of the way."

"Cease the bickering, hit the ball, and accept the eventual defeat that we shall mete out!" growled Worf from the other side of the net amongst the opposition. Will Riker rued the day he'd suggested that the Klingon try his hand at volleyball. Reluctance had rapidly melted away, to be replaced with a flashing warrior in kneepads, shorts, and T-shirt.

"Right," said Riker.

He lobbed the ball up and then pounded it over the net. Clean, crisp, and deadly, the ball caught an ensign unawares, bounced off an outstretched palm, and rolled away toward the illusion of waves in the background.

Worf snarled and gave chase.

"Pardon me, Commander," said Data, some yards away, still in uniform, observing the game.

"Yes, Data?" said Riker, accepting the kudos of his team and bowing mockingly to the opposing team.

"As I have said before, I mastered the rules of the game long ago. . . ."

"Yeah!" said Geordi. "And it's a damned shame you can't compete with us in the play-offs at Rigel II, Data. We'd win in an instant!"

Data cocked his head in bemusement. "But that would be unfair, Geordi. I would be able to exercise far more skill than a human."

Deanna Troi laughed, her curly, dark hair loose and draped down across the top of her turquoise one-piece bathing suit. "I think that's what Geordi means. He'd like to win the match by hook or by crook. It will take you a while longer, I think, to understand the importance of competition to younger, hormonally charged human males." She winked at Geordi, who simply shrugged.

Still bemused, Data turned back to Will Riker. "In any case, Commander, my question is: Why do you choose to play on a fabrication of a beach on a holodeck when it does not comply with the environment of regulation volleyball competition?"

"Well, we practice in such a court as well, Data, you know. . . ." Riker looked around at the absolutely splendid day. "As for why . . . Well, because it's *fun!*"

"Fun." The android nodded, his amber eyes gleaming. He seemed to absorb the information, but still not totally understand it. "I confess, the human preoccupation with absorbing harmful solar rays beside a briny body of water while playing on abrasive sand and rock is most fascinating."

Geordi said, "Maybe it's because our ancestors crawled out of the ocean with bottles of suntan lotion, wearing sunglasses, Data."

Data raised his eyebrows. "Ah! An excellent juxtaposition of incongruity, Geordi. A good joke, yes.

11

Still, perhaps if I study your reactions here today, I will understand better."

"Believe me, Data," said Troi. "You don't want to. Just call it a custom and be happy with that."

"Heads up, opponents!" called a deep voice, and a ball came flying toward Riker. He turned only just in time to catch the volleyball sailing his way at enormous speed. Worf hustled to resume his place amongst his team. "Serve again, and prepare for defeat." Worf looked particularly odd in swimming trunks, thought Riker.

Riker hit the ball directly at Worf, and immediately saw the move was a mistake. The Klingon leapt up into the air, snarling as though in battle. He pounded the ball back across the net so hard and at such a steep angle, the opposing team could do nothing to stop it. The ball spiked down into the sand.

Hands on hips, Worf called over to his opposition. "Our serve, I think."

The audience broke into applause.

As the other team moved around to take their places, setting up to serve, a man in full uniform stepped out from the crowd.

"A most curious game, Number One," said Jean-Luc Picard stiffly, brushing sand off his jacket with distaste and squinting, clearly not enjoying the bright sun of this holodeck scenario.

"Captain, you should join us sometime!" said Troi, holding up her hands toward the other team to signal a time-out.

"Riding, fencing, a few other sports—those are my diversions. And of course, curling up with a good book. Alas, team sports are just not my cup of tea," said Picard.

"Well, I hope you are there to root for us in the Federation competition," she said, still smiling but clearly taken aback by the abrupt response.

"Perhaps. I shall make an effort. But that's neither here nor there. Number One, I trust this game is not going to last much longer."

"We shall finish it shortly, I promise, Captain!" Worf growled, digging in on the other side of the fence, baring his teeth for fierce competition.

"That would be good of you, Lieutenant. I need to call a counsel in my ready room."

"Certainly, Captain. Do we have time to shower?" said Riker, sensing the seriousness of the matter.

"Yes. I wish to discuss the situation on Xerxes, and we will not be arriving there until tomorrow, so we have a little time left, I think." He joined his hands behind his back and examined the tennis shoe markers and gazed at the bent poles and slightly frayed net. "Tell me. This game . . ."

"Volleyball, sir," said Riker.

"Yes. 'Volleyball.' It hardly seems the pinnacle of achievement in Earth-derived sports. Surely there are other more sophisticated and challenging sports to occupy you." He looked around. "And on a beach?"

Troi seemed to sense the captain's light tone. "It's *fun,* Captain!"

Riker shrugged. "It's something to do in groups where everybody gets to participate. We're also practicing here to represent the *Enterprise* in that competition."

"'Team spirit' is the term, I believe, Captain," put in Data. "A mass psychological tool for a cohesive sense of community amongst disparate civilized beings."

It was clear to Riker that the captain was a bit bemused at the notion of "team spirit." Picard certainly valued teamwork, in textbook as well as real form. But Riker knew that while his family was stomping grapes in their vineyards, young Jean-Luc either had his head in books or in the stars. His sense of achievement was more personal.

Deanna Troi said, "Very true, Captain, and seeing as we're all a bit tense as to what may be awaiting us, I suggested that we have our practice in a relaxing atmosphere."

"Very good, Counselor. I bow to your wisdom as always. My ready room, Counselor, when it is convenient."

"Yes sir."

Picard nodded and strode away.

"Say, are you guys ready or what?" called a member of the other team.

"Tell me, empath," asked Riker. "Do you sense dissolution and fear amongst the opposition?"

"No, actually, I sense confidence and determination in them all, except for Worf."

"Worf?"

"Yes. He seems to be serving, and he wants blood."

"Prepare yourselves, opponents!" rumbled the Klingon behind the service line. He growled and proceeded to hit the ball so hard to Riker, it seemed as though he wanted to puncture it.

Chapter Two

Captain's Log, Stardate 45223.7:
I have called a briefing in my ready room, having previously assigned the appropriate crew members to research the appropriate material concerning Phaedra and Science Station Beta Epsilon. Preparation, when opportunity avails us of it, has always been a vital tool.

"THIS MEETING will come to order," said Captain Jean-Luc Picard, swiveling his chair around and sitting straight and alert at the head of the table. "We have an important matter ahead of us. I trust that you all are suitably relaxed after your interesting game. Doubtless I shall need every bit of your attention for what awaits us." For his part, the surrounding hum and muted lights, the Dopplering stars beyond the port, gave him a sense of control and well-being. He felt centered and ready to command—and to synthesize the information presented to him into decisions.

Worf frowned and looked even more dour than was

his usual wont. He looked at Riker, and though he did not growl, it looked as though he would have liked to.

"Lieutenant Commander Data has prepared a full report," Picard said. He nodded to the gold-skinned android.

Data nodded back in an exact mimic of the gesture and then began to manipulate the control panel before him. Cross-sectional graphics depicting a solar system appeared. Much of the nomenclature of the picture itself was self-explanatory, and there were letters of coding beside the bodies as well, but as a matter of formality, Data spelled the information out:

"Xerxes Gamma is a GO star in a cluster of the Cassiopeian system. Phaedra is the fourth of seven planets, and is Class M."

"Life?" said Riker, leaning forward intently, bearded chin propped on folded hands.

"No," said Data, "although curiously enough, the proper oxygen-nitrogen exists at about fifteen psi. Gravity is higher, at about one point three g's. The most unique aspect of the planet Phaedra, indeed the reason why a science station exists there, is its unique geological activity."

"Yes, Dr. Adrienne Tillstrom is renowned for her studies in the formation of planets, including her treatises on planetscaping," said Beverly Crusher. "I'm, of course, a lay person in that area, but I've read some of her articles. Quite fascinating. But what drew her to this planet, Data?"

"Essentially, the difficulty in the study of geology is of time," replied the android. "Planetary crusts change very slowly, particularly in late cooling stages of a planet's life. Mountains are formed over millennia, continents crawl over epochs along tectonic plates.

"Phaedra, however, is different."

He hit a button, and a multicolored graphic of the

planet came into view. "Phaedra, you see, has an extremely dense metallic liquid core. Although Phaedra is about the size of Earth, it is heavier, denser. It's gravity is greater, and it spins faster with a ten-hour day, which increases the convection currents in the core."

"Damn," said Geordi. "That would play hell with its magnetic poles, wouldn't it?"

"Precisely."

"Hmm," said Riker. "Well, the Earth's poles reverse every few million years, right? And as I recall, they drift a little, too. Is that what you're saying?"

"Precisely, Captain. Only the core of Phaedra is such that *its* poles reverse approximately every seventy-two point three Earth years. However, reversals are erratic and can occur at any time. Polarity field changes, causing quite a unique situation for the study not only of paleomagnetism's effect upon geology, but countless other aspects of planetary evolution. Science Station Beta Epsilon was established for just such a study, and Dr. Tillstrom's efforts have revolutionized our understanding not only of planetary formation but the laws of gravitation and magnetic physics in action."

"Well, if there's increased geological activity," said Beverly, "Wouldn't there be the danger of earthquakes?"

"The station was built to withstand earthquakes of high magnitude," said Picard, "and also constructed in the most solid and fault-free area available. Nonetheless, we cannot discount that possibility. Data, have you calculated the possible problems the station might be facing from the available information?"

"Yes, sir, and an earthquake is a possibility. There could have also been an equipment malfunction or a large electrical storm, or something else as yet unknown."

"Please report on the station, Data."

"Yes, sir." The android hit another button, and a schematic of a number of buildings built on what looked like large springs—clearly shock absorbers—came onto the screen. "Beta Epsilon science station is manned by twenty-two individuals, senior of which is Dr. Tillstrom. Its living quarters . . . here"—he pointed—"are separated from the structure housing the instruments of scientific measurements. There are vehicles which are used in the studies, both omni terrain vehicles and two flying vehicles. Here is the landing field."

"And that's what we're going to have to use to land a shuttle, aren't we?" said Geordi.

Picard smiled grimly. "Yes."

"I'm sorry, but you're running a bit ahead of us here," said Riker.

"I think what Geordi is concluding is what Data left out of the description of the planet," said Beverly Crusher. "A planet like Phaedra with a volatile paleomagnetic system . . . Well, the electromagnetic field there would be quite extraordinary, wouldn't it?"

"Very good, Doctor," said Data. Yes. The electromagnetic field of the Earth is point three one gauss. The electromagnetic field of Phaedra varies from five point two to three hundred one point two gauss. Transporters can be used at low ebb; however, general safety policy has thus far been to rely on shuttles."

Picard nodded. "We've got a Personnel Shuttle Type Seven being fitted and readied for rescue operations. I have another on call in case we have to evacuate the whole science team."

"I just pray they're alive," said Crusher thoughtfully.

"So do we all. Now then, standard rescue operations utilizing shuttlecraft are familiar to us all. I'm placing you, Number One, in command of the operation. Please review all materials and make appropriate preparations." Picard swiveled and focused on his engineering chief. "Commander La Forge, given the information on Phaedra, do you see any difficulties in establishing and maintaining an orbit?"

"Well, sir, no, we've faced far stronger electromagnetic phenomena before without any problem. However, you can bet I'm gonna review the history of orbiting that place."

"That is not necessary, Commander," said Data. "I have already taken the liberty of accessing computer memory on that issue. There have been no orbital problems in the five-year history of experience with Phaedra."

Geordi shrugged and grinned. "Well, saves my weary fingers. Thanks, Data."

"Nonetheless, I suggest you examine the records again, Lieutenant. An emergency suggests activity that could well affect us," said Captain Picard, dead serious. Levity had its place, but certainly not in a briefing.

"Yes sir," said Geordi, sobering.

"Now then. Rescue team will be Commander Riker, Dr. Crusher, Data, Geordi—"

"Pardon me, sir," said Data. "But perhaps, because of potential disruption in our mechanisms, Geordi and I should not be dispatched, given the emergency situation and the unpredictable levels of electromagnetism."

Picard responded levelly. "Do you see a real threat, Data?"

"No, sir. Frankly, I do not. However, there is a probability quotient of fifteen point nine percent that there will be."

Geordi opened his mouth to essay a quip, but then had second thoughts and shut it again.

Picard allowed himself a smile. "Yes. Excellent.

This is the reason for our briefings. Did you have something, Geordi?"

"I reluctantly agree with Data, sir. I hate to miss out on the action and the opportunity to help out, but I'd also hate to cause any complications with the old VISOR." He tapped the gold and silver device and shrugged.

"Your record in rescue operations is exemplary, Geordi. I hate to lose you on this one, but I see the wisdom of Data's thoughts as well. Very well. Number One, please select two suitable crew people."

"Yes, sir."

Picard looked around the room. "Comments, suggestions, thoughts . . . please."

"I just wish the message gave some kind of indication of the situation on the station—medical and otherwise," said Beverly.

"As do I. However, it wasn't even a vocal message from any of the station's members. It was merely an emergency subspace message lasting little over twenty seconds and then abruptly cut off." Picard surveyed the faces of his assembled people. "We'll have to face the very real possibility that there are no survivors."

"Well, sir, if what we've got is fierce electromagnetic activity, that could interfere with the signal."

"I have analyzed the composition of the beacon, sir," said Data, "and that would indeed seem to be the case."

"Or the ground could have opened up and swallowed them all," said Beverly. "Again, we're just going to have to be ready for anything."

"Just a moment . . ." said Troi. "If danger of geological activity exists, surely escape routes would have been established."

"The science station is indeed equipped with appropriate escape technology," said Data. "Coded distress beacons are records of whether or not escape transport has been used. In this case, it apparently has not."

"When the beacon was beamed, at any rate," said Geordi.

"Precisely," said Picard. "Data, we'll nonetheless have to do a sensor sweep upon arrival to detect any craft in orbit or ion trails of escaping pods."

"Yes, sir."

Picard regarded the assembled crew quietly. He was satisfied that not only did he have one of the finest assemblages of people in the Federation, but also that they were all rested and alert and at the top of their respective efficiencies.

"Excellent. I'm confident that if there is anybody or anything to rescue on Phaedra, we shall do so." Picard dismissed them, and everyone hurried on to be about their business. Commander Riker seemed to be particularly preoccupied, which was understandable. After all, he had to not merely assemble the rest of the rescue team, but attend to the details of the entire operation. Picard knew Riker would not have time for volleyball this evening.

However, as everyone left, Deanna Troi hung back. She waited a moment, and then pushed the door button. The familiar whoosh of the door closing sounded, and she turned around, the two of them in the room now enjoying complete privacy.

"Yes, Counselor," said Picard. He knew why she'd stayed behind, and not for the first time wished that Deanna Troi did not have the empathic powers she had.

"Captain, I'd like to have a word with you."

"Clearly," he said with a brief smile.

She smiled. "I do not mean to be intrusive as to your feelings and would not mention them, but it is my duty, and duty, after all, is more important than feelings, correct?"

"Touché, Counselor Troi." He granted her a brief pained smile.

"I sense that you have feelings toward this Dr. Tillstrom in danger on Phaedra." Troi's words were direct, prying and yet somehow not invasive. Per usual. The woman's perceptions were softened by her concern and genuine compassion, which made them hard to evade.

"I would hope that some feelings are allowed to be private, Counselor," he replied.

"Yes, sir, and normally I would not comment. However, that last speech . . . Well, I feel that in your efforts not to allow your feelings to enter this rescue operation, you may allow it to become too tentative."

"Continue."

"These are living beings whose lives are in danger. It is an important part of any rescue operation to feel a certain call and ignore danger. This is the stuff of bravery and courage, and it is the stuff that has made you strong, Jean-Luc, and Starfleet what it is today. I have served under your command for quite a few years." She smiled. "Do not panic, Captain. I'm sure I'll never understand you fully. However, I feel that in this case you may be bending over backward not to allow your own feelings to enter into this operation."

It was Picard's turn to smile. "You honestly believe that Commander Riker is going to turn his back on people in charge?"

"No, of course not. Perhaps I understand the commander better than I understand you. But it is not him that I am concerned about." She sighed and looked at him with those dark, beautiful, and penetrating eyes. "I think maybe that you feel frustrated that you cannot go along with the rescue team."

"The days of foolhardy risks to the commanding officer are over."

"As well they should be. But that doesn't mean

you're less frustrated. . . . You're worried about her, and you want to help . . . which is commendable. No reason to be ashamed or to hamper your rescue operation."

"Thank you, Counselor Troi. Point taken. I shall remember that in the future."

"I shall say no more . . . only that if you'd like to talk to me about it, if you'd like to share your thoughts about Dr. Tillstrom, I'm available to you as always." She smiled ruefully.

Picard nodded. "I hope you feel the respect I have toward you, Deanna. I'm sure you have only my best interests at heart."

"Good. Then my motives are cleared. Anyway, beyond my therapeutic abilities, Captain, I have to admit curiosity. A mystery woman in the life of Captain Jean-Luc Picard is always tantalizing stuff."

Despite himself, Picard felt himself go rigid. He felt a cool edge in his voice as he spoke. "Counselor, I thank you for your concern and your interest. Now if you'll excuse me, there are matters that I must attend to."

Counselor Deanna Troi nodded. "Very well, sir. I have appointments as well. Just remember . . . If you want to talk . . ."

"Yes, thank you."

She strode toward the door; the pneumatic door whisked open at her touch and she left.

We'll get you out of there, Adrienne, he thought. If there's any starship and crew that can do it, it's that of the *Enterprise*.

Chapter Three

Captain's Log, Stardate 45225.7:
We have arrived at Xerxes and have established a synchronous orbit above Science Station Beta Epsilon, which is situated on the equator of the planet. Communications attempts were met with failure. Life signs were sought; however, sensors met electromagnetic interference.
Commander Riker and his rescue team have been dispatched in a specially prepared shuttlecraft.

DESPITE HIS BEST EFFORTS, the shuttle landed with a jolt and shot Commander William Riker forward against his restraining belt. However, the shuttle landed reasonably well. They'd wisely chosen to land during daylight hours, in the landing field provided by the layout of the science station.

Riker got up and stretched his aching back. He wasn't as young as he'd once been, and the bumpy ride down had gotten to him. "Let's get a move on, then, folks. There are doubtless lives out there to save."

"I hope so," said Beverly, getting from her seat and unhooking her medikit, opening it to make sure nothing had been damaged in the turbulence. "Right. I'm ready."

"Ensign Fredricks," said Riker, turning to the man he'd selected to round out the rescue team. The man was a top athlete with a build on him like a champion. If he didn't have Data's strength and intelligence, Lars Fredricks had more agility and power than just about anyone else of the thousand-plus other members of the *Enterprise.* That, and plenty of mission experience in unusual situations. Riker had seen the blond, good-looking Nordic lad in action before and had been pleased. "Ensign Fredricks, have you got any life signs?"

"Yes sir. I'm showing at least vital functions of one . . . no, two people in there."

"Out of twenty-five . . . I hope you've still got interference there, Ensign," said Beverly. "Come on, we've got some serious work to do."

"Wait a minute. Any indication of what's happened?"

"Yes, sir," said Fredricks. "Sensors show complete collapse of many of the interior walls, and partial collapse of shells of all three principal buildings."

"Damn. What could have caused that?" said Riker.

"I suggest we monitor seismic activity," Worf said, looking at the visual monitor with suspicion. "Not only for recent tremblers but for indications of problems that may occur during the rescue operation."

Fredricks looked down, and his features bent into confusion. "That's the odd thing, sir. Sensors show no resonance of seismic activity within the past week here. And I took the liberty of scanning the foundations of the outpost." He paused and looked over to

Riker, and then to Dr. Crusher. "They're sound and show no signs of the damage they should have sustained in the nine point five Richter scale quake the damage approximates."

"And no indication of aftershock?" said Riker. His youth in Fairbanks, Alaska, gave him plenty of experience with the terminology of geologic movement. Although intellectually he was prepared for the ground to move beneath his feet, emotionally he was tensed and wary. Some things just drove straight to your instincts: Earthquakes were primal stuff.

"No, sir." Fredricks tapped the readout panel. "May I remind you, though, sir, that with the tectonic plate and fault structure, and, of course, the bizarre paleomagnetic phenomenon of Phaedra, we're entering an unpredictable arena."

"Let's enter it now," said Crusher impatiently. "There are injured people I need to attend to."

"Just a moment, Beverly. Let's take some precautions. . . . What have we got in terms of atmosphere out there?"

"Quite breathable, sir . . . A lot of dust, though, in the mix . . . but nothing harmful," Fredricks said.

"Dust. Hmm. And yet no seismic activity."

"No readings of it, sir. Our instrumentation may not be sufficient."

"Good enough. Come on, folks," Riker said grimly. "Let's open the door and see what's out there."

Auroras.

The word had not been mentioned in briefings, and Riker had been half expecting them. When a planet had a strong electromagnetic field, it almost invariably had auroras in the atmosphere. They did not impinge in any way upon the mission really, and so they had not been mentioned. However, stepping out into an open area, you could not avoid them.

26

Will Riker had grown up in the wilds of Alaska, and he was more than familiar with the stunning aurora borealis. But even he was impressed that this atmospheric phenomena should be so strong, especially during sunlit hours.

"Incredible!" said Beverly Crusher, her mission momentarily distracted by the stunning array of natural wonder spread on the horizon before her.

"Pretty amazing," said Fredricks.

Even Worf grunted with the display.

Shimmering colored lights danced and swayed in the upper air like curtains for exotic plays of gods. The flickering majesty was on such a grand, beautiful scale . . . an animated painter's palette of silent spectral enchantment.

Riker let them have exactly four seconds to register the sight before he ordered them forward to their duties. But even he indulged himself a moment to regard the phenomenon. He well remembered his father telling him as a youth, on one of their hunting trips in the wild, about what caused the aurora borealis. "It's this optical manifestation, son," the elder Riker had intoned when asked. "You see, the Earth is charged kind of like a magnet. In fact, it's got what scientists call a 'magnetosphere.' Now, the sun's got some pretty heavy-duty discharges from its corona. This is called a solar wind, and when the sun lets off a stream of ionized and magnetized gas flow, it interacts with the planet's magnetic field. Well, it's a little complicated after that, but essentially what you've got is a real electron frenzy. And you know what accelerated electrons do, don't you? That's right . . . they give off light. And what did I tell you about the spectrum? The different colors of the light's wavelengths. That's real good, Will. Maybe you're going to make something of yourself . . . maybe. . . ." Hmmm. Typical of the old man.

Well, Pop, thought Riker, gazing up now at the flickering majesty of the Phaedran sky, looks like I'm getting to see something on a hell of a bigger scale than the aurora borealis. . . . He felt proud of himself in a strange way, having proven himself to his own soul, and that nagging voice of Kyle Riker still bellowing at the back of his mind. Still, the little boy in him wished his dad could be here, just to see this incredible sight. All of this in just a twinkling: There were more important things to do now than reminisce.

"Come on, people. We've got a job to do," he said, and immediately they snapped to attention and went about their business, following him as he took the lead. He took a breath of the air. Oddly brackish, with definite mineral overtones. Riker was used to alien atmospheres filled with exotic tastes and smells. This one just smelled like a haunted rock quarry.

The shuttle had landed about fifty yards from the Beta Epsilon science station, the closest the runway would allow. The whole had apparently been cut and chiseled from a rocky plain which stretched around them into distant mountains. The entire world seemed to be contorted by mountains and volcanoes and other violent upthrusts of rock and shelving, except for where an anemic sea covered a mere thirty percent of the land surface, apparently the only source of vegetation and thus the contributor of oxygen to the atmosphere mix that made it breathable for humans. The sky against which the auroras moved was a dull gray with the large quantities of dust in the atmosphere.

Here, up against the sky like geometric pegs in fractal holes, were the grouped metallic and permacrete buildings of the station. Immediately Riker could see that they were not as they had been depicted in the graphics that had been presented at the briefing. Not only were they dented and partially caved in, but it looked as though they'd been splattered by large quantities of reddish brown mud. This stuff squatted on top of the ensemble of buildings and dripped off the side as though it were the droppings of some huge mythological bird-creature. Riker cringed at the simile.

"Just a second," he said, as they approached the closest building. "Dr. Crusher, how about trying another tricorder reading on that stuff, now that we're closer."

Beverly lifted her special medical tricorder and made the appropriate adjustments for that duty. After a few moments of scanning and flashing of lights, she reported the results. "There's quite a mélange of stuff, Commander. Magnesium, alkalis, basalt, quartz . . . quite an array of small crystalline compounds, silicates . . ."

"But inorganic."

"Yes, sir. It's mud, sir. This planet's version of plain old clay mud."

"It looks as though it's been hurled at the structures by something," said Worf. "And yet, sir, there's no other sign of life on this planet, nor the mechanisms for the hurling. . . ."

"I think we can safely conclude that it's the result of geologic activity of some sort. . . . We just don't get any readings of lingering resonance," said Riker.

"Could be a flood," said Fredricks.

"That it could, but I don't see any water, and there wasn't any sign of a river anywhere nearby, as far as I could tell. Fredricks, please check again on your tricorder for any alien life signs."

Fredricks did so. "Nothing alien. The possibility of human life signs . . . flickering, sir, so I can't be entirely sure."

Riker cleared his throat. This really wasn't getting them anywhere. What they needed was *action*. "There must be an explanation, and I should think that we'll get it from inside. So then, Lieutenant Worf, would you be so kind as to try the door."

"Yes, sir." Worf had his phaser out and ready. The chief security officer cautiously approached the door. It was built into a bulkhead, and the whole arrangement looked reinforced with heavy-duty duranium alloy. It was clear that this installation had been built to withstand a lot of punishment. However, when Worf stepped up to it, he registered a grunt of surprise. "Sir, the exterior door . . . It's not even closed!"

"The interior door is, however," noted Fredricks.

"Let's go, Worf," ordered Riker.

The Klingon stepped down into a well, his boots sinking into a layer of the reddish clay mud. He traipsed forward toward the open door . . .

And roared.

Before there was anything that they could do, the big officer seemed to be pulled off his feet. He went off to the side in a skid, slamming down into the muck.

"Worf!" yelled Beverly.

"Damn!" said Riker.

"I am all right," said Worf, fighting to maintain his dignity as he lifted himself up. A good portion of his uniform was covered with the thick mud. Some of it glopped off back into a pile, but much clung. "I slipped."

"For a moment I was in the middle of a horror movie and you were being sucked under by some awful creature," said Beverly Crusher, breathing easier.

"Nothing so noble," said Worf, wiping some of the stuff off. "Fortunately my phaser still works perfectly." He leaned against the other wall for a moment at an angle that the sun reached, and the sun sparkled strangely in the myriad crystals within the mud. An odd combination of beauty and ugliness, thought Riker.

"Well, let's hope we don't need it. Onward, Worf."

"Yes, sir." The Klingon slogged through the mud more carefully this time, reaching the open door without further indignity.

They passed through an anteroom where they found the closed door. Inset was a door handle, and Worf pushed it down. It clicked and began to roll open slowly. Then it jammed.

"Not locked, sir, but apparently it's electronically assisted, and the power seems to be off," reported Worf.

"You need some manual help there?" called Fredricks.

"Thank you. I believe I can deal with this."

The Klingon inserted his arm into the opening, wedged himself in, and pushed. He growled with the strain and for a moment the door held . . . but then gradually it gave way and slowly slid back. With one more grunt, Worf heaved it fully back into the wall, giving them full entry.

Riker looked through. He could see that though the rooms beyond were dim and filled with dust and gloom, spears of daylight punched down, illuminating the areas sufficiently that their portable lights would not generally be needed.

"Looks like we should have brought our galoshes," he said grimly.

"It's just mud, sir," said Beverly. She stepped through the mud, her boots squelching, carrying her medikit gingerly. Worf turned around and helped her through.

Lieutenant Fredricks followed, and Riker brought up the rear. Just mud, they'd said, and most certainly it was, quite similar in consistency to the mud he'd played in when the Alaskan steppes would thaw briefly in the long days of summer. But alien mud nonetheless, as those glittering pieces of crystal attested.

For some reason he felt uneasy about the structure, even though sensors had still shown the supports to be sound. It didn't seem likely that it was going to collapse on their heads, but still . . .

Nonetheless, there were people still alive in here. People who had to be rescued, and as soon as he saw Beverly's concerned eyes when he stepped through the door, he recovered his aplomb and went into action.

"Okay, Doctor. What's the prescription?"

They stood in a kind of anteroom. There were lockers on either side of the room, with a bench in the middle. Boots were lined up in a neat row under the bench. Clearly this was the changing room for outside expeditions.

Beverly was looking down at her tricorder. "In here," she directed, and quickly went ahead of the rest, unheedful of the general rule that the away team individual with a phaser went first.

"Oh God," she said the moment she disappeared from Riker's view. Her upset voice drove a shiver of concern through him.

Fredricks was even faster than Worf in responding. He leapt through the open doorway, pulling out his phaser. However, Worf was not far behind, nor did Riker dally.

He sprinted forward.

Riker found himself in a large room with machines grouped on all walls. Dead machines, with nary a flash of light or a hint of digital readouts on computer array. And something more was wrong with these machines, Riker noticed peripherally. His first duty, however, was to be certain of his medical officer's welfare.

Dr. Beverly Crusher was bent over a fallen man, her

medical tricorder humming and flashing. The woman was perfectly fine, he was relieved to see, but the man was not. You hardly needed a telltale device to see what was wrong. The man was in gray khaki coveralls and he was sprawled at an angle, neck crooked and head against one of the machines. His eyes were open and staring into infinity, dulled by death. He lay in a large pool of congealing blood.

"Massive skull concussion and brain trauma," said Crusher in a monotone. "Skin and vein rupture."

"Looks as though he's been hurled against that machine there and split his skull."

Worf grunted. "He died in combat. But with whom?"

It was Riker's turn to draw out his phaser. "I don't know, but let's not take any chances." He turned the setting up to heavy stun. As he did so, he looked around at the machines. They all looked wrecked . . . and from the floor cracks there oozed that same reddish clay that had been in the entrance well. "Looks like there's been a break in the wall, too . . . that mud again."

"Yes, sir," said Fredricks. "I've taken the liberty of comparing the composition of the mud with the surrounding environment. It's exactly the same all around, sir. It's just normal material."

"Hmm. And do you read a breakage in the walls?"

"Yes, sir. And considerable water content, so that would explain it. Maybe there *was* a flood, only the ground absorbed it on a water table."

"Whatever it was, it happened fast, and it's doubtless a phenomenon that could happen again. Looks as though the violence here could have been man-made, anyway." He nodded down at the dead body. "Nothing we can do for this fellow now."

"I'm afraid not." Beverly sighed. Her fingers danced on her medical tricorder. A red-blue-white

33

light sequence and then a *bleep* and a pointing arrow. "Life signs through the next room, sir. There's someone still breathing there."

"Do me a favor, Doctor. Let Worf go first this time?"

Crusher nodded distractedly. She gave the Klingon a look of impatience. Without expression, Worf turned and, phaser slightly ahead of him, entered the adjoining room. They advanced in single file.

The next room was much the same as the one they'd just visited, only it held larger machines, a table, and no corpses. The following room, however, bore fruit. More machines, none working. Splayed over one, his arms outstretched, a projectile weapon in one hand, blood rivuleting down from a cut in his forehead and ear and some other wound, was a young man wearing identical khaki coveralls as the dead man.

"Source of the life signs," said Beverly. She hurried over and allowed her machine to perform a hasty examination. "Concussions, but nothing fatal, I think. Some brain edema, though. We need to relive the intracranial pressure before permanent brain damage occurs."

The man jerked. He gasped, and his eyes opened. He gazed up blearily and reached toward Beverly, trying to stand up.

"No, don't strain—"

The young man tottered and then keeled over, straight into Beverly Crusher's outstretched arms. A smaller woman might have toppled as well under the weight; however, Dr. Crusher not only was a larger woman, but she kept herself in good shape. She caught him with a little gasp of surprise and somehow maintained her grasp of the tricorder as she let him down onto the ground.

The young man was still conscious. Riker recognized him from the pictures he'd seen. "That's Mikal Tillstrom," he said.

At his name, the young man—he couldn't have been more than twenty—opened his eyes and looked at them. "Ah . . . rescue party . . ."

"That's right, son," said Riker. "What happened here?"

The boy's eyes rolled about a moment, unfocused. "Mother . . . Dr. Tillstrom . . . in sickbay . . . Must save . . ."

The boy's head lolled back into the crook of Beverly's arm. She gentled him down to the floor and then passed the med/tricorder over him. "Situation stable, I think. He'll be all right for a while. Just let me deal quickly with this wound so he doesn't loose any more blood." She pulled out the septic equipment and the dermaplast dispenser, hands moving quickly and expertly.

Meantime, Riker ordered Fredricks to see about more life signs.

"Well, sir, we've got some readings a few rooms away, and that pretty much matches up with the sickbay location on the schematics I've got stored here."

When Crusher was finished with her "Band-Aid" effort, as the procedure was still dubbed by human medics, Riker ordered Worf to stay with the fallen young man while he and the others struck out for the sickbay. "Maybe there are some things in there you'll be able to use."

"Not if the machines are in the state I've seen here."

"Funny that there don't seem to be any machines working here, Captain," said Fredricks. "I don't know what happened to them. Some were apparently destroyed—others . . . well, they're just not going. . . ."

35

"You are recording all this, aren't you?" said Riker.

"Oh, yes, sir."

"Good. We'll save what lives we can. The rest we'll be able to examine from a little safer distance." He shivered despite himself. "This place gives me the creeps."

"It's like a submerged basement with the water gone . . . but the man's clothes weren't wet. . . . And that mud . . . Look . . ." Dr. Crusher pointed to a corner where the stuff was packed, and also to piles of it independently stacked on the floor, sometimes with trails leading to walls or other piles, sometimes not. "I'm looking forward to full computer analysis on *this* one."

"So are we all, Doctor. How are we doing, Ensign?"

"According to the plan I have here, Commander, the sickbay should be just adjacent . . . Yes, right here, through this door."

The indicated door was closed. Fredricks tried it.

"Electronic door, sir. Mechanically jammed."

Riker could see that if they tried hard enough, both of them might be able to force the door open. But there really wasn't sufficient angle for purchase. They didn't have the time, anyway.

"Use your phaser, then, Fredricks." He pulled Dr. Crusher back from the door. "Now."

The ensign had his phaser on the proper setting within a matter of moments, and almost immediately after, a pulsing red beam of energy burned a hole in the side of the door. Fredricks had guessed well. His phaser stream had triggered the door release spring. The door trundled open fully.

"Excellent." Riker peered through the smoke into the dimness. He made out some forms beyond. "Yes, I think I see biobeds." Crusher leapt forward, but Riker stopped her. "What did I tell you, Beverly?"

He smiled grimly and stepped forward through the

smoke hovering at the portal. The stuff was acrid, and the interior was little better. There was the harsh, brackish smell again, like a sour sea. The dimness inside here was unrelieved by any windows or holes punched through the roof. Riker pulled his light from his belt and directed the beam about him. The light splashed on dead instrumentation against the wall. He played it across the forms that had been suggested before: Yes, biobeds. One, two, three . . . and upon the fourth he made out a human form, lying faceup.

She was a woman with long, graying hair sprouting from beneath a large bandage wrapped around her head. She wore a smock, and Riker could easily see her chest rising and falling with respiration.

"It's a woman, all right, and she's alive. Come—"

Then the stuff dropped hard upon him from the ceiling.

Chapter Four

How can a mirror reflect itself?

Data looked at himself in the looking glass, pondering the question, trying not to access computer files. He just wanted to *think* about this, reason it, try to *feel* it out if possible, rather than use any kind of predigested statements or theses. Certainly there were plenty in his memory banks. He'd made a study of human philosophies from Sartre to Socrates, as well as alien philosophies, and hopefully he'd learned from them all. However, accessing and comprehending, deep down, were two different areas entirely. Data wanted to understand his material, than rather merely hold it in his fingertips a mind's touch away.

"Well, Data," said the girl. "What do you think?"

Data looked at himself again in the old-fashioned hand-held mirror. He cocked his head quizzically. How fascinating. Yes, there was that slicked-back hair, those golden eyes, that largish nose, that Adam's apple . . . all this a reflection not of natural selection, and a mother and father's genetic mix, but rather a copy of his creator, Dr. Noonian Soong. But all these features and characteristics, even past the artificial skin to the positronic brain—amidst all of this, what was truly the essence of Data?

He handed the mirror back to Penelope Winthrop and answered her question. "Given the existence of another mirror, then certainly a mirror can reflect itself."

Penelope laughed, her eyes sparkling. She was a young girl of eighteen years with long, tawny hair that swept down past the collar of her ship's uniform. She had a small button nose and green eyes and somehow had managed to effect freckles on her round cheeks, despite having spent most of her past couple of years aboard the *Enterprise,* away from any natural sunlight. Her body was slender but clearly a young woman's, its curves highlighted by the shape-accenting lines of her uniform. She was not a member of the ship's crew, however, but a daughter of a family amongst the more than a thousand beings who worked and lived on the survey and diplomatic vessel. She was a fascinating and bright person, and although Data was spending time with her as a favor to a friend, he altogether enjoyed the experience. As the saying went, Penelope "kept him on his toes."

"I'm not talking about the mirror's frame, Data," said Penelope. "I'm talking about the mirror itself. The surface."

Data mused, pursing his lips in a way that he knew Penelope found comical. "Well then, the question is, is the mirror a glass—or is the mirror merely the light which it reflects?"

Penelope giggled and fell onto her back on the blanket, allowing herself a full-throated laugh. They were on a bluff overlooking a beach of white sand, ridged by a foam-surfed ocean. An earth scene, one of Penelope's favorites . . . one that relaxed her. Holo-derived, of course. They were on Holodeck Three. But even Data found it all so interesting that he tried to "suspend his disbelief," as the English poet Samuel Coleridge put it, and pretend he was actually there amidst the sweet-smelling tranquillity of it all.

A breeze whipped Penelope's hair as she lay back, and Data looked down at her. He knew theoretically that Penelope was an attractive young woman. Indeed, everything about her image was aesthetically pleasing. However, not actually being human, he did not respond to her as another man might, which was probably why Troi had requested these sessions with her. Nonetheless, as he looked down at her, at the joy and pleasure on her face, a part of him wondered what it would be like if he had an endocrine system and he could feel desire and emotion toward her. Much as he envied humans their humanity, that aspect of it still baffled him. Besides, he well knew the trouble it all caused!

"Data, I just can't pin you down, can I?" She got up onto her elbow and regarded him, smiling. "It's such fun talking to you, though. It's so refreshing. . . . You know, Counselor Troi warned me not to fall in love with you, but I love you anyway, okay? Platonically, okay?"

"Yes, Penelope, I consider you my friend as well."

"Good. Then we can continue to verbally torment each other with philosophical conundrums?"

"If you mean talk to one another, yes, of course, although I hope the subject is not always philosophy. I should like to broaden my panorama." He tagged that with a quirk of the mouth that humans called a grin and gave the appropriate tilt to the meaning of the sentence.

"Of course, of course."

"Perhaps you have much to teach me about life."

"You, Data? You know everything."

"I did not know how appropriate this holodeck selection would be. The rhythm of the waves, the heat of the sun on my sensors. Yet I find the experience intriguing."

"Oh good!" She clapped her hands, clearly pleased. She reached into the picnic basket and drew out a bottle of cold Berninian cola, which she poured into cups. She gave him one. "Let's toast!" The stuff effervesced agreeably.

Data obediently clinked glasses with her. "Yes! Let us toast!" He raised his eyebrows. "Penelope? To what are we toasting?"

"To *us* of course, silly!"

"You mean to our relationship."

"To our . . . our friendship." She frowned. "Our . . . f-f-friendship." She brought the cup up to her full lips and was about to drink when suddenly she stopped as though she, too, were an android and someone had just cut off her power supply. She stared off past Data, as though through him, her eyes empty, her face blank. Data knew that she got like this sometimes; he'd seen her do it before in the three or four times they'd spent time together. Troi had said to expect it. However, it was most disconcerting to be with a human who acted this way, and most especially when it was a . . . well, a *friend*. It wasn't as though she was distracted. She simply wasn't there, as though some force had sucked her up back into the hard shell surrounding her mind.

"Penelope?" he said softly, patiently. "Penelope, it would seem that I have gotten you upset. I am sorry."

Nothing. She seemed frozen, like a statue. When this sort of thing happened, Troi had said, it is best just to ignore it and continue talking . . . albeit what you would have then wouldn't be a dialogue, but a monologue.

Data shrugged, still in his human gesture program mode. He could do that.

He rambled for a time. He spoke of what they could do together in the future. He spoke his thoughts concerning his relationship, as an android, to the crew and to the *Enterprise* itself.

Abruptly he stopped.

He looked at the girl.

"Or am I simply exercising the tendency of an interconnection of patterned systems which is a sentient mind to superimpose patterns where they are inappropriate?"

Penelope spoke suddenly, as though she'd been listening all along. "You are full of the most fascinating ideas, Data."

"Thank you. Are you well?"

"I left again, didn't I?"

"Yes."

She nodded and sighed. "I think I got scared. But don't be upset, Data. Believe me, it's not as bad as it is with . . . others. Especially young men who I happen to . . . uhm . . . you know."

"To whom you are attracted."

"I'm afraid so. Plays havoc with my social life. Do you think, Data, that I could *ever* be good socially, with strangers?"

"May I say, from my reading of societies and particularly social novels, you display a sensibility and an intellect that, with the proper instruction, would put you in good stead in just about any society that involves any display of manners."

"Why . . . why, thank you, Data. I believe that is one of the most interesting compliments I've ever received. Shall our next holodeck excursion be onto a cotillion in Regency London?"

Data did a quick computer access on that one. "Ah. Early-nineteenth-century pre-Victorian England. A fascinating period. A dance? I would be honored."

"You're so silly, Data!"

Data affected a chagrined, confused look. "I have been called many things before, Penelope, but never silly."

"I hope you're not hurt."

"You forget. I do not feel pain. Emotional pain or otherwise."

"Well, be certain I would never knowingly cause you pain if you did, Data." She leaned over and kissed him on the cheek, and smiled warmly at him.

"Thank you," Data said.

"You're welcome."

"Well, I see that you two are getting along swimmingly!" said a voice approaching them.

Penelope swiveled around, her long hair carouseling. The sun picked out the highlights, and Data noticed a bit of a blush on her cheeks at the arrival of the visitor. "Oh. Counselor Troi . . ."

"Deanna, Penelope. I told you, you should address me like a friend . . . which I most certainly am." The brunette Betazoid walked the rest of the way up the bluff and joined them. She surveyed the view. "Delightful. You worked this up, Penelope?"

"Yes. That was what you suggested, wasn't it, Counse—Deanna?"

"Quite right. And a marvelous choice of color, scent, temperature . . . Quite invigorating. I believe even Data looks happy."

Data was about to speak up in contention, since these, after all, were things he did not feel. However, he caught himself in time. Penelope might be hurt.

"Yes, Deanna. If I could be happy, then in this delightful young woman's company, I would be."

The ladies just looked at each other and laughed.

"Thank you, Data," said Penelope. She got up and essayed a curtsy. "Do practice your dancing for that Regency cotillion date you promised to take me on sometime."

"Hmmm. I believe that will have to wait. Dr. Crusher will doubtless be quite busy with the survivors of the Beta Epsilon crisis and will not be able to give me dancing instruction. May I"—he accessed quickly—"take a rain check?" He smiled.

Penelope laughed. "Of course."

"I can see that this is working out very well, Penelope."

The young lady looked down sheepishly at her boots. "I'm afraid I zoned again, Counselor."

Data said, "Yes, Penelope entered her reverie period for approximately two minutes, nineteen seconds."

Troi licked her lips and nodded. "Well, you seem none the worse for it. . . ."

"I got a little excited, a little frightened. . . . My feelings got going, I'm afraid."

"But you came out of it easily. This is good. Excellent progress."

"Yes, right . . . Put me with a guy who wants to kiss me, though, and God knows what might happen. . . ." She sat back down on the blanket, looking slightly vexed. "What a pain! Miss Nil Social Life. I'm sure the guys must have all kinds of names for me. Miss Space Cadet. Stoney. Oh dear." But she didn't seem terribly distraught, Data noted. Which was a positive step.

Human psychology was certainly one of his weak points, and it appeared as though Troi had stuck him smack dab into a psychological therapy situation.

Penelope Winthrop had been born on Xerxes Three, a colony quite distant from the Federation and far from the usual medical and psychological aid of modern times. She had suffered a prenatal trauma and though she had splendid, nurturing parents, her childhood after the age of three had been troubled with autism.

Since it was so rare in these times, Data had not been familiar with the term and had to dig deep in the main computer's archives for specifics. Essentially autism was a human mental illness that involved a withdrawal from reality. Her problem was superficially similar to the problem that Barclay experienced, but in reality, it was actually quite different. Barclay's had been more of an obsession with the unrealities he had propagated on holodecks. The mental fault displayed by the younger Penelope had been far more fundamental. Her parents had finally had to return to the mainstream of the Federation to get her the proper treatment. It had taken a few months, but Earth doctors had almost entirely cured her.

Years later her parents had enlisted aboard the *Enterprise*, bringing Penelope along. However, in her adolescence some of her problems resurfaced from time to time, particularly in moments involving stress or the opposite sex. Troi was treating her, and after a degree of limited progress, had asked Data to have "conversations" with her.

One of the interesting side effects of this condition, Troi had told him, was an unusually high psi-quotient. Apparently, Penelope had powers of the mind that were rare in humans. Troi sensed the potential, and yet the girl kept this potential even more tightly wrapped than her conversation. It had been Troi's hope that with Data she might sometime talk about it.

So far, however, she'd not said word one on the subject.

"You're such an unthreatening yet attractive male figure," she explained. "It will be practice for her, do you understand?"

Data had sort of understood, but it was really all beside the point. He was all too happy to help out, especially after he found that his partner in conversation had such a nimble and imaginative mind. Perhaps, he thought, she was helping him as much as he was helping her. . . .

"Nervousness is something that I confess I do not understand," Data said. "Like fear, it is a function of the adrenal gland, which I do not have. However, if it is of any help, may I observe that your beauty most likely causes far more nervousness and upset in the young male hormonal system than you give yourself credit for."

"No way! They don't go into orbit around Black Holesville!"

"I think that Data has an excellent point," said Troi quite seriously. "In my experience in counseling humans utilizing my special Betazoid abilities, I have always been surprised at their lack of understanding of one another. . . ."

"What do you mean?"

"Well, naturally there are differences in everyone . . . but there are more similarities than they generally take into account. The opposing army is generally just as afraid in their foxholes as you are in yours. However, fear is something that defies logic. Humans become far too involved in their own problems to notice that those around them have not only similar problems, but similar feelings. I have always wished that I could impart some of my abilities to my patients. It would go a long way, I think, in their counseling."

"Yes. I understand," Penelope said.

Their conversation was interrupted by a voice over a loudspeaker.

"Counselor Troi . . . Commander Data. If I may have your attention, please." The voice of Captain Picard.

"Yes sir," said Troi.

"The shuttlecraft has returned from the surface of the planet," said Picard. "Your assistance may be needed."

"Coming, sir," replied Data.

Chapter Five

THEY WERE A MESS.

Picard had never seen quite the like of it in all his experience with shuttle rescues.

Normally Jean-Luc Picard would have overseen the procedures from the main bridge, but this seemed to be a time when his presence on the shuttlebay floor could be required. That was why he'd called in Data and Troi as well. They indeed could be useful in this situation.

For his own part, he'd been down here at shuttlebay Ops to view the return of the craft as soon as it had neared the *Enterprise.* He'd watched the door open and the craft sail smoothly in. It had been hell waiting for the doors to close and the big deck to repressurize so that the shuttle doors could open and its passengers could be attended to.

But then, Jean-Luc Picard had been trained to take hell. *And* high water, after all, if need be.

When it was safe, he and a crew of security men stepped out. Gurneys rolled along behind them.

The door of the shuttlecraft opened, and Picard was able to see what had happened to his people.

Yes, indeed, they were a mess.

The clay they had spoken of was everywhere inside, but most of it seemed to be on Dr. Crusher, Ensign Fredricks, Lieutenant Worf, and Commander Riker. Mostly on the latter two, from the looks of them. It was also spread out on the seats and interior of the shuttle. Apparently ascent from the surface through the atmosphere had not knocked off what had gotten on the shuttle in its landing. There were still specks of the stuff on the housing, as well as the rudders.

A little dirt wasn't the important thing now, though. What was important were the two survivors whom the rescue operation had saved. Nonetheless, even as Dr. Crusher jumped off and began directing the placing of her patients on the gurneys, Captain Picard thought it best to take precautions.

Peripherally he noted the arrival of Data and Troi.

"Captain," said Data. "I would like to analyze the content of that clay our rescue team has brought back with it before it is disposed of."

Just as the transporter was equipped with a biofilter that destroyed any incoming bacteriological and viral forms known to be dangerous, so the shuttle area had its detectors as well. Detectors that had not gone off.

"Proceed, Mr. Data."

Data took a nearby tricorder from a supernumerary crew member, and his fingers danced expertly on its face.

"I can tell you what you're going to find, Captain," said Commander Riker, looking peeved and uncomfortable. "Mud. Lots of clay mud."

"I've recorded the composition on my tricorder, if you'd like to compare, sir," offered Fredricks.

"It's just dirt, sir," said Dr. Crusher impatiently. "I

need to get these people to where I can do some good!"

"A few more seconds won't hurt them," stated Picard, face immobile.

"Sterile, sir," said Data.

"Composition?"

"Sir, I'd be happy to list them in their entirety, but that would take quite a while. Basic components seem to be silicate-based basalts, quartz . . . quite an array of inorganic minerals, sir. A most remarkable mix. But from all apparent signs, simply clay mud as reported."

"The geology lesson can wait," said Dr. Crusher. "These people are *hurt.*"

Picard mulled this over for a moment. "Very well. Take the injured to sickbay." He turned to his officers.

"You received our comm report, sir. You know what happened," said Riker.

Picard nodded. "Yes. Clean yourselves up, gentlemen. I want a full debriefing in thirty minutes in my ready room."

"Yes sir," said Riker.

Captain Picard swiveled to address the on-duty flight deck officer, a Lieutenant Montgomery. "I trust you can deal with this mess."

Troi stopped him as he was about to walk away. "Will you require me, sir? I have the end of a session to attend to, if not."

"Can you postpone it?"

"Yes, of course."

"Good. Do so. I want to make absolutely certain of something before we leave this place."

He turned and strode briskly away toward the lift.

Will Riker still ached a little, and not just in the body. His ego was a little bruised as well.

I really should have been a little more cautious, he

told himself for the hundredth time as he entered the ready room, clean, and received a nod from Captain Picard.

When he'd walked in that chamber, the whole roof seemed to fall on him. Actually, it had been just more of that damned reddish clay mud, seeping through the ceiling and falling on him. He'd nearly lost consciousness there, floundering beneath the stuff on the floor. It had been good he'd brought along a man of Fredrick's strength to dig him out of that stuff.

Afterward, he'd been just fine, though. As usual, he'd save any trauma for later. Blow some tunes through the old trombone and knock that damned mud out of the spit hole in the process.

"Very good," said Captain Picard as Riker took his place at the meeting. "We're all here now. And considerably cleaner, I am happy to say."

Worf grunted. Riker had never thought of Klingons being particularly fastidious, but Worf hadn't seemed to enjoy wallowing in that muck. As shimmering and interesting as it looked when hit by light, mud was mud, and Worf seemed just as happy to be rid of it as was Riker.

Picard leaned forward and punched a button on a comm unit. "Dr. Crusher. The meeting has convened. I am sure that we'd like to start with a report on the progress of your patients."

"Dr. Tillstrom and her son, Mikal, are in stable condition," reported the doctor. "I've done what I can, and only time can tell."

"We are certain that the male is Mikal Tillstrom?"

"Yes, sir. Photographic and DNA identification identical. Absolutely no doubt."

"Excellent. And what caused the damage, Doctor?"

"Violence apparently, sir. Both sustained bad head wounds. There are bruises all about their bodies as well."

"Nothing more?"

"Well, sir, the mediscan shows that Mikal has an engram-circuit implant in his neocortex which seems malfunctional. It poses no danger to him, so I'm going to let him recover from his concussion before I do anything about it. Though actually, I'd like to ask him personally about its function."

"Sir," said Data. "Engram-circuits are generally utilized in an experimental form to store extra ROM memory. They have also been successfully shown to augment the human intelligence quotient—though they are not a hundred percent infallible."

"I see. Dr. Crusher, in lieu of your presence here, can you continue to monitor our conversation?"

"I don't see why not. I can monitor my patients from here with no problem."

"Thank you." Picard swiveled his gaze, which lighted finally on Riker. He could feel the penetrating, demanding gaze hard upon him. He returned it with equal power. It was a little game the men played often. A kind of benign stare-down. "Number One, what went on down there?"

"Sir, we don't know. We've taken a recording of everything, which is available for examination and scrutiny."

"Yes, we've received your verbal reports . . . and we will certainly take the visuals and computer material into account." Picard leaned forward. "I'm talking about what your call is, Number One. Two survivors, both suffering from head wounds. Two men discovered dead from similar blows . . . and the rest of the scientific team . . . Twenty-one people . . . gone. No life signs, either, so we must presume them to be dead."

"Yes, sir."

"But what happened to them?"

"Croatoan, sir," said Data. "Similar anyway."

"What, Data?"

" 'Croatoan' was a message left, the last remaining sign of the Roanoke colony in Virginia during the colonization of America. The people simply vanished. No evidence as to what happened or why it happened."

"We have evidence of foul play here," Worf said. "And survivors as well as dead bodies. Survivors who will hopefully awaken soon and tell us what happened."

"I trust you brought along the dead in the shuttle for autopsy and proper burial, Number One?"

"Yes, sir. That's been taken care of." Riker cleared his throat.

Fredricks jumped in eagerly. "We talked about just that on the way up from the planet's surface, sir! We were speculating—" Riker felt a surge of pique, but then allowed it to pass. It was his duty to make this part of the report, but he well knew the eagerness to participate that the ensign must be feeling. Nonetheless, Fredricks got a glimpse of the emotion of his face and stopped in midspeech. "Oh. My apologies, sir."

"That's all right, Ensign," said Riker magnanimously. "I'll merely fill in anything you leave out, as will Worf and Dr. Crusher."

"Thank you, sir," said Fredricks, clearly grateful to be allowed to participate at all. "Captain, there were no signs whatsoever of any other craft landing. No evidence of alien interference; of course, such could easily be covered up. But the question has to be . . . why? Why would anyone attack a science station, kill and kidnap most of its people, and then leave? Dr. Crusher speculated on the possibility of some kind of madness taking over the crew of the station . . . a mental illness caused by the environment."

"Is that correct, Doctor?"

"Yes, sir," came the voice on the comm. "It would

also explain the lateness of the emergency call. Perhaps Dr. Tillstrom thought it was under control when in truth it was not."

"What course of action do you recommend, Number One?"

Riker straightened a little bit, feeling pride that his opinion was being sought. "For that I need to ask Dr. Crusher a question. Doctor, are our resources sufficient to treat your patients?"

"Yes, I believe so."

"Then you expect them to revive soon?"

"That's hard to say, but diagnostics would indicate that at least in Mikal Tillstrom's case, it won't be more than a few days. His mother is a little more questionable, but she's out of danger."

"Sir," said Riker. "We have to consider our previous destination of Micah IV. They are still waiting for their shipment of the Jovian antiviral serum that was our mission. And while their supplies are still holding out, we still have our orders. We can examine our tapes in transport and can return if need be, after successful completion of our mission."

"My thoughts were along the same lines." Picard nodded. "Make it so, Number One. But Worf and Dr. Crusher. If this violence was internal amongst the members of the science station, it does not behoove us to leave our unconscious guests as they are. Some kind of restraining measure might be in order."

"Easy enough, sir," came Crusher's voice. "I'll have an armed security officer on guard at sickbay at all times, sir."

"Excellent. This meeting is adjourned, and we shall prepare for departure from orbit around Phaedra. Please keep me informed on the state of the injured, Dr. Crusher. Awaken me if necessary. I want to talk to them as soon as either is conscious."

"Yes, sir."

Riker watched his captain's face as he made these orders. Stone. Pure lack of registering any emotion but a calm devotion to duty and to the Right Thing to Do. A sense of admiration filled Riker as usual, but also a wondering. What was the captain really feeling? Troi would know, of course, and not for the first time did Will Riker envy her Betazoid abilities. He knew that Picard must be feeling *something* about the fact that his old friend Dr. Tillstrom was lying unconscious in the sickbay of the ship. But what? And how did he keep everything so under *control*? This was a talent that Riker knew he'd have to achieve before he could even think of being worthy to be captain of the *Enterprise*.

They filed out quickly from the ready room and took their places on main bridge. Riker, as executive officer, took his seat on the right-hand side of Captain Picard. With feminine poise, Counselor Deanna Troi settled in her usual position, attentive and yet clearly tuned in to much more than just what normal senses took in. Lieutenant Lars Fredricks, Riker noted with amusement, had been dubbed to play pilot today. Perhaps as a reward for a duty well done on Phaedra. Maybe. Even though he wasn't an empath, he could almost feel the pride that radiated from the young man.

"Ops report," requested Picard.

"Ship functioning under normal parameters," said Data, after a quick review of his controls.

"Engineer report?"

"Running smooth as Alabasterian moth silk, Captain," replied Geordi.

He leaned over, clearly feeling in charge again. "Ensign Fredricks, lay in a course for Micah IV, cruising speed warp six. We've got some catching up to do."

"Aye, sir."

"Data, time necessary for flight?"

"That should be two days, nine point six hours, sir," said the android with hardly a pause.

"Course plotted and laid in, sir. *Enterprise* ready for warp," reported Fredricks with considerable élan.

Riker leaned back, almost feeling the course of power mounting and throbbing through this vessel's engines, subtly vibrating everything in it. Ah, it was even better than his boyhood dreams. Flying across the starscape, sailing through the solar seas with the gusts of adventure in their metaphorical sails.

He sat back to enjoy the ride, but something niggled at the back of his mind. Something was bothering him. He turned almost from habit and looked over to Troi.

She was frowning.

She felt him looking at him, and she turned to face him. There was something troubling her as well, though those deep, delicious eyes were confused.

Something *felt* wrong about this whole business with this planet called Phaedra.

"Engage!" said Captain Jean-Luc Picard, and they were on their way.

Chapter Six

Captain's Log, Stardate 45225.7:

We are a day into our continued journey to Micah IV, and caught up in our schedule. The operations and routine have returned to normal. Dr. Crusher reports that while Dr. Adrienne Tillstrom is still in a deep coma, her son, Mikal, is much closer to consciousness.

I look forward to speaking with him, hoping that his report will solve some of the puzzles that have been presented us. Having sent off a report on subspace to be relayed to Federation Headquarters, I am prepared to be ordered back to Phaedra after successful delivery of the serum.

DR. BEVERLY CRUSHER was fortunately in the sickbay when it happened.

Of course, her monitors and telltales would have alerted her immediately, and since she was never terribly far from her place of duty, she could have returned there quickly enough. Nonetheless, she was glad she was actually around when the alarm sounded.

She'd been monitoring the readings on Dr.

Adrienne Tillstrom, wondering if there was something more she could do. With the help of her machines, she'd repaired the cellular damage in the brain, and done an excellent job on the skull fracture and skin as well. The doctor was healing up quite nicely, physically. However, even all the technology and knowledge available at her fingertips didn't seem to be able to pull her out of the coma. It was almost as though she wanted to stay there, as though she'd pulled the blanket of her neurons over herself and had settled in for a long sleep of escape. Nothing could nudge her; not one of the EEG descendants could peer down into the dense folds of her gray matter and suggest that she might come up and say hello.

It was frustrating, particularly since it was apparent that Jean-Luc was troubled. Not just about not knowing what had happened back on Phaedra, but about Adrienne Tillstrom. Oh, he didn't say anything, and goodness knew you couldn't get even a facial expression of concern out of the man, but Beverly knew him well enough not to need Troi in the matter. Nor did she need to sense the concern. The captain knew that he'd be contacted the *instant* there was any recovery of consciousness, and he'd not only checked in several times over the comm, he'd actually come down and *looked* at the patient.

"She was a friend of yours, Jean-Luc," Beverly had finally said, breaking the silence in her usual forward and confrontational way.

"Yes," said Jean-Luc, ever articulate on matters of the heart.

"Long ago?"

"Hmmmm? Oh, yes. Before her son was born, that was for certain."

"Would you like to talk about it?"

He had turned to her and speared her with those hazel eyes. "No."

"The captain of a Galaxy-class vessel surely has more important things to worry about than personal memories. And I've always found it therapeutic to discuss troubling memories with a friend."

Picard was thoughtful for a moment and then spoke. "Doctor Tillstrom is a friend of long ago, with whom I had lost contact. Suffice it to say that I would very much like to renew acquaintance, particularly in light of recent events."

"Yes, of course."

"Orders remain as before, if you please," said Picard. He marched out, and the door opened. He stopped in middeparture, turned, and said, "I thank you for your concern, though, Beverly. As usual."

She shrugged. "I can't help myself, Jean-Luc."

He nodded, straightened up, stiffened, and walked out, carrying his thoughts tucked safely away to himself. Oh, she'd find out soon enough, Beverly Crusher knew . . . but it was galling to her that she had to wait . . . and even more galling that she cared so much.

When Mikal Tillstrom woke up, it wasn't just the chime that Dr. Crusher heard. It was Mikal Tillstrom as well, calling out the moment he awakened.

". . . help . . .!"

Then all sorts of instruments went off, causing a cacophony. Beverly Crusher hurried over. Fortunately, the restraining force straps had also been triggered, so that Mikal had not fallen off the biobed. His eyes were wide open, though, and he lay inert, looking to be a threat to no one but himself. . . . His blood pressure had risen incredibly.

She quickly injected him with a sedative and touched a vernier on the special restraining field on the biobed to loosen the bonds a bit. She didn't really expect any kind of violence, but Worf had insisted that she be cautious.

The security officer stationed at the sickbay charged in, phaser at ready. She was a young pale woman, lithe but well built, with short blond hair. Beverly had been uncomfortable with her at first; she reminded her a good deal of Tasha Yar. But as she got to know Metrina—Metrina Harcourt was her name—she reminded her less and less of the ill-fated and much missed security chief of the *Enterprise*.

"Are they awake?" she asked.

"The man seems to be. But he hasn't come after me with an ax yet."

The tenseness melted from Harcourt's face. However, she kept her hand on her phaser as she stepped over to the biobed. Mikal Tillstrom's eyelids were fluttering. His head turned back and forth, and he was moaning softly, as though still mired in some nightmare. "I hope he's all right," said Metrina. Beverly had noticed before that the young security officer had been studying the man's face as though she found it interesting. And she'd asked an inordinate number of questions about Mikal Tillstrom, showing quite a bit of concern for a person merely stationed to make sure that the survivors didn't run amok upon awakening.

Beverly nodded, glancing at the bio-readouts. What they were showing was not only good life signs, but a marked improvement in just about everything. Except for a curious anomaly in the brain readings, which she'd have to check in detail later. Nothing to be alarmed about—it was in the neocortex as opposed to the R-complex and brain stem, which might indicate violent or destructive tendencies. "He's quite healthy and he's coming out of his coma."

"Obviously."

"Do me a favor, would you, Midshipman?" said Beverly, making some adjustments in the cortex-stim mechanism. "Notify the captain. I've got my hands full, and he wants to know immediately about any significant change. I'd say this is significant, wouldn't you?"

"Yes, Doctor." The young security officer stepped away two meters so as not to interfere with anything, and then hit her comm button with her hand, delivering the message as ordered.

Meanwhile, Mikal Tillstrom was indeed becoming conscious. The fluttering of the eyes stopped, and he opened them fully. He gasped and started to get up with a moan. Terror flooded his face. The restraint kept him back, but he did not struggle against it. Instead, the sedative seemed to overtake him, and he relaxed, falling back into the headrest, a clear lack of understanding showing on his face as he began to take in the surroundings.

"Where . . . where . . . am . . . I?" he said. But it wasn't so much a question to anyone as a statement of confusion.

"You're safe, Mikal," said Beverly Crusher. "You're safe aboard the USS *Enterprise*. And right now, you're in my care. I'm the doctor here."

His eyes turned her way, blearily. "Doctor . . . numb . . ."

"Yes, you might feel a little numb for a while. I've given you something to relieve your pain. You've had some kind of accident, from the looks of it, but you're going to be all right. I promise." She spoke with quiet authority, imbuing her words with just the right amount of gentleness to comfort. She knew she had a good bedside manner, a requisite of a doctor even in the twenty-fourth century . . . and she used it as skillfully as she used any of her machines. "Just relax and don't worry."

His eyes were still full of apprehension and chaos. They were disbelieving, as though not only did his surroundings not register, but nothing was right. "Epsilon . . . station . . . work . . ." He looked over at her again. "Mother?"

"Your mother is here as well, Mikal. She's asleep" —best not to be too truthful immediately—"and she'll be fine, I'm sure." She paused a bit, looking down at him, searching his face and his eyes as though for answers. None seemed forthcoming, and so she asked the question. "Mikal . . . what happened on Epsilon Station?"

The young man opened his mouth to answer and then suddenly turned totally puzzled. "I don't . . . I don't remember," he said. He seemed extremely upset and agitated by this revelation. "Why can't I *remember!*"

"Shhh. Shhh! You'll remember soon enough," said Beverly. She'd suspected this might happen. It didn't make the situation any easier, but she'd been prepared for memory loss. The neocortex stuff. There was no doubt some sort of damage there. . . . "You're safe now, you're with friends, and that's what's important, isn't it?"

"But I should remember. . . . I *have* to remember!" he said, his brown eyes ablaze with earnestness.

"Why do you have to remember now, Mikal? Can't you just let it go for the moment, be glad that you're alive?"

"I'm . . . alive," he repeated, eyes glassy. "I'm . . . alive." A long pause. "Is . . . this . . . life?"

"What do you mean . . . ?"

"Life." The young man's mouth twitched, and his dark, troubled eyes traveled to his hands, which he held up, wiggling the fingers. "Life . . . it's so very . . . strange, Doctor. It's not what we think it is, is it? Not at all! We're so wrong! So very *wrong!*" He moaned, and then his face changed. "Why am I saying that, Doctor?"

"I was about to ask you the same question, Mikal. But please . . . can you just put all this thinking off for a moment? . . . Speaking, too, if you like. We'll work it all out later. Let's just take things one step at a time!"

Metrina stepped back alongside Beverly, a good pace away in deference. "The captain's on his way."

"Who . . . who are you?" demanded Mikal.

"Ensign Metrina Harcourt, security," said the woman, working hard to keep her voice hard and stern.

"That's . . . that's a *phaser* you have there, isn't it?"

"That is correct."

"A security person . . . a phaser . . . these restraints. Have I done something wrong, Doctor?" asked Mikal beseechingly. The pain and anguish in his voice made Beverly's heart go out to him, and she was about to answer when Midshipman Harcourt spoke up first.

"Just precautions, Mikal . . . I mean, Mr. Tillstrom. Ordered by the captain . . . and . . . oh . . . I have spoken out of turn. It's not my place."

"That's all right. I like you. You have a nice face, nice eyes . . . and a beautiful voice."

It was clear that Ensign Harcourt's presence, phaser or no, had calmed her patient rather than inordinately alarming him.

"Well, it appears we have a new Florence Nightingale in our midst. Ensign, it looks as though our guest would like to talk with you a moment while waiting for the captain to welcome him," she said without any rancor. "Carry on. I've got to attend to something else anyway."

There was a new diagnostic report coming through on the readout display, fruit of the excellent work the medical sensor array was doing above Mikal. Hopefully it would have some of the information on his cerebral activity that would clue her in to what was going on inside his skull.

"Oh," said Harcourt. "Yes . . . of course." She turned to the patient. "Hello, how are you?"

Beverly listened to them as they talked.

"They say my name is Mikal. Mikal Tillstrom. I'm afraid I've got a touch of amnesia."

Metrina smiled faintly. "Well, at least you remember the name of your problem."

"It's term. Yes . . . I guess so. I seem to have a vocabulary, though its rather patchy. I remember something about working with my mother . . . at a science station on a rather odd planet. My mother . . . Where is she?"

"She's sequestered behind that curtain over there."

"Why?"

"Privacy, I guess."

"May I go see her?"

"You'll have to ask Dr. Crusher about that. For right now, why don't we just talk?"

"You know, I don't remember if I had a wife or a girlfriend or anything," stated the young man quite baldly.

"You seem to be a little too young to be married."

"It does seem unlikely, doesn't it? At any rate, I know I like women."

"I'm glad." She smiled. "That happens to be what I am."

"I hope we can be friends. That is, if I get things straight in this head of mine . . . And, Doctor . . . you know, Doctor . . . really, not only am I amnesiac . . . I'm beginning to get a headache. That pain reliever, I think, is wearing off."

"Just a moment," said Beverly. She was peering down at the schematic of the young man's brain. A portion seemed to pulse with its own peculiar rhythm. How odd . . . something that should definitely be examined more carefully, especially the area in the frontal lobe where the engram-circuit was. The spectrography showed a deep orange, indicated a greater temperature in that area. That could be causing an irritation in the blood-brain barrier. . . .

She forced herself away from the examination and back to the needs of her patient.

Just as she approached, Captain Jean-Luc Picard walked into the sickbay.

It was the boy who'd awakened, not Adrienne.

Hard not to show a reaction of disappointment, but Picard managed to pull it off. The ensign had only mentioned that one of the patients was awake, and of course, the captain realized that it was much more likely for Mikal to recover first.

He walked up and nodded curtly to the young man, forcing a mild smile. "Welcome aboard the USS *Enterprise.* I hope the doctor is seeing to your needs, Mr. Tillstrom."

"Thanks, Captain." Mikal tried to lift a hand, but the restraining field caught it.

"Doctor, I don't think the restraint seems to be in order."

"No, of course not," Beverly replied. She turned off a switch, and Mikal immediately thrust out his hand. Picard could do nothing but shake it.

Mikal said, "Once Dr. Crusher gets rid of this headache, heals my mother, and gets my memory back, I think I'll just be peachy keen." He grinned at Crusher. "I'm afraid I had a bit of a shaky awakening, and I'm still not entirely steady. Still, I seem to have made a friend."

The security officer seemed to stiffen. She looked away, her face reddening. Picard felt amusement, but of course, he didn't show it.

"Actually, Captain," Beverly said, "I attribute

Mikal's quick readjustment, considering his state upon awakening, to the ensign."

"Absolutely!" Mikal shook his head sadly. "Although I do wish I'd get *something* back. I've got a feeling it's pretty important."

Picard nodded. "Indeed. You remember nothing of the events at Beta Epsilon . . . ?"

The young man turned grim. "It was something bad, wasn't it? I can feel part of me pushing it away. . . ." He paused and then looked up directly at the starship captain with a penetrating gaze. "You're going to tell me anyway, aren't you?"

Picard opened his mouth and then caught himself. He looked over to Dr. Crusher for guidance. She nodded, but her eyes said, be gentle. He tugged at his uniform and stared straight at the man, his gaze filled with unflinching honesty. He told him the events as he had experienced them, from the reception of the emergency beacon to the rescue of the survivors. He saw the pain in Mikal Tillstrom's eyes, but the young man took the news straight and without comment.

"So, as you can surmise, we had hoped that you might be able to help us in discovering what happened at the station. . . . We found only two dead, and the rest of your colleagues are missing."

"Awful!"

"Yes. Not a shred of memory on the subject?"

"No, I'm afraid not."

"It was you, we believe, who tripped the emergency beacon."

"That could well be, Captain, but I don't remember it."

"Do you remember any of your life before the time on the station?" said the captain, probing.

"Yes. But not so well the time approaching . . . Captain, if you'll just give me time . . ."

"Of course. Nonetheless, I had to ask these questions. How's that headache?"

"Better, sir."

Beverly stepped forward. "I think that Mikal should have some rest now—"

"Captain Picard!" said Tillstrom. "Captain Jean-Luc Picard!" As though he'd just had a revelation.

"Yes." Prompting him. Hope rose up in Picard. . . . Maybe the memory was flooding back.

"My mother . . . my mother spoke of you!"

Beverly looked at Picard. He felt a little odd, but was happy that at least something new was filtering into the young man's head. It boded well. "Did she? Well, I hope?"

"Oh, yes, sir! You were friends, I think, before she met my father."

"That is . . . correct."

"The Star Wanderer, she called you. Jean-Luc Picaresque!"

Beverly chuckled. "What a name!"

Picard smiled ruefully, despite himself. "Yes, we were friends. We lost . . . touch. I am sorry. But I look forward to her regaining consciousness, and not just for information. It will be good to renew our friendship again."

"Well, I must say, disoriented as I am . . . I feel as though I'm in good hands. Thanks for rescuing me, sir. And thank you on behalf of my mother."

Beverly said, "I'm sure she'll be able to do that soon. Now why don't you get some rest, or that headache is going to come back."

"You won't forget our date, will you, Mikal?" said Metrina.

"I'll remember it as soon as you're off duty."

She smiled warmly. "I'll let you know."

The security officer was dismissed, and after Beverly saw to her newly awakened patient's comfort, she took Picard aside. "Can you come into my office? I want to show you something."

Dr. Crusher sat him down and swiveled the computer monitor so that he could see it. Her hands played over a control panel calling up the scan of Mikal Tillstrom's head.

She pointed. "Are you familiar with these?"

"That would be the engram-circuit you mentioned earlier. I have heard of them, of course."

"Engram-circuits are essentially ROM chips developed for implantation in the human brain. They augment the intelligence, but mostly they hold and filter in an immense amount of data. They can only be used with special permission of Federation Medical and Political because they can easily be abused."

"Yes, we studied the situation that occurred on Carstairs II. The colony that controlled much of their population with the things."

"Precisely. Some of the more tyrannical political groups had been secretly discussing utilizing them to enslave whole races."

"And yet the technology involved led to Geordi being able to see."

"Technology in itself is never bad. It is the applications. In any event, I think it is safe to say that this one was not implanted in Mikal to hurt him. Here's a close-up." She stepped up the image. "Can you read that?"

"Manufactured by Digital Bio-Ap, it would seem."

"You recognize the symbol."

"Of course. I daresay Geordi's got that symbol on his implants as well. Digital Bio-Ap is purely scientific applications and a respected company."

"Yes. It's my guess that Dr. Tillstrom wanted to bring her son along as an assistant on this mission, but cut through the necessary education involved by having him implanted. I'd bet that the information on that chip is purely scientific—geology, what have you."

"Why are you showing this to me, Dr. Crusher?"

"Two reasons. It seems to still be working. The batteries are operational. But Mikal doesn't seem to be able to access it. Look here, Jean-Luc." She showed him a picture of the brain. "Scar tissue."

"Yes. So?"

"Modern medical technology uses methods that generally preclude scarring. This, sir, shouldn't be here."

"Maybe there was a complication and the implant had to be adjusted."

"There are a lot of possibilities, sir. But let me also point this out. . . . The sensor array was able to weigh the circuit. It's about a gram heavier than it should be, according to our records. I don't know what this means, and I'm not necessarily alarmed. But I think it's something that bears scrutiny."

Picard considered this for a moment. "You are so ordered . . . and perhaps it is to the good that our young charge has shown an interest in Ensign Harcourt."

"Ah, yes. Though I hesitate to place spying in the middle of a blooming romance."

Picard shook his head impatiently. "Nonsense. Merely inform the ensign that you are concerned about Mikal, and the reasons you are concerned. She will come to you of her own accord if anything unusual happens. Now, if that is all, there are other matters that need to be attended to." He got up to go, but then a thought struck him. "Beverly . . . Dr. Tillstrom. Any further prognosis?"

"No. I'll let you know the moment I find out."

"Yes. Of course. Thank you."

He wished he hadn't asked that. Of course she'd let him know. Redundancy was something that he usually avoided. Yet he could not deny the eagerness with which he wanted to solve this puzzle and help his guests.

He really wanted to talk with Adrienne.

Interlude

It was not awake yet, and yet it knew.

It was not aware, not conscious, and yet it was beyond the Barrier, and its molecules were freed from their chains.

Its body was dispersed. To the winds between the suns, it seemed. And yet with instinct below instinct, quantum interactionics took place. Energies on a subatomic level shuddered through its various formations, kicking up to first atomic and then molecular level. The ladders, the lattices, the configurations . . . they rumbled and they spread, from the central matrices out, out, on wings of crystal.

It sensed the Holy.

First it created cohesion amongst its parts and then it adhered to whatever it was closest to, integrating itself, assuming that form, and yet also subsuming that form.

For it also sensed a Danger, here in the New Sacred.

It was not awake, it was not aware . . . but it knew it would be. . . .

Soon. Very soon . . .

Chapter Seven

DATA SAT ON A CHAIR beside Penelope Winthrop, watching the volleyball game.

Today it wasn't on a beach, it was in a regulation gym, and the players meant business. They wore their uniforms and kneepads, and there weren't as many cheers and as much laughter as when the game had been played on the beach. He had to admit that watching the earnestness with which the players attacked this sport was fascinating. And he also found that through using statistical averages, he could often predict probabilities in the scoring. More complex and not as exact a science as baseball, true—but a worthy effort for at least part of his multileveled mind.

The other, more conscious, aspect of him was engaged in a conversation with Penelope.

"You seem to be so interested in the game, Data."

"I am indeed, Penelope. Human games of all varieties fascinate me. Have I told you about the time I played baseball on the holodeck . . . ?"

"Baseball? Data, isn't that an ancient sport? Nobody plays baseball anymore. . . ."

"I do not believe it is much older than volleyball," stated Data. "But it really doesn't make much difference. There are many different sports involving balls in a structure of rules. They all most certainly have their peculiarities, and yet they all are a combination of skill, intelligence, athletic prowess, and, in cases involving more than just two players, teamwork. My tenure aboard the *Enterprise* has certainly taught me the importance of the latter, and I applaud the psychological practice that this encapsulates." He cocked his head, following a particularly effective spiking maneuver perpetrated by Geordi La Forge. "I am also assured it is fun. Sports are something you might try, Penelope."

"Me? I have absolutely *no* reflexes, Data."

"Hand-eye coordination is essential, of course. However, that is a human ability that, according to studies, is perfectible. I think that Counselor Troi would approve of any sports activity. I know for a fact from my studies of the psychology of male/female relationships that couples engaged in sporting events have a mutual conversation topic as well as nonthreatening play."

"Data, I think—"

Data, though, remembering that one of Penelope's big problems was nervousness around the opposite sex, decided that this lecture was just the thing she needed.

"This, I believe, is a phenomenon called 'breaking the ice.' It allows relaxation and easy flow of conversation, allowing the pheromone accumulation and natural nonvocal intercommunications called 'body language' to strike up the necessary ease of interplay. This frees either the male or female to make the initial move for intimacy. A successful kiss, at one point or another, depending upon the moral code of the osculators, will no doubt lead to sexual intercourse as well as physical and emotional fulfillment."

He looked over to Penelope, expecting an expression of thanks for this elucidation. Instead he found a teenager blushing furiously. "Data," she said. "I *do* know the facts of life, okay? I'm not ignorant, I'm just a little mental!"

"If I have caused embarrassment, I am sorry. But do not be embarrassed. I am your friend, Penelope."

"Yes, Data. But you're a *male.*"

"I am made to resemble a fully functional male human. And yet, I should remind you, I am not human."

"I know, I know," she laughed. "But you're sweet and gentle and unthreatening and brilliant. You're too much of a fantasy to be a *real* man."

"Oh, but I am no fantasy, I am quite real. . . . I am simply not . . . a man. I am an android. That is, derived of man and resembling man."

"Come on, Data. You're as much a man as I am," asserted Penelope.

Data gave her a quizzical look. "You are a girl . . . I mean, pardon me . . . a woman!"

"Precisely, Data. Derived of man and resembling man . . . or actually, you know, man is derived of woman and resembling woman, too. So I guess that makes us both forms of humankind."

"No. You stretch the definition. I should like to be human, but I am not. I have neither flesh nor blood . . . but most importantly, I am not equipped with an analogue endocrine system tied in to my reasoning process."

"You're more human than some people I've met, Data," said Penelope, looking on him with great affection.

"You are confused by the devices I utilize to blend

in with humanity on a social as well as intellectual level. Do not mistake me . . . I should like to be human. However, I cannot lie to you, a friend, and to have you believe I am would be just that. A lie."

"Data, Data, you're taking this all too *seriously.* I know!" She leaned over and hugged him.

Data's response was even. "It is a serious subject, is it not?"

"I'm just making a philosophic point, I guess. There are so many different varieties of mankind. Can't you see that you might consider yourself as just that? A variation on a theme?"

"An interesting theorem," stated Data flatly. "Perhaps we might carry on our philosophical dialogue at a later time . . . and watch the volleyball game now."

"You're right. I'm sorry. That's what we're here for, isn't it?" She subdued herself slightly, and that was that.

They turned their attention back to the game.

The team that would represent the *Enterprise* in the Federation competition had already been winnowed down to its core members, and this was one of a series of games to not only practice the individual players but to perfect their collective force as a team. To play against them, the players who had been cut from the final team had formed their own team—and were bent on proving themselves. They were playing very well indeed, noted Data. The score was eight all. Perhaps Team B, as it had been dubbed, would like to defeat Team A, he thought, and use such to argue that *they* should go on and represent the *Enterprise.*

Team A included Riker and Geordi, while Team B included Worf and Troi. They were friends, and yet now they played as though they were enemies. Human competition was something that Data knew he needed to study more to comprehend.

He and Penelope watched for a while quietly.

Curiously, she seemed to be rooting for Team B. Data inquired about her behavior.

"I like to cheer for the underdog, Data."

"Underdog?" Data accessed his banks. "Ah! A person or group in an inferior or subordinate position. I am confused, Penelope. You wish for the representative team of the *Enterprise* to win the competition in the games. Team A has already been selected for that. Why do you wish for Team B to defeat them, thus perhaps bruising their group spirit?"

"I don't know, Data. Do I have to explain everything? Besides, my cheering can't hurt Team A's chances, can it?"

"An argument can be made for crowd collective conscious society and its effects on the outcome of a competition. Perhaps if you seriously want Team A to go on and win the games, you should cheer for them now."

"Data, let me ask you a question. Do you want the *Enterprise* to win the games?"

"Hmmm. I have never considered that. Let me do so." It took a full second or so. "I have concluded that it makes no real difference who wins. However, given that, and since I am a loyal member of the *Enterprise,* it is my 'duty' to desire our team to achieve victory."

"You'd be an excellent volleyball player, Data. Why don't you play?"

"My skills and abilities would be an unfair addition in competitive sports. Therefore, I am not qualified to play."

"Too bad. But if you want Team A to win now . . . why are you just sitting like a bump on a log? Why aren't you rooting from them?"

"Rooting?"

"You know . . . cheering. Becoming part of the crowd psychology that might help them win."

Data considered this. "You are right." He turned

and called out. "Go, Team A. Go!" He turned back to Penelope. "Is that sufficient, or should I do a search for more complex cheers?"

"No, Data," Penelope said, struggling to keep a straight face. "I think we should start organizing a cheerleading team. I think we would both look quite good in pom-poms."

"Ah . . . you are teasing me. I see. Quite . . . funny!"

"You picked up on the teasing part, Data. You must get teased a lot. Doesn't it bother you? . . . no, wait, don't tell me. You aren't bothered because you don't have emotions."

"That is correct."

"And it doesn't bother you that you're so predict-able?"

"The correct answer to the obvious is generally predictable."

"You know, Data, the thing is . . . if that's the truth . . . then why aren't you boring?"

Data considered this. "I assume that is a compli-ment. Thank you."

"Oh, let's just watch the game!" she said, cheerfully frustrated.

"Very well."

Team A defeated Team B, to the obvious chagrin of Worf, who demanded an immediate rematch. Since there was sufficient time, a rematch was agreed to and begun.

It was just after Will Riker served the first ball of this match, pounding it into the opposite court with extreme authority and panache, that Metrina Har-court came in, with Mikal Tillstrom by her side.

Data was surprised enough to see that Mikal was out of his biobed, let alone well enough to attend a sporting event. He looked well, but his head was partially shaved.

Data noted this and was about to turn his full attention back to the game, considering the possibility of accessing some banks for some traditional cheers that might aid the appropriate team in their endeavors, when he was approached by Ensign Harcourt.

"Data, I'm sorry to bother you, but my friend here would really like to meet you." Metrina Harcourt was not in uniform, and she looked a little ill at ease, as though her companion had insisted that she introduce them, rather than merely requested. Data knew Ensign Harcourt only slightly, because she had requested his help once in a science class project she was participating in through a university extension course on the *Enterprise*.

"Yes. I'm terribly sorry to be so forward . . . but you know, it's really funny . . ." The affable character stepped up to him and shook the android's hand firmly, then let it go. "I don't remember much of my past, and I don't remember anything of my time at that science station. . . . You do know what I'm talking about, don't you, Data?"

"Yes, I know about you, Mikal Tillstrom," responded Data.

"Anyway, I did remember something about the *Enterprise* . . . and that was you, Data. I remember that the *Enterprise* had, as an officer, the only known android. . . . I studied what there was to study about you, Data, and I really *had* to meet you as soon as possible."

Data slanted his head, quizzically. "Why?"

"Admiration! You're really quite splendid. In the flesh . . . or pseudoflesh . . . And your mind! What a splendid creation. But I'm sorry, I'm being quite rude, I know. . . . I just thought that, well, you might help me."

"Help you?"

"Yes. Recover my memory. So that I can figure out what happened on that station."

"I have already done some work on the matter. I would be happy to do anything I can to help you, Mikal Tillstrom."

"Data, may we sit down and watch the game? Say, these seats aren't taken, are they?" he asked Penelope, smiling.

"No," said Penelope in a meek voice.

"Hi. I'm Mikal Tillstrom." He took her hand and gave it a warm shake. "This is my friend Metrina Harcourt."

Penelope, Data noted, was looking at Mikal as though he were some kind of cosmic revelation. "Hello," she said quietly.

"What a lovely friend you have here, Data," said Mikal. "Have a seat, Metrina, and let's watch the game."

They sat in silence for a moment. Penelope was still looking in an odd way at Mikal. Data was concerned. He recognized the potential for psychological difficulty in his young friend, and he wasn't entirely sure that he could handle any adverse reactions she might have. Nonetheless, there was nothing he could do at the moment, and he reasoned that he would best serve Penelope by remaining observant and ready.

Suddenly, after a few minutes of watching the game, Mikal exploded into a frenzy of questions about this game he was watching. What was its name? Who was playing? What did it mean? What were the rules and what were the dynamics? And most of all, what was the reason that glowering Klingon was bellowing so much?

Some of these questions, he asked to his date, some to Data, but some he directed at Penelope. He looked at the young girl with obvious interest.

At first, Data thought for certain that Penelope was going to retreat into a fugue or something similar. The ingredients for this catastrophe were all too apparent. A handsome young man, a social situation, the clear nervousness and sexual interest in Penelope's mannerisms. And yet, somehow, such was the prestidigitation of Mikal Tillstrom's body language and verbal abilities that he kept the young lady so interested that he somehow drew her out of herself, and kept her from going into her usual retreat. Data recognized that he was not qualified to deal with the delicate situation—or the consequences of this kind of excitement in a previously wounded psyche.

However, nothing happened.

Nothing negative, in any case. Data watched carefully, noting the way that Penelope reacted. There was no wandering of the eyes, no loss of focus. She seemed centered directly on this animated, absorbed, and clearly lively young man. Data, because of his nature, examined the other data available from the situation. This youth's voice was mellifluous, yet deep, owning a profoundly comforting timbre. His face was smooth, the lines of his nose and chin would be aesthetically pleasing to females, particularly in conjunction with the dark brown eyes. Data also detected a rich and complex texture of pheromones. Not jolting at all, but quite subtle. Finally, his movements, though expressive, were not wild and bullying but rather soft and illustrative. A distinctive young man indeed. Worthy, it would seem, of a young female's attention. And Penelope was responding. Doubtless her estrogen levels were presently elevating. He detected female pheromones reaching out already.

Fascinating.

The game concluded. Team A indeed proved worthy of its ranking. They beat Team B by a full five points. Worf was clearly upset. However, afterward

Data noticed that Commander Riker made sure to go over and congratulate the Klingon for the quality of his play.

"It is not, after all, a Klingon game, Worf. I doubt there's much honor in it, anyway," said the smiling Number One.

"Someday I shall challenge you to a game of Klarg!" said Worf, eyes blazing.

"Let me get through the volleyball championships before you decimate me, eh?" Riker clapped his friend on the shoulder. "I'm going to need every bit of my considerable ego to properly captain this team . . . so I shall need your cooperation and consideration."

Worf grumbled in his distinctive way, but agreed this was the best course.

Data turned his attention back to the renewed conversation around him.

"What a fascinating game. I hope that somehow I'll be able to see the Federation games you're talking about," Mikal commented.

Ensign Harcourt, who had not said much up to that point, nodded. "So do I. I just hope that you haven't overexcited yourself here. The doctor will never forgive me if I bring you back in worse shape than when you left.

"Anything's got to be an improvement over the way I was before. You've done a marvelous job, Metrina . . . an absolutely terrific job." He turned to Data and Penelope. "Don't you think she's done a wonderful job? See this smile?" He grinned and pointed at the grin. "This delightful lady put this there. And I shall always be in her debt."

"Mikal, I really think I should take you back. Besides, I have a shift that starts very soon."

"Ah. Duty calls. Well, Data, I can't tell you how satisfying it's been to finally meet you. And Penelope." He turned his full attention on the girl. He took her hand and kissed it. "Charmed! Absolutely charmed. I hope I'll be seeing you around the ship. What was it that Miranda said in *The Tempest?* 'Ah, brave new world, that hast such beauties in it!'"

"I believe that Shakespearean quote read, 'O brave new world, that hast such *people* in it,'" Data corrected.

"After being around Metrina and Penelope, can you blame me for my mistake? See you later!" He strode off arm in arm with Metrina, but he cast a lingering glance back toward Penelope.

Penelope stood, frozen, for several moments after they left, staring after the young man.

"Well, Penelope, I believe that I should embark on my analysis of planetary samples."

Penelope grabbed him firmly by the arm. "Data. You've got to help me."

Data blinked. "Are you ill? Shall I call for the doctor? Do you need Counselor Troi?"

"No, no. I'm fine, Data. I've never felt better in my life!" Looking a little stunned, she sat back down in her chair. "Oh, I wish I were more clever!"

Data was confused. "But you *are* clever, Penelope. You are a very intelligent person."

"Not really. I'm just a lump. He was so nice. . . . He says I'm beautiful. But I'm not really. He was just being nice."

"You seem well within the human aesthetic parameters for 'beauty.'"

"You're sweet, Data." She sighed sadly.

"What is it you wish me to do, Penelope?"

"Can't you guess? You saw my pathetic performance back there."

"Performance?"

"Well, at least I didn't zone out, Data. He was just so . . . so . . . wonderful!"

Data nodded. "Ah. I perceived your . . . attraction. Excellent. Troi will be pleased."

"Deanna mustn't hear a *word* of this. Not now, anyway!"

"But why not!"

"She won't let me be around him. She might think it'll cause a relapse."

"That's very doubtful."

"You *mustn't* tell her. That's part of the help I need, Data."

"Very well. If you insist."

"No no. You're not getting off the hook that easily. You *are* my friend, aren't you?"

"Certainly."

"Friends do favors for friends, right?"

"I believe that is part of the description of a friend," Data readily agreed.

"Data, you've got to help me talk to Mikal Tillstrom! You've got to make him see me as desirable . . . I want to be *around* him."

She looked indecisive for a moment.

"Data, I don't know if Troi's told you this or not, but I've got . . . special powers."

Data nodded. "Yes. Psi powers. An inclination toward telepathy and a range of other things, so far unclassified. However, you keep them tightly wrapped and closeted."

She bit her lip, pushing through her embarrassment. "Something in him touched me. When I was a child I once was angry at a man who tried to hurt me. I reach out, reached into his mind . . . and twisted. He was unconscious for days. It scared me so much I've kept this part of myself very tightly contained. But with Mikal . . . I couldn't help but reach out and touch him. Inside. It was as though I *belonged* there, in his mind! Of course when I realized what I was doing I withdrew immediately. I don't wish to intrude. The mind should be a private place. But still, I want to *know* him better, Data!" She took a deep breath. "But I'm so afraid he's not really going to like me if he sees me get all . . . all, you know . . . tangled in my head. He'll think I'm a freak or something."

"You're not a freak."

"Everybody else on this ship is so well adjusted! Everybody is so perfect. Except for me! He's bound to find *lots* of much more wonderful women here to be around. He'll forget all about me!"

"How do you propose that I aid you in this endeavor?" Data said.

"You'll help me! You'll *do* it? Oh, Data, what a good friend you are."

Data found himself in an embrace.

"I appreciate your show of appreciation," stated Data. "But you still have not told me what you want me to do!"

Penelope looked thoughtful for a moment. "I haven't quite figured that out yet, Data. But I know you're going to be a great help. I just *know* it!"

Data felt nothing, of course.

However, he discerned a great probability for potential trouble in this matter in the days ahead.

Interlude

It was not awake, it was not aware, but it planned.

Its Time was not now, but its Space was in preparation, and the molecular instincts and chemical energies moved like a tide drawn by an invisible moon.

Its pieces settled, selecting the closest appropriate material to adhere to and bond with.

In a swarm, the part of it that had been flung from the Enterprise *spread in a patina all across the underside of the Saucer Module, and down the fuselage of the Battle Section.*

The part of it that had seeped into the cracks and crannies of the shuttlecraft grew faster, penetrating into the shuttle's computer.

The part of it that had been sluiced into the wastewater section adhered to pipes all along the sewage system. With the presence of H_2O and abundance of other needed chemical compounds, it, too, slowly stretched out.

The other parts, the smaller parts, grew as well, though more slowly.

In the second day of its presence on this new source of potentiality, the Thing That Was Not Aware had sufficient networks built up to sense the powerful engines of the starship.

Tentatively the growing stuff, undetected as yet because of its thinness and camouflaged state, reached out for the mighty pulse of the engines.

Soon, it knew unconsciously, it would Be.

And then it could reject the bad life it sensed all around it like toxin, slough it all off. . . .

And grow . . .

And grow . . .

Chapter Eight

"So, Doctor. What's the prognosis? You can tell me the whole truth. Why am I getting these headaches?"

Beverly Crusher studied Mikal Tillstrom for a moment. "You're still feeling pain?"

"No, but I would if you weren't giving me medicine. Which means that you're covering over the effects of something rather than healing the cause. Am I wrong, Doctor?"

He was bright, there was no question about that. Slightly annoying, too, which made it all the harder to bear. He reminded her a little bit too much of her son, Wesley, for comfort. He had that astounding combination of know-it-allness and naïveté that used to drive her up the wall with Wes when he was on the *Enterprise*. Now, of course, she missed him quite a bit.

Still, this was a most definitely different personality here—and most definitely some other mother's child.

"No. You aren't wrong."

"Could you tell me something about it? . . . I think I might understand."

It wasn't a bad idea, really. Besides, she was meaning to ask anyway. . . . He might have some memory in that area now. Memory was such a peculiar thing, and when it returned, it could come back in dribs and drabs—or all in a rush. There might be a drab waiting around now to be discovered. A drab that could eventually turn into a rush.

"Mikal. Have you remembered anything about the station?"

"No, Doctor, I'm afraid not."

"How about your life before the station?"

The young man concentrated on that a moment. Beverly had noticed that below that glib and happy outward persona that he'd been using to deal with others, there was a confused and wretched man, and some of that showed through now as Mikal let down some of his facade.

No. Strike that. Confused *boy*. Beverly felt like taking him in her arms and comforting him. But of course, she did not.

"Not too much, Doctor. Vague things. Stuff about my mother, mostly. Our life at Stanford University, on Earth."

"Well, that's something, isn't it? Mikal, I'm convinced that these headaches are caused by something that's been added to your neocortex. Frontal lobe. Are you familiar with these terms?"

"My brain. Right." He did not look alarmed, he just looked extremely interested.

"Yes, of course. Have you heard of a digital engram-circuit before, Mikal?"

"You mean I've got one of those in me?"

"You know what they are?"

"Sure. I remember some people getting them in Stanford. That's a tough school, Doctor. You need every aid you can get. . . . Engram-circuits are quasi-legal on Earth. You've got to have the right strings pulled in the bureaucracy, or you can get them on the black market. Anyway, they boost your knowledge and intelligence most of the time. . . . Sure, I know what they are." He held his hand up to his head, as though feeling for a bump or a bulge.

"But you don't remember getting one."

"No. Not at Stanford. And not at the station." He suddenly pounded a fist on the arm of the chair. "God! It's so awful not *knowing.*" He rubbed his head again, and then looked up at Beverly, a kind of pleading in his eyes. "You think you should take it out?"

"Mikal, if I don't know why it's there, I'm not going to take it out. It doesn't seem to be life-threatening . . . just oddly active. I think observation would be the best course in this case." She thought about this, almost out loud. "I saw the medical equipment on your base. You had the facilities for the operation. That could explain the scarring."

"What are you talking about, Doctor?"

"I just wonder when and where you had that augmenting circuit placed, Mikal, not just why. That's all."

"You can't analyze the codes and information stored on it?"

"Not indirectly. There would have to be a direct link, and frankly, I don't want to hazard a probe into your brain after your concussion. It could wipe out *more* of your memory. What we can do here is amazing—but there are still limits."

Mikal nodded. "I'll try to remember, Doctor. It's there, somewhere; I can feel it lurking."

"An interesting image, Mikal."

"How's my mother doing?"

"About the same."

"She'd remember. I can't see my mom with amnesia. She remembered everything."

"Well, there's something you definitely remember, Mikal."

"Why, yes it is . . . and I don't think I remembered it before. That's an improvement, isn't it, Doctor?"

"Yes, it is." She got up to attend to something, and that was when she noticed Data standing at the entrance of the sickbay, watching them and looking painfully tentative. "Data. How long have you been there?" she said, not able to hide her surprise.

"Two minutes and sixteen seconds, Doctor. I did not wish to interrupt what I perceived as an important conversation." He paused, as though considering the matter further. "May I speak to Mikal Tillstrom, please?"

Mikal, looking excited, bounded out of the room, eyes alight at the sight of the android. "Data! So good to see you. Have you come up with something in your researches?"

Data, Beverly noted amusedly, was clearly taken aback by Mikal's enthusiasm. "Nothing of relevance, I think." He looked directly at Beverly as though for help—but since she didn't know why he'd come, there was nothing that she could do or say. She gave him a leading sort of expression, but Data didn't pick up on it.

"That's too bad. Anyway, it looks like we've got something in common."

"Oh?"

Mikal tapped his forehead. "I've got computer circuits in my head."

"Oh? You mean the engram-circuit. Yes, of course. Are you able to access it now?"

"No. That's the funny thing."

"And yet it seems to be working, from my discussions with Dr. Crusher."

Beverly turned to Mikal. "I consulted with Data on the subject."

"Hey, I think that's great. Like I told you, one of the things I remember is a huge regard and interest I had in the android aboard the *Enterprise.*"

"I am available for consultation at any time." He paused, as though shifting gears in his head. "Although that is not why I am here——"

"So go ahead, Data! I'm all ears."

"You must pardon me. I am not trained in these things, and these kinds of discretionary matters are hardly second nature for an android. For example, I could never be a diplomat. There are far too many subtle social nuances and feints involved."

"Well then, just be yourself, Data," said Beverly, "and tell us what you have to say."

"My mission here is in regard to Mikal. I am not sure if you are aware of it, Mikal, but there is a social function this evening in Ten-Forward."

"Our recreational lounge," explained Beverly. "Hmm. Yes, that would be one of our special dances, I believe."

"Yes, and it is my understanding that the Federation Horns, including Commander Riker, will be playing as well," said Data.

"What are you fishing for, Data?" said Beverly, crossing her arms suspiciously.

Data turned to Mikal Tillstrom. "My friend, Penelope Winthrop, whom you met earlier at the volleyball competition, would very much like to talk with you further. She thought that not only would you be entertained by the social function, but that the dance would provide the context to talk further and enjoy one another's company. I might add that I shall be along if you wish to converse with me further."

"Sounds to me like this Penelope Winthrop is asking you out, Mikal!" said Beverly, amused—especially by this business of Data playing John Alden!

Mikal Tillstrom seemed tickled at the thought. "Well! She's a quiet thing, but attractive enough. Can she dance?"

"I believe not," said Data. "However, thanks to Dr. Crusher's excellent instruction, I can and would be happy to step in as a surrogate."

"Data, I think that Mikal would far prefer dancing with Penelope, whether she can dance or not."

Mikal laughed. "Of course! And I'm pretty good at teaching a few dance steps, too. You can tell that to Penelope. . . . But my question is, why isn't she here?"

"I believe that the reason is severe shyness. This is why she has enlisted my help," said Data. "Please do not relay that I have described her as such, for she would be upset. However, I have decided that to tell the truth is the best policy."

"Well, she is quite young, I suppose," said Beverly. "But still . . . a dance. Loud music."

"Perhaps if you are worried about the effect of loud music, Doctor, then earplugs might be the answer," Data suggested.

"Sure. That's it. Give me some earplugs, Dr. Crusher," said Mikal, obviously pleased with the solution. "I'll use them if I have to."

Beverly regarded them both skeptically. She was amused and yet also concerned. She wondered what Mrs. Tillstrom might say in this matter. Then again, a woman who would allow surgeons to stick microcircuitry in her son's brain probably wouldn't be against earplugs. Or loud music at a dance either (although truth be told, she well knew that Federation medical regulations aboard starships kept the decibels well within the safe range in lounges and theaters). "You know, I find it very interesting that you should be such a social gadabout considering your state—and that of your mother," she said.

"Doctor, is sitting by my mother's side holding her hand going to bring her back to consciousness any sooner?" Mikal spoke this quite seriously after a moment of thought. Then his face split into a sly grin. "And as for social proclivities . . . I understand that you've got a son of your own. I can't imagine that he doesn't enjoy the company of young women."

"Touché, Mikal." Beverly nodded. "Well, you can't blame me for putting in a concerned word. Please don't overtax yourself."

"It might actually do me some good. Jog my memory." He turned to the android who'd delivered the invitation. "Please tell Penelope that I'd be happy to come to the dance, and I understand about shyness. I used to be terribly shy once." Mikal blinked, and was suddenly quiet. He turned to Beverly. "You know, come to think of it, I *was* shy. That's something I didn't remember before, Doctor. In fact . . . I recall being quite . . . aloof. Withdrawn, even."

"Good . . . good . . . Is there anything more . . . anything else you remember?" Memory tended to come in chains. When you got one new item out, if you yanked it, other things would often come out as well.

"No. Nothing right offhand."

"Do me a favor, Mikal. If you remember anything else—and I mean *anything*—tell me. And if you can't tell me immediately"—she went to her desk, pulled open a drawer, and took out a data PADD—"I want you to record it. Okay?"

"Fair enough."

"I don't care if you're dancing, eating . . . pitching woo at some girl. Write it down. It could be what we need to get the rest of it back."

Mikal nodded with great gravity. "I understand, Doctor. I will do as you ask. Now, if you'll excuse me . . ." He turned back to the android. "Data . . .

perhaps you might tell me a little more about Penelope and the particulars about this dance . . . and maybe you can even tell me some more about yourself."

Data looked over at Beverly, as though for permission. Beverly nodded.

With appropriate adieus, they left.

That Data, thought Beverly. Hardly what you would call a guarded personality. So honest and so open . . .

Of course, he had nothing to hide.

Despite herself, Beverly Crusher wondered if Mikal Tillstrom *did*.

Chapter Nine

SOMETHING WAS WRONG.

Captain Jean-Luc Picard was a practical, sensible man. He was a man of amazing leadership abilities who had the intelligence and skills with which to back up the respect he commanded from those who served above him, and most of all, those who served below. He was, above all, a pragmatic man, a rational man who did not pay much attention to anything remotely like superstition or the outré.

And yet, like every good captain of a ship of the sea, a ship of the air, or a ship of the void between interstellar reaches, Jean-Luc Picard had a sixth sense about his ship, the *Enterprise.*

And something was wrong.

He'd gotten this irksome feeling the second morning after the rescue on Phaedra. He'd woken up in his Spartan cabin. Normally his trained senses brought him alert immediately and he would give himself a few moments to adjust his consciousness, whereupon he would get out of bed and call for his Earl Grey tea, hot, more out of habit than for any needed stimulus.

But that morning, he'd woken with a groggy head pierced by a nameless fear. He'd allowed himself to just lie there for two minutes and rid himself of this, but finally he had to get up and take a hot shower in the attempt to sluice himself of foreboding.

After his shower and his morning routines, he sat in his chair of command and asked for a systems check of everything aboard the *Enterprise.* When his officers returned with a report showing that everything was running smoothly, he shook his head. Something still felt wrong.

He went into his ready room and commed for the main computer.

"Computer, I want a point-by-point function check of the systems aboard this ship. Place the results also on-screen."

The computer, naturally, did precisely as requested. Together they went through the hull system, the structural integrity field system, and the inertial damping systems. Nothing came up amiss, even though Picard had ordered the computer to stop on *any* irregularities.

He went through the command systems from guidance systems all the way through engineering. He allowed the computer to quickly show him everything, and everything seemed fine, including a computer self-check.

His first check had been a level-five diagnostic. He'd done a level-four diagnostic himself. There were three other levels of testing, but they were not routine as the others had been, and they involved a large number of crew. He did not wish to alarm his ship members unduly when he had no real *reason* for worry or suspicion. He'd done a thorough check, and that should be enough.

There were other things to deal with, most particularly preparation for the diplomatic routine when they arrived at their destination. Captain Picard retired to his cabin and began, still feeling ill at ease. He took his midday meal there, and emerged only for a spell of solitary exercise. For this he chose a simple treadmill so that he could read a manual on the computer stand beside the exercise machine.

It was here that Counselor Deanna Troi appeared, toward the end of his session, ready for a workout herself.

"Counselor, could I have a word with you later?" Picard asked.

"Certainly, sir . . . I sense you are . . . troubled? How about now?"

"Yes, if you don't mind putting off your exercise. I should like to talk with you."

Back in his cabin, the captain ordered up tea for them both. He sat down uneasily, sipping at his perfumed astringent choice, and sighed. "You know, Deanna, I'm not given to premonitions or other psychic phenomena. However, a competent captain generally develops a certain so-called sixth sense about his ship, and I suppose I have developed such about this one."

"You are more than competent, sir, and by no means should you ignore your feelings and senses about the *Enterprise.*"

"The truth is, I feel something is wrong. I've done fifth- and fourth-level diagnostic checks, and the *Enterprise* is operating well. Nothing seems wrong, Counselor, and yet you are right. . . . I am troubled. . . ."

"I'm glad you're willing to talk. Perhaps it is the worry you feel for your friend who is still in a coma. Sometimes worry and guilt express themselves in anxiety in wholly unrelated areas."

"A possibility." Picard said.

"Regardless, if that is the case, and I sincerely doubt it is, then there is no real threat to the *Enterprise*. I must, however, not take any chances that my instincts as a captain are not true."

He told her of the precautions he had taken and why he was concerned about taking others. Troi listened carefully, with those limpid eyes softly attentive.

"I see," she said finally. "And I understand. A full level-one diagnostic would take time and energy, and cause concern amongst the crew. You do not wish to cause alarm. . . . You would keep the anxiety to yourself." She took a thoughtful sip of her chamomile tea. "Before I advise, however, let's talk a bit about the 'sense' you have. I can feel it, of course . . . or at any rate, your fear and concern. . . . It is difficult to differentiate. What do you think, qualitatively, this fear represents? What are your thoughts on the matter?"

"My father . . . the vintner, you know . . . back in France . . ." Picard smiled fondly. "I remember him saying, 'Jean-Luc, I can feel wine going sour in casks. . . . I can see it in the color of this crop's leaves.'"

"He saw his business as a whole, then."

"Absolutely. Whole . . . an organism. Bugs in the vines, rats in the cellar—they resonated through the whole thing." He tapped his drink thoughtfully. "Have you ever read the play *Hamlet,* Deanna?"

"Yes; are you speaking of the 'Something is rotten in Denmark' speech? The poisoning of a king poisoned the whole land."

"Something like that, yes. In Shakespeare's day, a king was a living extension of his land . . . and if you poisoned the land, presumably the king was poisoned as well." He cleared his throat. "I think it quite amusing, really. Here we are in a league of mostly free worlds. A universe of progress—where we have created wonderful equality and opportunity for everyone . . . and yet here, on our starships, we have little medieval worlds, little kings . . . kings who must rule wisely, lest they become tyrants."

"An interesting analogy, though I hate to think of the crew of the *Enterprise* as serfs and vassals."

"No. Princes and barons and royalty all." Picard grinned ruefully. "That's the best analogue I can present to you about how I feel. My duty, here in this little kingdom, is to see that it all functions well. I have tools at my disposal . . . fabulous tools. And yet ultimately it is something beyond those tools that makes a good captain. However, Troi, this particular captain is above all a rational man."

"He pays attention to his instincts, though. And often instincts are beyond reason, beyond psychic processes. Captain, if you feel something is wrong, then you should ascertain whether the ship is well or not. . . ."

"It could be some kind of foreboding concerning the future that may be nothing you can diagnose."

"My prescription stands. . . . Follow your gut feelings and check the ship. As much for your peace of mind as for the benefit of the *Enterprise.*"

"And what about the psyches of the crew?"

"Currently quite sound and able to take it, I believe. And if not"—she shrugged—"I'll just have to work overtime, won't I?"

"Thank you, Deanna. You've helped me make up my mind. We'll have a level-one diagnostic this evening, utilizing the appropriate people."

"Oh dear, sir . . . the musical affair in Ten-Forward."

"Ah yes . . . Well, there would only be the tech crew involved in a diagnostic. I myself was going to attend.

. . . Ah well, there's no reason to reschedule. We'll just have to have an encore performance next week for all who missed it, and all who care to attend again."

Troi smiled glowingly. "I think our particular king may have the wisdom of Solomon!"

"Just don't bring any swords and babies my way, Counselor. That will be all. You are dismissed."

A cloud passed over her face. "Oh dear. This is awful. I forgot. Data usually participates in that sort of thing, doesn't he?"

"Yes. Why?"

"Well, sir, he's been helping me with a patient. And he has a very vital service to perform at the dance this evening. Might he possibly be excused?"

"I don't see why not. We can always call him if we need him." For the first time that day, Picard smiled without affect. "Data at a dance. I'm sorry I'm going to miss that. Very well, you are dismissed."

"Yes, sir." She got up and began walking out. "Oh, and by the way, Captain. I'm more than willing to take a few minutes out of my schedule again if you should care to talk about any other matter."

Picard knew exactly what she was talking about, but he didn't really think acknowledgment of the subject was necessary. "Thank you, Counselor, I'll remember that."

When she left, Captain Picard immediately ordered the level-one diagnostic for 1900 hours, with news of the addition of another dance for the following week.

Then he went to his bed for a short catnap.

These things took a few hours, and could be grueling. It would be best if he was well rested for the event.

"A level-one diagnostic?" said Geordi disbelievingly as the captain's voice faded away into the recesses of Ten-Forward. He was there, helping to decorate for the special event that night. "Damn! Great timing."

Riker shrugged and handed up another brightly colored streamer for his friend to put into place. "Tough luck, Geordi. You get to miss out on my playing."

"I had a date!" Geordi exclaimed. "What am I going to tell her?"

"You've got a real good excuse. . . ."

"And tonight was going to be our special night. . . . Damn and double damn."

Geordi stepped down from the ladder and regarded his handiwork. "Hardly state of the art, I guess."

Riker laughed and patted his friend on his back. "Maybe I can convince her to come down and check the warp field nacelles with you. I understand things can get pretty hot down there."

"They're going to be hot anywhere we are that I give her the bad news. Oh well. Lucky in cards, unlucky with love."

Geordi noticed Data coming in. "Now, there's an android that looks like he wished that a good stiff one might affect him."

"I think you're projecting, Geordi. Let's get this finished up. You've got work, and I've got a little rehearsal time to put in." Riker looked over to the case that held his trombone, eagerly anticipating assembling it, holding it in his hands, sliding it, blowing it, making lovely, happy jazz.

Before they could do anything, though, Data came up to them. "Pardon me, Commander and Lieutenant. I seem to have a conundrum, and perhaps you can give me some advice before I seek to solve it myself."

Riker took another rolled streamer from a box the computer replica had prepared. "Go ahead, Data. We're listening."

"I have just heard the news about level-one diagnosis. To begin with, I am puzzled. I myself noticed the results of lower-level diagnostic tests done just today. All systems seem to be functioning normally."

"Tell me about it," Geordi said disgustedly, taking the end of a bright orange streamer and climbing a ladder.

"I would never question the wisdom of the captain's actions," said Data. "Although this puts me in somewhat of a dilemma. I have promised to chaperon a young couple to the dance tonight, and my presence seems very important to one of them. And yet my duty is clear. I must participate in the testing of systems. Tell me, how may I excuse myself from the chaperon duties?"

"You're concerned about hurting someone's feelings," said Geordi, gingerly stepping down the ladder to get another streamer.

"Yes. More to the point, in this situation, 'hurting someone's feelings' may seriously damage the individual psychologically and impair a friendship I value." Data looked vexed.

"Talk to the captain, Data," said Geordi. "He may understand."

"I'm sure your contributions to a level-one diagnostic are invaluable—but I am sure it can be accomplished without you," said Riker. "So tell us. What's going on?"

Data briefly explained the situation.

Riker's eyes lit up. "Well! This should be quite a dance, then! Data, I think clearly you belong here. Penelope . . . right, I saw her with you at the volleyball games today. Look, I guess maybe I'm not the best matchmaker in the world, but maybe I can give you a hand. At the very least I can dedicate a song to the couple."

Data looked thoughtful. "In the event, Commander

Riker, that I am unable to attend the dance, I would most appreciate your occasional intercession. As I said, Penelope is most concerned about her shyness inhibiting the success of her interaction."

"I'll do what I can . . . but a little bird tells me that you'll be here tonight."

Data's eyes darted about as though in search of the aforementioned avian creature, but then he got it.

"Yeah, Data. We're not serving under Captain Bligh here." Geordi marched back up the ladder.

"I should consult him immediately."

"Pardon me, Data," said Riker. "One more question. How did you get the job of dealing with the girl's shyness?"

"Counselor Troi asked me to hold a series of conversations with her. She felt I might be an unintimidating male to practice conversation with."

Riker put a hand on the android's shoulder. "Good luck, Data. I know you'll do well."

"Thank you, sir. I will now go and speak to the captain."

"Just a hunch, Data. Maybe you should talk to Counselor Troi first. I've got the feeling that since she's heard about the diagnostic as well, she may already have intervened."

"Ah. That would be fortuitous. An excellent recommendation, Commander Riker. I will do so."

Chapter Ten

CAPTAIN JEAN-LUC PICARD SLEPT.

And as he slept, on the verge of his dreams, the memory of his time with Adrienne Tillstrom nibbled at his heart of hearts, past the walls of defense he'd built up over the years.

He'd gone to Cal Tech reluctantly.

When he'd enrolled at the Academy, he assumed that he'd study hard, work hard, and graduate in record time to take his place amongst the ranks of the chosen, the officers of Starfleet. However, he'd had a few problems here and there, and one of those had been in the mathematical side of the sciences.

"Jean-Luc, you're going to make a fine officer one day," his adviser had told him. "I know it. However, there's no reason to hurry through like an angry bull in a china shop. You've got excellent marks in all your subjects save one of the most important. Mathematics. And I suggest that you not spend the summer vacation trying to take extra courses to graduate early, but review the substance of the work in your math courses. And I know just the program to suggest, and some of the very best professors to essentially tutor you." He'd smiled then, wistfully. "Cal Tech. I did some work there. I know the right people, and I've got the hunch it's the place for you, Jean-Luc."

Picard had balked. "But, sir, I'm just fine until I hit Boolean algebra and the more advanced math past it. And I've been told that my marks will do just fine." Hell, he'd worked so hard to do *that* well.

"You don't seem to understand, Jean-Luc. I'm more than aware of what your goals are . . . but maybe more aware than you about how to achieve those goals."

The truth was, Jean-Luc loathed higher mathematics, and the thought of spending a whole summer immersed in them, anywhere, was not one he cherished much. . . . However, he was gratified that the Admiralty was so interested in his performance. He agreed.

Cal Tech was perched in bright metals and plastics upon the ruins of Old Pasadena; it shone resplendent in the bright sun, its campus an example of the technological achievement of the powerful minds that studied and researched there. Jean-Luc Picard was impressed. He was given a private dorm room, a ticket for free meals at the cafeteria, and precious access to the place's formidable libraries.

He was also given a simple schedule of classes and, most important, his own tutor.

She was a geology student at the university, looking to earn a little extra money, and at first the two of them loathed each other. Each of them thought the other a terribly stiff prig. However, on the second day of their lessons, the tutor admitted to being "charmed" by his slight accent. On his own behalf, Jean-Luc admitted to being very impressed with the tutor's abilities to simplify and explain certain principles of advanced mathematics that had eluded him before.

He said nothing to her about the fact that he also found her dark hair and features very attractive, and that when she'd leaned over to correct an equation he'd just completed, her nearness had made his heart jump a little.

"Well, then, Jean-Luc," said Adrienne Tillstrom on the fifth day of the tutelage, as she reconnected the computer stylus they'd been using back onto its board, "I suppose you're going to have a high old time this weekend in Los Angeles. Check out the clubs, catch some sun at the beach, pal around with some friends."

He gave her a blank look. "Nothing of the sort. I have a full semester of new courses this fall at the Academy that I must prepare for. Many books to read. I also intend to make use of the gym on both days. An officer-candidate must stay in peak form." He raked his hand through his mop of thick brown hair. "I believe I need a haircut as well." He smiled faintly. "And then, of course, there is the small matter of the mathematics homework that has been assigned."

She looked at him as though for the first time. "My God, I hate to say it, Jean-Luc, but you're a lot like me."

The softening of her expression made him appreciate that she, in fact, in her severe way, was quite a striking female. There could be no doubt that she had a razor-sharp mind, and Jean-Luc appreciated that quite a bit. And her dedication to her work was clear in everything she did and said, indeed in the very way she held herself. He admired that tremendously.

"I take that as an extreme compliment."

Adrienne laughed, and it made her eyes sparkle. "Thank you; I suppose it is. You know, Jean-Luc, I warn you . . . last year I got ulcers from worry and overwork. I was properly repaired and my diet was adjusted—but the medical consultant suggested that friends and the occasional social activity would go a long way to preventing a recurrence."

"I have no friends here. My gastrointestinal system is just fine. And I do exercise and eat quite balanced meals."

She sighed. "Smart people can be so stupid. I'm trying to get you to take me to dinner or a show or something this weekend, Jean-Luc. You don't want me to get ulcers again, do you?" She smiled, slightly nervously.

"Of course not. I suppose I could set aside a few hours—for entertainment. Though I would prefer if it were something educational or at the very least culturally enlightening."

She nodded soberly. "Absolutely."

They went to the Hollywood Bowl and listened to Mozart and Beethoven under the stars. Afterward, they had a late dinner. The evening ended with only a handshake, but their relationship had clearly warmed up quite a bit at that point, and Jean-Luc found himself asking if she'd like to have dinner the next night. At that dinner he learned more of Adrienne Tillstrom, and he told her something of himself.

She was the daughter of a scientist, a xenobiologist. However, her own interests lay in geology and xenogeology. She excelled at mathematics, and her advisers had encouraged her to perhaps work in computer science or theoretical physics, but her love was for the study of planets, their births, their lives, their deaths.

"My father was away all the time when I was young. I missed him terribly, but when he came back, it was like he brought back every day we'd lost, and more. He spent time with me and told me of his travels and gave me relics and rocks and pictures . . . and most of all, he gave me the sense of wonder and mystery that's out there. . . . He made me want to go there myself, and study other planets."

"Sounds like an interesting and compelling man."

"He is. He's still doing it. I only see him for a couple weeks every year . . . but it's almost enough."

"Almost?"

She shrugged. "No. It's fine. It's given me something that not a whole lot of people have, and something that I see you have, Jean-Luc. Strength. Independence. The ability to *live* without leaning on others. It's a noble kind of loneliness, don't you think? Necessary, for what we want to do with our lives."

"Yes. Yes, I guess you're quite correct."

There was a kiss that night. What followed was an odd romance. Not Jean-Luc's first, by any means, but the first he'd had with a woman like himself in many ways and sharing his ambition. They saw each other every day, and enjoyed each other with a kind of aloof passion, a cold heat that comes with a meeting of analytical minds. Jean-Luc, with Adrienne Tillstrom's help, began to understand mathematics not only as an intellectual rigor that had to be hurdled to achieve his goals, but as the underlying necessity for the appreciation of science . . . and a marvel of beauty in its own pure form.

His adviser had been right. His summer at Cal Tech gave him exactly what he needed to attain his full potential—at least intellectually.

One night, toward the end of the summer, Adrienne drove him up Mullholland Drive atop the Santa Monica Mountains. Much of the area was park preserve, and there were stops along the way where you could stop your ground-effect car and look out over great views of L.A. or the San Fernando Valley.

The romantic purposes of such views were not lost

upon even so practical a soul as Jean-Luc's, and after a time of gentle physical affection, he looked out upon the intersection of the grid of city lights meeting with the sparkling of the stars like jewels in oil, and for a moment was lost in it all.

"Nice, isn't it?" Adrienne had said, after giving him a few moments.

"I'm most grateful. You've given me so much, Adrienne." He said that with a depth of sincerity that clearly stunned the woman.

"There's greatness in you, Jean-Luc. That you've permitted me to touch it . . . Well, perhaps I should thank *you*."

"After you, Alphonse."

"No, after *you*, Gaston!"

They both laughed and the tension was gone.

After a moment, Adrienne said, "Once when I was a little girl, my father brought me back a sea creature from Stromgren Ten. It was like a living rainbow one moment, and then, after it fed, it would change into an entirely different creature. It had the oddest eyes, and it *responded* to you when you looked at it with odd signaling motions and ripplings of its dorsal antennae and facial muscles that made it look like a creature from a cartoon. It was very funny and very beautiful, and amused me greatly. The next time my father came home, he asked me if I had learned anything from the *mongefish*—that's what it was called. Well, I'd learned responsibility. . . . I tended it well. And I'd learned a great deal about animal behavior, because it had interested me enough to read about it in books, and to read other books on animals. But what pleased my father the most was what I said finally. I had learned that the universe must be a fascinating and mysterious and wonderful place to have such a strange creature in it. He smiled and said good, that was what he had hoped it would do, because that started us talking about all the things he'd done and what he'd learned. But you know what else he said, Jean-Luc?"

"No. What?" said the young cadet, forgetting everything but this woman and the stars.

"He said, you know the *mongefish* probably finds you as strange as you find it. That made me laugh, Jean-Luc. It delighted me more than I can tell you. To be as strange and unique as a *mongefish!* To be me and shine so full of colors and the exotic breath of alien worlds!"

"And shine you do, Adrienne!"

"Thank you. But I've finally found a stranger creature than myself or a *mongefish!"*

"Oh?"

"Yes. My future starship captain!"

He laughed and kissed her and they had a splendid evening.

After the summer session was over, they corresponded, and she even came up once to visit him. However, as much as they enjoyed each other's company, they both knew, deep down in their bones, knew and *respected* the fact that there were other far more intense topics on their agendas than each other.

The correspondence continued intermittently through the first couple of years of Jean-Luc's service with the Federation. Then, after Adrienne married a fellow xenobiologist, the correspondence slowly faltered and finally he lost track of her, save for the occasional article he'd read by her or about her in the science journals he followed.

It had not been the most intense relationship Jean-Luc Picard had ever had, nor perhaps even the most meaningful, but in many ways it was the most positive one he'd enjoyed with a woman. Often, at times of loneliness, he wondered if perhaps he'd not made a mistake in not pursuing something more with the xenobiologist, if only because she alone of all his women had understood his dedication to his goals and ideals and dreams. She could, perhaps, have lived with that, where for other women it had been anathema.

He was surprised at the regret that remained in him about the matter over the years. And was even more surprised how his heart had lurched at the thought of her endangerment.

And now, seeing her, aged with the dust of a hundred worlds on her hardened hands, but still striking and even beautiful, like a sleeping *mongefish,* he could not help but remember their time together, or the fondness he'd felt for his mathematics tutor at Cal Tech.

Jean-Luc Picard awoke from his brief nap, not rested at all.

With an effort of his formidable will, he pushed the dread and upset he felt to the back of his mind.

He got up, washed his face, and went to prepare for the level-one diagnostic that he hoped would at least clear his mind of worry about the *Enterprise.*

That, at least, would take his mind off his other concerns.

For a time, anyway.

Interlude

It grew.

It spread.

It cohered, it bonded, and it replicated itself over and over with the ample, excellent material it found.

Soon its own version of RNA built a complex neural system through its body. Soon all manner of electronic communications from its "parts" would be in effect.

Nonetheless, instinctually it knew there would be opposition. It sensed the bad life inside this shell and it sensed the energies that it instinctively drew away from.

It had no fear, it had no conscience or intellect, only the blind urge to grow and create and change . . .

. . . and strive toward the Consciousness that was its Destiny.

Chapter Eleven

GEORDI LA FORGE consulted his PADD checklist, and then looked up at his engineers.

"All right, folks, what have we got?"

"Status report monitors have shown absolute top functioning of warp engines, sir," reported Ensign Andrews, looking up from his monitors.

"Well, that's good, but the stasis reports are hardly the stuff of level one." He looked around at the engineers. "Come on, guys. Time to roll up our sleeves and get to work."

"And the captain wants to maintain this warp speed as well?" said Andrews.

"Yes, sir. Level one is usually done when in orbit or in open space. Not in warp drive," chimed in Second Lieutenant Oblata, not particularly vexed, just stating fact.

"Yeah? No kidding."

Geordi well knew that this couldn't exactly be a full level-one diagnostic. He wasn't sure why the captain

had ordered it, but there must be a good reason.
. . . Actually, proper preparation was just as good a
reason as any, he supposed. He'd just rather be at that
dance. His date had been understanding enough, but
she was in a position to be—she was going and he
wasn't. Oh well . . .

A level-one diagnostic required that systems be
taken off-line, while a team of crew members physically verified operation of system mechanisms and system readings, rather than depending on automatic
readings. This way you could be sure the automatic
self-checking systems were accurate. With certain
systems, of course, there would be no problem. You
didn't need the impulse system when you were in
warp space. What you *did* need, though, was the warp
drive system, so they'd have to rely on the usual
checkers for that, and just ask for a deferred diagnostic when they arrived at their destination.

They'd just have to make the best of what they had,
and with his crew's experience, Geordi was confident
they'd be able to do so.

"Commence operations, fellows," Geordi said.
"The sooner this is over, the better we'll all like it, but
that doesn't mean we can slack off on our duties. Let's
make this as excellent as always."

His under lieutenants nodded and bent down to
their work on their particular work stations at the
master systems display, keying in the necessary orders.

Ensign Andrews went over to another work station.
Geordi looked up and was gratified to see the speed
and efficiency of the man, signaled by the impulse
propulsion systems status display. "Main impulse
engines off-line, sir."

"You've got the auxiliary on as backup?"

"Yes, sir."

"Good work. Okay, get your team together and go check it out. I'll monitor from my office."

Geordi, as chief engineer, had his own office, which included smaller-scale repeaters of most displays in Main Engineer, as well as extra work stations. He went to his own station and commenced his own work.

After a couple of minutes of intense work, he glanced up at the result on the display board.

Everything optimum. Nothing wrong as far as he could see.

Eventually he knew they'd have to go over the navigational systems and weapons systems, but for right now, he figured he had a few moments to spare, so he'd check the structural integrity of the ship, along with lesser systems.

On first processing, everything was normal, and in a lesser diagnostic, the answers on the board would have been taken as enough evidence of the integrity of the hull and structure of the *Enterprise*. However, since it was a level one, Geordi took things to an extreme. On one screen, he processed the material again, personally examining the figures and readouts. Function was just fine . . . but there was something here in the mass distribution, something that the sensors were picking up . . . the merest point digit off, a reading that would not throw anything off normally. During a level-one diagnostic, though, it had to be checked out.

What the screen was showing was a readout on the complex and massive amount of coordinates for the *Enterprise*'s skin: the hull. Marginal, almost infinitesimal, gradient irregularities.

Hmm.

Geordi La Forge nimbly thumbed off the sensor scan and pushed up for the camera array, the "eyes" posted on the exterior of the hull, to visually examine.

Sensors weren't showing any damage, which was why there wasn't any kind of alarm. But why did the readings look wrong? A visual was necessary here.

He swiveled to another pair of screens, and waited. Nothing came up.

"What the hell?"

Static. All he was getting was static . . . and now there was a MALFUNCTION reading coming. He switched from starboard to port views. These appeared fine. The aft, the others . . . they seemed okay as well. The starboard cameras, though . . . a definite washout. And these systems didn't have auxiliaries!

There was only one way he was going to get a visual on the starboard hull.

Lieutenant Commander Geordi La Forge hit his comm button.

"I need a Theta Structural Team," he said. "Get the suits ready. We're going outside."

It was not in Data's nature to be nervous. And, as it was not a particularly attractive human trait, he had not programmed himself to appear to be nervous at any given circumstance. However, in this situation in which he found himself, he could well understand why and how human beings entered into that state. The confusion, the uncertainty, the pressure . . . Although he marked it all analytically as it transpired, he could see that, were he human, he'd be a wreck.

"Oh, Data . . . Data . . . do you think I look all right?" Penelope twirled in front of him, showing him her chartreuse dress and her new hairstyle.

"All your tabs and zippers seem to be closed," Data said. "Your makeup appears properly applied. I detect perhaps an overabundance of perfume." He took her arm. "And your pulse is somewhat high."

She took his hand away. "No, no . . . do I *look* all right?"

Data finally got it. "Yes. Yes, of course! You are most aesthetically pleasing."

"I don't know about this dress. . . . Maybe I should have gone with that other design. I think I'll go back to the replicator and get another."

Data consulted his internal chronometer. "If so, then we will be late."

"Well, isn't it a woman's prerogative to be late?"

"I am not aware of that social convention. Actually, it seems rather facetious, particularly in that you are the initiator of this 'date,' and the agreed-upon time of meeting Mikal Tillstrom is approaching, and if we leave now, you will be precisely on time."

"Serves me right for asking a *machine!*"

Troi had warned him that insecure young women tended to strike out verbally, but he'd assured her that this would not be a problem. After all, he had no feelings to hurt. Nonetheless, this label was a bit irksome.

"I am an android. A machine lacks self-awareness, Penelope."

"Data, we're not here to discuss philosophy, and I am sorry. Well, I guess I'm just going to have to live with this incredible mess that I'm in and hope that Mikal isn't too turned off."

They left and began the trip to the quarters adjacent to sickbay where Mikal had been placed since his discharge. There, he could not only be close to his mother, but could be monitored as well.

"I have a question," Data said in the turbolift, seeing that Penelope was getting awkward and withdrawn as they drew closer. He hoped to thus pull her out of her shell. "Mikal Tillstrom seemed to think you were quite attractive in your appearance at the volleyball game. He made a reference to it again when I spoke to him last. He seemed to like you as you were. Why have you changed your appearance?"

"Because . . . it's a dance, Data. I want to look *better!*"

"I see. So you will be more attractive and he will pay more attention to you."

"Yes, of course."

"Why do women 'dress up' and 'make up' in unnatural colors and clothing to attract men, when they know that this is not their usual state of attire or looks? Is this analogous to the display of plumage in the peacock?"

"Data, it makes me feel . . . well, more self-confident. Okay? Does that make sense?"

"I see. The theory, then, is to attract men, ensnare their interests . . . and then return to the quotidian?"

She looked annoyed at first, but then she thought about it for a moment. "I don't think it's a particularly logical theory, Data. I guess it's just human nature." She smiled. "Though when you think about it, I guess it is pretty strange."

"This is true. As Troi told me to remind you, you are not the first eighteen-year-old who has been nervous at a dance."

"Maybe the first to worry about going catatonic!"

"That is why I am there, true?"

Sometimes, Troi said, having a crutch around, even if you didn't use it, made you feel better.

At the very least, this would be an interesting exercise in human social interaction, and potentially of great value to Data's study of humanity.

But then, on the other hand, was this not the same as dressing up and wearing makeup for a dance? This was a troubling thought. He'd have to speak to Troi about this. But not now . . . later.

There were other dilemmas to deal with now.

At first, it went very well.

The meeting with Mikal was fine. As before, Mikal's

friendliness and verbal abilities seemed to deflect Penelope's nervousness.

The difficulties did not develop until later, at the dance.

"What a *wonderful* place," Mikal said, clapping his hands with glee at the sight of the room known as "Ten-Forward." Data regarded the familiar space with its elegant lines and underlighting, its soft, soothing colors, and its comforting decor. This was, of course, the place where crew members came to relax and socialize. Tonight, though, the lighting was a touch brassier, and the decorations festive. It reminded Data slightly of the wake that Riker had held in memory of Geordi La Forge, when everyone thought that he and Ensign Ro were dead.

They were early, and only about twenty people had arrived, but even with the level-one diagnostic, quite a few more would arrive. The diagnostic demanded the work of only about fifty crew members on the tech staff.

"I believe that it has been prepared in a 'New Orleans Party' atmosphere," Data said, seeing that Penelope was not chiming in immediately with conversation. That was, after all, one of the reasons he was here—to fill in the dead air.

"No. No, good shot, but I'd say it was more a New York, New Year's Eve, atmosphere. How enthralling. New York really is an exciting place now that they've remodeled it. I've been there quite a few times. . . . You know, it's too bad," Mikal said, after surveying the decorations and the bandstands, the instruments in their cases all ready for playing. "I wish I could have helped decorate. I'm pretty good at that kind of thing." He turned to Penelope. "How about you, Pen?"

She nodded, eyes trained on Mikal.

Data, expecting the conversational tennis ball to be

returned by his player, was caught short for a moment. "Yes, I believe that Penelope has shown quite a penchant for artistic things. Don't you think she did a marvelous job on her face and in the selection of her dress?"

"Data!" Penelope blushed.

"Oh, I agree, and that is no small talent. But you know, Penelope clearly has a face that is suited for any kind of occasion, makeup or no. . . . But I do believe that makeup gilds the lily, don't you, Data?"

"'Gild the lily' . . . Oh. A most appropriate analogy. Yes. Yes, I do agree."

"Well, where do we get our drinks then? And food? I must admit, I may have lost much of my memory, but very little of my appetite."

"You remember that you had a good appetite before the time of Epsilon station?" said Data. "Is this a breakthrough? Shall we report it to Dr. Crusher?"

"No, Data. I was just playing with words," said Mikal, laughing. "Look, you know, this item over here looks very much like a bar. And I'd wager quite a bit that attractive lady behind it is our bartender. Come on, folks. Let me buy you a drink."

"That is not necessary, Mikal," Data said. "Everything is free aboard the *Enterprise.*"

"Well, thanks, Data." He turned and stepped up to the bar, leaning on it and looking at the array of drinkables wistfully.

"Hi," said the exotic, black woman behind the bar. "I'm Guinan. You look like a kid who just stepped in a candy store for the first time, after a trip to the dentist."

"This is one perceptive lady!" said Mikal to Data and Penelope. "I believe I have the memory of quite enjoying bitter-tasting, mood-altering beverages—but don't tell my mother. Anyway, as interesting as the array of possibilities is, I'm afraid that Dr. Crusher has limited me to weaker things—drinks that will not affect this troubled noggin of mine." He tapped his skull. "But I'm being impolite. I should ask what my friends want first. My name is Mikal, Guinan. It's nice to meet you." They shook hands lightly, and Data noted that Mikal managed to extract a large smile from the bartender, something not always forthcoming.

"Yes. You're the fellow we picked up at the science station. Nice haircut. I hope your mother recovers soon."

"So do we all."

The smile turned into a frown. "Yes. Now then . . . I'd better get your drinks. Then I've got to get the punch bowl out."

"Excellent. I think I'll wait and have that. Penelope? Data?"

"I presume by 'punch' you mean a collection of fruit juices mixed with a syntheholic beverage?" Data observed.

"Psuedorum."

"I think that would be just fine. . . ." He looked over to Penelope, who looked as though she'd rather have a Saurian brandy, but of course, she wasn't old enough. "And a punch for Penelope, too."

"I think I can handle those orders now. You won't have to wait. Hello, Penelope. You look really beautiful tonight."

"Th-th-thank you, Guinan." A genuine smile broke through the rigid mask, and Penelope looked indeed radiant. Guinan went off to get the drinks. When she returned with the cups, and handed them around, she said to Mikal, "You are a very lucky fellow. You have excellent company tonight."

"Oh yes, I know, I know . . . and I wouldn't be here

except that they made sure I came. . . ." He looked around as more people walked in, and brightened as band members began to move up to the stage, checking their instruments and preparing for their session, Riker amongst them. "My God. That guy has an old-fashioned tenor sax. Will you excuse me? I've got to talk with him for a moment. I'll be right back." As though to prove it, he put his drink down on the bar. Then he hurried up to the temporary bandstand.

"Data, Data," said Penelope after heaving a sigh. "It's a disaster! I can't seem to say anything. Oh, when is Troi coming?"

"Am I proving insufficient in providing conversation?" Data asked, internally reviewing the last fifteen minutes.

"No. It's me. I'm a total stiff." She turned to pick up her drink, and noticed that Guinan was still there.

"You know, it's never easy," said the bartender sympathetically, "trying to make someone like you. In fact, in my experience it's absolutely impossible."

"Oh, thanks!" laughed Penelope. "You're a great help, Guinan."

Guinan shrugged. "It's kind of like the monkey and the peanut and the bottle."

Data accessed. "Oh! The parable. Ingenious. The monkey's hand is caught in a bottle because he will not let go of the peanut he has made a fist to take! I believe what Guinan is suggesting, Penelope, is that you have done everything possible to achieve your goals, and you should just let go and let them move in their natural course."

"Right! Total disaster." Penelope was unconsoled.

"You know, Penelope, one of my jobs here is to dispense perception and wisdom, and they say I do that pretty darned well . . . in my inscrutable way!" She laughed. "I suppose I've got a few unusual talents.

And goodness knows I like being inscrutable. Mystique helps a lot. It makes people take even stony silence as eloquence."

Penelope turned a puzzled expression toward Guinan, who had to say good-bye.

"What was that all about, Data?"

"I believe what Guinan was saying was that silence is not always bad, if utilized properly as a tool. It is more than apparent, Penelope, that you are presently incapable of conversing in what you feel is a normal fashion with Mikal Tillstrom. Therefore, perhaps you might utilize what you perceive as a weakness as a strength, and not let it trouble you so."

"You mean . . . it's okay not to talk?"

"In my preparation for this evening, I quickly accessed many books on human social interaction on a psychosexual level. There are many more entries than simply 'Conversation.' There is eye contact, pheromonal exchange, tactile stimulus, visual display, body language—"

"What Data is trying to say," said Guinan suddenly from behind them, startling them both, "is just *dance* with the guy, Penelope."

"But I don't dance very well!" she said.

"Just move your butt a little; that's all it takes."

Guinan was gone again.

"Okay. Okay, I'll try," said Penelope. "At least I don't have to talk when I'm dancing, right, Data?"

Data nodded. "I do not believe that conversation is required."

Within a moment, Mikal was back. "This is going to be just great! They're going to do some old swing numbers from the twentieth century. I asked if they could start off with some slow ones. The fast dances are kind of hard, and I do want to dance with you, Penelope."

Penelope nodded. "I'd like that, Mikal." She sipped at her drink.

By now, the room was filling up. Guinan, along with some helpers, put out the punch bowl and the trays of cheese, crackers, and such.

Data was about to address Mikal when Penelope began speaking. "I'm afraid I don't know much about 'swing music.'"

Data immediately accessed and began to report. "Swing music. A form of jazz popularized in the thirties and forties of the twentieth—" He stopped as soon as he felt her step on his foot. He was about to ask why she was doing this when he looked at her and was able to distinguish the message clear in her eyes. "Ah—you know, I realize that my banks are curiously barren of good information on the subject. Mikal, could you assist me in answering."

Mikal, delighted to show off something that he did indeed remember, continued. "Actually, you know, it was started in the twenties with the groups from Harlem, New York City. Ellington, Count Basie—people like that. They took blues and jazz and synthesized it into large ensembles, more resembling orchestras than simple pickup bands, which were common in the South and Midwest. But then in the thirties, it caught on in a big way with groups led by people like Benny Goodman and the Dorseys. . . ."

The information simply poured out, and Mikal seemed intensely involved in its telling, gesturing dramatically as he spoke. Penelope seemed to have no problem simply listening, becoming enthralled with the young man's enthusiasm. So much so that Data noted that her expression and gestures and manner were much more the normal Penelope than the upset Penelope. In fact, when Mikal finished his lecture,

Penelope was so excited that she actually spoke a paragraph to him.

"I've heard the music before, here and there, but you know, I've got so much a superior *appreciation* for it now. Thank you so much, Mikal. I'm really looking forward to hearing tonight's music now. You must really have a very perceptive ear to be so wide-ranging in your appreciation and critical analysis."

The onslaught of words from the previously monosyllabic girl clearly surprised Mikal. He grinned, and Penelope smiled sheepishly.

"Then I hope you'll dance with me."

She nodded, a little withdrawn again, but nothing serious.

"Excellent," said Data.

"Tell me something about the music that *you* like, Penelope," Mikal suggested.

"Classical," she said shyly.

"Oh. Pre-twentieth-century, you mean?"

"Yes. Romantic, mostly, I guess."

"Dead on. My sympathies exactly. Beethoven, Brahms, Liszt, Chopin. Terrific stuff. Ageless!"

The girl looked frightened again, and out of her depth. Mikal, Data noticed, had moved in a little closer, and stood beside her, his arm almost around her. She seemed quite relieved when Riker and company arrived at the bandstand, and turned to their first piece of music.

"As a request," he announced, "we're going to start off with a number called 'Begin the Beguine' . . . and this is for a young lady named Penelope. I hope that you all realize that you're not just here to listen. You're here to dance."

Riker turned and directed the band to start, using only his finger to initialize conducting.

Mikal offered Penelope his arm. "Shall we?"

125

Data gave Penelope a significant glance.

"Yes, we shall," said the girl.

Riker started the downbeat, and the band commenced.

To Data's trained ears, the band's music was not quite professional, but it did have something that he had difficulty putting in his own music—heart and feeling. He could imitate styles of play on his violin and the other instruments he attempted, certainly, but he couldn't get the emotion and passion that gave live music its special touch.

At first, Penelope moved with marked awkwardness. But under Mikal's expert and sympathetic tutelage, she was soon moving along with him in a nice rough rhythm. And as she relaxed with the next number, a more uptempo "Take the A Train," she seemed to actually enjoy herself tremendously. Data noted her eyes were large with a clear sexual excitement. Mikal seemed to be equally taken with his partner.

They stepped out of the next dance, a fast swing number that demanded fancier footwork. Data had retrieved cups of punch for them and offered them when they were finished.

"That was such *fun,*" said Penelope. "I should take dancing lessons, don't you think, Data?"

"I have found them necessary," Data agreed.

"Well, I think you've got the stuff, no question. Too bad you haven't had them before. I'm itching for a good workout!"

Data noted that Mikal seemed slightly tense despite his relaxed sense of fun. Clearly he was worried about his mother, even though he'd been assured by Dr. Crusher that she would recover.

His eye seemed to catch sight of something. He turned around and noticed a single woman walking into the room, wearing not a dress but a casual uniform, as though looking for someone.

Data recognized her. It was Ensign Metrina Harcourt of security, the woman who had taken Mikal to the volleyball game.

That was when the trouble began.

Chapter Twelve

LIEUTENANT COMMANDER Geordi La Forge hit the comm button.

"Captain. La Forge reporting."

"Yes, Lieutenant."

"I've got some marginal hull irregularities. Nothing significant, but I'd like to check them anyway."

"Yes. By all means."

"Not in warp, sir. If you want the full inspection, we need to get an EVA team out there."

"What's wrong with electronic visual analysis?"

"It hasn't picked it up, sir. I did a composition scan. I'd like to go out and have a look, sir. We're going to lose some time, but I know that if you ordered a level one, and we've got something, you're going to want to be comprehensive."

"Yes. Thank you, Lieutenant. Please proceed with your inspection team. Keep this line open, though. I want to follow your checkup."

"Yes, sir."

"Geordi. What did you find?"

"I don't know, sir. Could be nothing, could be just a patina of dust or something. We'll find out soon enough."

"Make it so, Lieutenant Commander."

Geordi could hear the captain ordering the pilot to take the ship out of warp.

Lieutenant Geordi La Forge was ambivalent about the EVA. On one hand, this was the kind of stuff that dry-dock workers did. The crew never actually got much of a chance to get out on the hull in deep space, which was exciting but could be dangerous.

That, of course, was the other side of the coin. You spend all your time inside a magnificent ship like the *Enterprise,* you get the feeling of security, of *home,* even in the middle of the farthest-flung reaches of space. A shuttle flight was almost an extension of that. But to actually get into an environmental suit and step out onto the skin of that home, beyond the protection the mighty machine offered . . . that was something else entirely. Fear was something you learned to live with when you served aboard a starship. Your ability to handle it was one of the reasons you got picked for the job, anyway. But fear inside of the *Enterprise,* and fear *outside* the *Enterprise*—those were two entirely different varieties of that prickly, snarly animal.

La Forge pushed the beast back in its cage and told it to shut up. Then he went to organize the EVA team. As he stepped out of this office, he noted the lights of the engine display dance their way out of warp.

He hit his comm. "Control, get me a sensor reading of the area of space we're in. I don't want my guys to fry in radiation or get hit by a meteor shower."

A pause, and then the appropriate bridge operator answered. "Lieutenant Commander La Forge, that would be unlikely. We are a full light-year from the nearest source of radiation—and sensors show no form of danger."

"Thanks. Just checking." He turned to his fellow engineers. "Okay. As long as we're off-line, I want you to do a visual check of the warp engine components."

"Yes, sir."

The irregularities on the hull fortunately were quite close to an airlock. Wouldn't be too far to hike. Geordi trotted to the turbolift and called out his locations. Moments later he was on his way. Well, he thought. This shouldn't take long.

The drill was a routine that snapped into immediate effect. Four other men were in the locker room, already suiting up. One of them was Ensign Lars Fredricks, who'd been spending a lot of time on the bridge lately.

"Captain sent me down. Thought since I was down on Phaedra . . ." said the big man, slipping into the special material and readying his air tanks.

"The captain thinks the irregularities have something to do with that Beta Epsilon stop." Geordi pulled open a locker, quickly checked to make sure that the suit there had been inspected recently. A-OK. He did a quick review of the routine of suiting up first, and then he took off his boots.

"He doesn't know. But it would stand to reason, wouldn't it?"

"True. Sounds more like a gut thing." Geordi pulled the bright material up his body, then slipped his arms into the sleeves. He never stopped marveling how light this stuff was. He sat down on a bench to put on the boots.

"That's why he's captain, I guess."

"Yep," said Geordi. "Sometimes I feel a malfunction in the engines somewhere in my kidneys first."

Fredricks smiled as he started to put on his helmet.

When Geordi was finished and all the rest of the team were suited up and breathing bottled atmosphere mix, he sealed his own helmet and pointed toward the airlock. The controller helped them in, and cycled the door behind them. As the air was pumped out of the lock, Geordi swallowed down the anxiety he was feeling and allowed the grid of his training to lock onto his mind. In this kind of situation, you just go through the prescribed moves and use the rest of your brain only when called on. That kept things a lot safer.

They were all then outfitted with phasers and tricorders. As the air gushed out, Geordi checked his comm, chinning it on. "Captain. Testing. You hear me, sir?"

Captain Picard's clear and confident enunciation crackled over the tiny speakers by his ears. "Loud and clear, Lieutenant Commander La Forge. Let's see what's out there, eh?"

The reprise of the familiar refrain was dryly funny. Geordi turned to the exterior door as it started to crank slowly open. His VISOR registered a fantastic new display of lights, unhindered by the interference of glass or any other kind of instruments. "Stars so far, sir. Lots of 'em. Makes me wish I had normal eyes."

"Pretty majestic, sir," said Fredricks "But you know what they say . . . you seen a trillion stars, you seen them all."

"That's what it looks like out there," said Ensign Michaels, a young, thickset hull maintenance engineer. "Lots of stars all staring at you."

"Well, let's go stare at the hull some," said Geordi. He gave them the coordinates. Ensign Michaels was the field guide. He knew the hull like the back of his hand, and beckoned them to follow.

Finally they eased their way out into raw space. Geordi felt a simultaneous stab of wonder and vertigo. The grav field cut off as they achieved full exit, and

Geordi could feel himself go weightless. He'd go drifting off except for these boots. He felt as if he were a streamer, attached to the hull by Velcro.

He stepped forward, still overcome with the hugeness of everything out here. It was one thing to look at your ship through monitors, and an entirely different affair to actually stand on its hull and see it all round you in full dimension.

Huge. Absolutely *grand,* as Jean-Luc Picard might say.

They were standing now on the side of the Battle Section, and the Saucer Module reared before them like a huge mechanical mushroom. Behind them, of course, were the warp nacelles. And though he certainly knew what they looked like, Geordi couldn't help but turn and stare. The effect, standing there in the middle of the enormity and majesty of the *Enterprise* bathed by starglow, powered by the incredible engines that *he* commanded, *he* knew and perfected every day, was awe-inspiring, breathtaking. Geordi had always felt a strange, almost proprietary feeling for those engines—but now he felt as though he somehow owned the whole of the enormous spacecraft.

Or it owned *him.*

The combination of adrenaline, his sense of duty, and the buzzing words of Michaels in his ear prompted him out of his fugue. "Okay, we all out?"

"We're all here," returned Geordi. The lock door, its lambency streaming out into space like a comforting night-light, a buoy marking their way back, was still open.

"Terrific." Michaels ordered the artificial gravity on, and the team stood waiting for it. When it came on, it fortunately came on gradually. Geordi could feel himself softly progressing from weightlessness to just below one g.

"Okay? Everybody's stomach under control?" Geordi said.

They started walking.

Michaels consulted his instruments, then looked ahead. "Hmm. That's odd."

"What's wrong?"

"I'm not getting any bounce-back. Grid points aren't responding to my signal. They respond fine on the other side of the hull. My apologies, sir. I thought we were snipe-hunting out here. Looks like we got something on . . ." His brow furrowed. "On a significant area within the sector. Let's go have a look. It's just a few meters away."

As they walked, Geordi wondered.

He looked out in the direction they were traveling, but for the life of him, couldn't see anything abnormal.

It just looked like the hull of the *Enterprise,* complete with sensor pods, bulbs, nodes, antennae, and what-have-you. Windows shone with light, people moved within. It didn't even look *dirty,* for heaven's sake.

And yet something wasn't right. That had been borne out by two separate methods of analysis.

The "hull" of the *Enterprise,* as such, was actually complex strata of different elements, the main component being interlaced microfoam duranium filaments. The pressures of this technological giant were so great under warp and impulse speed, however, that just as important as the physical elements were the "structural integrity field systems," the special forcefields that kept everything adhered and bonded, especially when under stress.

However, the stuff they were actually walking on was a 1.6-centimeter sheet of AGP ablative ceramic fabric chemically bonded onto a substrate of 1.15-centimeter tritanium foil. This was the equivalent of paint. What with meteorites and contact with enemy fire that the *Enterprise* faced, sectors occasionally needed to be stripped off in dry dock and then replaced.

This stretch looked pretty good, though. They hadn't actually gotten a new refitting since they'd visited the Earth after that incident with the Borg, but as far as Geordi could tell, this section was barely pocked or burned at all.

In fact, he didn't notice anything visually troubling. What was showing up as irregularities, then, in the readings he'd taken, and why couldn't Michaels get a read-back on his tricorder?

"Lieutenant Commander La Forge, do you find anything amiss?" The captain's voice was formal and demanding in his ear.

"Not visually, sir, but we're still checking."

"Very well. Report anything immediately. If there's nothing wrong, I don't want to linger in the middle of nowhere."

"Well? You still not getting your read-back?" Geordi asked Michaels.

"A few, but I don't get anything from the ones planted in the primary stratum."

By then they were right in the middle of the sector that had showed the irregularities. Geordi did a 360-degree scan, visually and with his own instrumentation. In one way, things looked all right . . . but there were still those irregularities.

"Funny thing," said Fredricks, looking down at his tricorder. "I'm getting crystal lattice structure readings here. . . ."

"Well, could be the graphite weave," suggested Michaels.

"No . . . it's sort of similar to the stuff we were looking at back at that science station on Phaedra. . . . Altered, but some of the same patterns."

"Well, I don't know, but this looks damned suspicious to me," Geordi said. "But we're not going to get anything more on the tricorders. Michaels, would it be possible to use a phaser to slice off a section of this top layer for analysis inside? Wouldn't do any harm, would it?"

"Absolutely none, sir."

"Let me check with the captain."

Quickly Geordi commed the captain and reported their finding, asking permission to take a sample.

"It's going to take a little longer, sir, than planned."

"Well, wc've got to see what's going on. Continue, Lieutenant."

"Okay, Michaels. You heard the man. We don't need much. How about just a square half meter?"

"You got it, sir. We've done this before on much larger sheets, so it won't take long. We just cut out a section and then release it from its bond." Quickly Michaels radioed in the exact coordinates so that the structural integrity field could be damped in the area.

Geordi watched as the men pulled out their special phasers and adjusted the levels to laser-cutting levels.

Geordi suddenly felt odd. He just wanted to get this sample and get off the hull. Space suddenly didn't seem so wonderful, and the *Enterprise* had a cold feeling to him, as though it were some stranger, some alien impostor.

He wanted to get back to the warmth of his engines.

Two of the men took out their phasers and made the proper adjustments, while Michaels pulled out a marker and drew a quite respectable square without a straight-edge along the hull in an area free of appurtenances.

Michaels put the marker back in the tool belt he wore, then pulled out a pair of strong, old-fashioned pliers.

"Okay, guys," said Geordi, "cut me out that square

there, and give me a hold. Then we'll use just one of those to separate the specimen the rest of the way, while I peel off the skin. We've done this before, so it shouldn't be any problem."

The phasers came alight, and slowly and methodically, with almost surgical precision, cut along the lines that had been drawn, the blooms of light glowing like arc welders. Halfway through the task, Geordi thought he felt a fluctuation in the gravity—as though it plummeted from nearly one g to something quite a bit less.

Quickly his checked his magnetic boots. Still firmly in place. "What was that?"

Michaels responded, "A fluctuation in the artificial gravity. Happens out here sometimes."

Geordi took the opportunity to report. Picard suggested they proceed with caution.

Again, the gravity fluctuation. Geordi felt as though he were in a roller coaster just cresting the top of a hill and starting to go down. And then the full gravity took hold.

"Cripes," said Fredricks. "What's going on?"

"That's funny," said Michaels. "Never happens so often. Geordi, could you check with the guy in charge, plea—"

What happened next occurred so quickly that there was absolutely nothing that could have been done about it. In fact, there was no way that the men on their EVA mission could have possibly been prepared.

The hull *rolled.*

Like a wave in the sea, it bowed up and rolled under them, nearly knocking them off their feet. If not for their magnetic boots, they would have spun off into space.

"What the hell!" said Geordi. He turned to follow the wave.

Just as suddenly, the wave stopped just before the edge of the airlock, freezing for a moment. Beneath the starlight, Geordi could see that the hull no longer resembled the hull in form—it also seemed to be composed of something entirely different.

Crystals winked and shone in light, as though of their own accord, not through any reflection. And Geordi La Forge felt a primitive fear run like wildfire through him.

"Emergency!" he said. "Get us—"

With great speed, the wave changed. The stuff elastically extruded a pseudopod, and struck at the men, hard.

Instinctively Geordi ducked. He fancied he felt the batlike thing whizz over the top of his head. Ensign Michaels was not so lucky. The tip of the club extrusion caught him, striking him hard. It lifted him up, tearing the magnetic boots from their grip on the hold. Michaels's scream shrilled the comm speaker. He was hurled up off the surface of the hull, and then past the gravity field, into the emptiness of space.

"Phasers!" cried Geordi, and it didn't take much more prompting than that for the two armed men to aim their weapons and fire. The beams struck the psuedopod extruding from the hull in the middle. It reacted first by withdrawing, and telescoping back into an amorphous blob, glowing a dull red. . . .

And then, suddenly, its surface became a mirror and the phaser beams were reflected away.

"Turn them off!" screamed Geordi. "Turn them *off!*"

Before they could do anything, though, the beams they shot were swung back on them, striking the nearest. He was thrown to the hull. The other man cut his beam off and flung himself down as well.

The hull moved again.

Geordi could feel the gravity go entirely, as though that cresting roller coaster he was on had just reached the top of the hill and was rolling now not down a railed track, but into raw nothingness.

The hull of the USS *Enterprise* became like the canvas of a trampoline then and simply hurled him off toward the stars.

Chapter Thirteen

THE STARS CHANGED.

Ten-Forward had a nice panoramic view of the stars, and before, they'd been in their strange Dopplering dance of warp drive. Now they'd slowed down and were still.

The band kept on playing, though, not noticing, but Data noticed immediately.

Mikal, sitting at a table alongside him and Penelope, noticed as well. "We've come out of warp," he said.

"Why are we stopping?" Penelope wanted to know. She didn't seem particularly interested. She seemed concerned and preoccupied with other matters.

"A diagnostic, level one, is being performed," replied Data. "The captain must have decided to take the warp engines off-line to check them."

"Makes sense," said Mikal. "This sort of thing happens all the time. Diagnostics, I mean."

"Diagnostics occur automatically every day," said

Data. "Level-one diagnostics occur only at monthly intervals or when trouble is suspected."

"And this isn't a monthly interval."

"No."

"Nothing we can do, right? Might as well enjoy the party. But, Data . . . I would think that you would have been asked to participate. I mean, you'd be perfect for that kind of analysis."

Data opened his mouth to reply truthfully, but received a kick in the shin from Penelope, along with a significant glare. He knew her well enough by now to recognize the signal. It was good that she was so reactive, given this social interaction. Nonetheless, Data was concerned about her aggressive nature. He would have to speak to Troi about this. Again, he wondered why Troi was not there. According to his calculations, she was a full ten minutes late. Her presence would not doubt go a long way to ease the situation.

"I am being trained in human social interaction and being helped by Penelope here. As such, I received special dispensation. My presence is not required for this diagnostic. However, I can be called to assist, if necessary."

"Data's such a good student. But he's got a long way to go," said Penelope, patting her "pupil" on the shoulder. "But you must tell us more about yourself, Mikal."

"Oh, I've been blabbing away too much anyway. Perhaps you could tell me something more about your—"

He was interrupted by Metrina Harcourt. "Hello. Well, Mikal, I didn't think I could make it . . . but here I am."

"Oh. Metrina! Glad to see you."

She nodded to the others. "Can I steal him for just a

moment? I want him to meet a friend. I'll bring him right back."

Data didn't know what to say. Penelope was speechless. But the most shocked person was Mikal. "Well, I don't know. . . ." he said.

"Just a nanosecond, and we'll come right back."

"That's all right, Mikal," said Penelope. "We'll be right here." Mikal, bemused, allowed the young woman to lead him off. They walked over to the other side of the room to where a knot of people were standing by the refreshment table.

"Data!" Penelope said immediately. "Data, this is just *disaster!*"

Data looked around, startled. Seeing that everything appeared to be all right, he turned to Penelope. "I'm sure that the diagnostic is well in hand. We have an excellent crew and they are dealing with whatever the matter is and—"

"No! I mean, Mikal and that girl. . . ." Penelope looked absolutely stricken. "She's going to keep him all to herself. This is just going to be terrible!"

Data considered. "He is not abandoning us. He is merely participating in that conversation. Why should that be threatening to you, Penelope?"

"I wanted him to come here so that he would pay attention to *me,* that's why. It's your fault. You shouldn't have let him go with her! You should have been more *interesting.*"

Data was confused. "I am sorry." He was sorry; however, he was also pleased. There was a moment there in which Penelope was clearly teetering on the edge of her condition. How easy it would be for her simply to not deal with this, to cut herself off again in that safe little world. As primitive and as selfish as these emotions that she was expressing were, he could almost hear Deanna Troi saying that she was releasing them, which was a healthy thing for her. "But perhaps you should wait and see what happens before you make any more judgments as to the eventual outcome."

She seethed, but calmed down. She had a good mind, and ultimately she saw the wisdom of what he was saying. "Very well. But you must help me keep some of his attention!"

"I will do my best."

Penelope sighed. "Okay, okay. I'm being really immature. But do more than just stand there like a lump next time, Data. You're here to help."

Data nodded. "I will do what I can, Penelope."

"You're such a sweetheart. Data, you know, if all men were like you, women would be a lot better off."

Data cocked his head. "But if all men were like me, they would not be men, would they?"

"You are so exasperating sometimes!" she said. She looked up, and immediately pasted a smile on her face. Data turned and saw that Mikal was returning, with Metrina Harcourt in tow.

"Guess who I found," said Mikal, gaily.

Metrina nodded politely. "Thanks so much for letting me borrow him. I hope you don't mind if I linger here a moment."

"No, of course not!" said Penelope.

Mikal laughed. "Isn't she a sweetheart, Metrina? Penelope wanted to make sure I felt welcome here on the *Enterprise,* so she and Data invited me to this dance." He pursed his lips. "But, Metrina. I thought you were on security this evening."

"My shift was let off early, and I had nothing much to do. I thought I'd sample some of the music. I'm rather a fan. I have many recordings of the old bands."

"Excellent. We were just talking about the history, weren't we, folks? Isn't it funny that this particular kind of music has lasted so long?" commented Mikal.

"Good music tends to linger through the ages," said Metrina.

There was a moment of uncomfortable silence—a "conversational lull" was the term, Data believed. He did his best to fill in.

"Do you not think that Penelope is one of the most beautiful women here this evening? According to my understanding of human aesthetics."

Penelope's eyes widened. "Well, thank you, Data."

"I'm diplomatic enough to agree that she's absolutely beautiful—but each woman shines in her own way," Mikal said. That drew a slight smile from Metrina. "I mean, you must admit, Metrina, this outfit you've got on now's a lot nicer than a security outfit!"

There was another conversational lull. However, before Data could step in to pick up the pace, the band ended the song they were playing. Will Riker put his trombone down and stepped up to the mike. "Hope you all are having a good time!"

The crowd cheered and clapped.

"Normally, as you know, I'm partial to Dixieland jazz, but tonight's music is a lot of fun, don't you think?"

The crowd generally agreed.

"Good. Well, we're going to step it up quite a bit with a quick dance number. So don't worry about looking stupid—just move around a little bit and have a good time. This is called 'Jumpin' Jive.'" To a smattering of applause, he moved back to his place, picked up his instrument, moved the slide back and forth in preparation, and then waved for the downbeat.

The band launched into a fast, peppy dance number.

"Great. Who's for dancing then?" said Mikal.

Penelope went white. "This really isn't something I can do, I don't think."

"Mikal," said Metrina. "You seem to know the music. Do you know how to dance to it?"

Mikal shrugged. "I can try." She nodded toward the dance floor. "I don't see anyone out there doing anything particularly special."

"Good. We'll be right back." Metrina didn't even look at them as she said it. She dragged Mikal out and immediately began twirling and swirling up a storm.

Penelope slumped into her chair. She didn't look as though she was going to check out of reality, observed Data, but she didn't look particularly happy, either.

He was at a total loss as to what to do or to say. This was something beyond his depth.

Fortunately, Deanna Troi chose that moment to arrive. She made her way through the crush, holding a cup of punch in her hand. "Oh, there you two are! Sorry I'm late. I had some writing I had to finish up . . . and . . ." Her face changed as she picked up on her patient's emotions. "Oh dear. What's wrong? Where's Mikal?"

Penelope pointed out to the dance floor. Troi turned and immediately saw the young man dancing with Metrina, clearly having a marvelous time. Data noted her face changing to an expression of understanding. She gave him a significant look, and then sat down alongside them.

"Have you and Mikal danced?" she asked.

"Yes. But I can only do slower numbers."

"And so he found someone who could do something faster," observed Troi.

"I believe that I was an unacceptable choice," said Data.

"Hmm. And you'd hoped to have him all to yourself." The trombone hit a wrong note, and Troi cringed. "Will always does better with Dixieland, I think." She patted Penelope's knee. "It's only a dance. It's not the end of the world."

"I don't think he likes her as much as me," said Penelope.

"I think the young man just wanted to dance with someone. You really shouldn't take it too personally. And you know, you're doing very well. I can see that being with Data has taken you long strides. . . ."

"Yes," asserted Data. "She carried on quite an excellent conversation with Mikal."

Penelope beamed. "I did! I was shy at first . . . but I generally spoke my mind."

"Excellent. I'm so pleased with you. And no spells?"

Penelope looked surprised. "No, I guess not."

"Good. I think that we've won a real victory here, dance or no dance." She seemed thoughtful for a moment. "Data, you dance, do you not?"

"I have had lessons. And of course, I have access to the dance steps."

"You know, you might as well just jump in and give it a try, Penelope. Far better than sitting around moping."

Data said, "This is true, Penelope. No one out there seems to be executing any difficult moves. We could just call it a lesson."

Penelope looked doubtful, but then when she glanced over at the dancers, Mikal chose that moment to twirl Metrina around. The security officer laughed and seemed to be having a wonderful time.

"Teach me how to do *that,* Data," said Penelope, "and you've got a dance partner."

"Data, I believe you've found a new calling in life," said Troi.

"I am uncertain of my suitability," said Data, standing up and offering Penelope his hand. "However, I will view it as a challenge."

"Good. Go to it, you two!" said Troi, laughing.

Data and Penelope moved out onto the dance floor. "Have you been observing the movements of the people out here?" Data asked her.

"Yes. It seems a little chaotic."

"Yes; however, there are always basic patterns to the steps, which can be played with. The play, Dr. Crusher informs me, is as important as the pattern. However, you must know that pattern to understand the parameters."

Penelope looked lost.

"Stand here and watch me."

Data stepped back. He held his hand out, miming the presence of a partner. And then he began showing her the necessary movements of the feet.

"That doesn't look too difficult," said Penelope.

"Let's do it together. You just do as I do." He took her hand, and they moved, woodenly at first, Penelope following Data's steps precisely.

"Very good!" called Troi. "Very good, Penelope!"

"Now maybe a little faster, Data?" the girl suggested.

"Very well."

It wasn't the best of dances, but they did it, and suddenly Penelope seemed to be having a good time. The band went right into another quick swing number, and the dancers just kept on dancing, Data and Penelope amongst them.

"Okay, Data," said the girl. "Now swing me!"

Data swung her.

She twirled around, laughing. It wasn't the most graceful of moves, but neither was it out of control. Penelope seemed to exult in it, laughing almost gaily. A few meters from them, Data could see that Mikal noticed them. He seemed slightly perplexed, but mostly happy that Data had gotten Penelope out dancing. Doubtless he would ask her for another dance . . . a fast one this time. Emotions were all very well, thought Data, but clearly, often as not, humans paid far too much attention to them.

Perhaps he was teaching Penelope more than dancing.

When it was over, she seemed radiant with confidence.

"Excuse me, Data." She stepped over to where Mikal and Metrina were standing. "Pardon me, Metrina. But I think the next dance is mine!" She smiled as she caught Mikal by the arm and pulled him away into the sound of the next number, leaving Metrina with an astonished look on her face.

"Funny," Data heard Mikal tell Penelope. "While I was dancing with Metrina . . . it was as though I heard your voice in my head, calling for me."

Data stepped back to Troi.

"I do believe you're getting the knack of it, Data," said Troi, smiling.

"Dancing?"

"Yes," the counselor said. "That, too."

They watched the young couple. They danced excellently and seemed to be having a wonderful time.

The song was just coming to an end when the whole deck of Ten-Forward shook as though the *Enterprise* had been hit by a photon torpedo.

The music stopped, and the dancing stopped.

People screamed.

And things, thought Data as he lurched toward the ground, having lost his balance, had been going so well. . . .

Chapter Fourteen

THIS IS IT, thought Geordi La Forge. This is how I'm going to die.

It wasn't his training that made him think that as he hurtled away from the hull of the *Enterprise*. It was the incredible sense of helplessness.

He twirled head over heels in space, squirming about to get ahold of something, grab something that might be of help.

He could taste his own sweat, smell his own fear. Beyond him, he could see the other members of the team flounder away.

A globule of blood hung in the vacuum.

Below, the skin of the *Enterprise* crawled.

He had just gotten ahold of his phaser, and for that matter, himself, when the scene changed.

One moment he was in the midst of vacuum, radio crackling in his ear; the next, he felt a familiar shiver and found himself on the transporter platform.

Two of the other workers were with him.

Transporter Chief O'Brien peered up from behind his assemblage of controls, motioned them off.

"I'm locking on to the others!"

Geordi hopped off the platform, tearing at the top of his environmental suit, getting the helmet off. He felt claustrophobic. Even as he did so, the yellow-alert Klaxon began to sound, and the ship began to shudder.

Geordi banged into a wall.

The ship steadied, and O'Brien brought in the other men he'd managed to lock on to.

Two were all right. Shaken but alive.

The other was Michaels, who was a mess. Geordi could barely bring himself to look at him. What the flailing pseudopod had apparently done was more than just crack his skull. It had destroyed the helmet, and the vacuum had done the rest.

A medical team hurried in, but Michaels was past help.

Geordi adjusted his VISOR. He could feel the sweat dripping from him and onto the controls. He hit the right button. "Captain. La Forge here. Did you see any of that?"

The captain's voice was stern and somber. "Yes, Lieutenant Commander. I've aligned phasers toward that portion of the hull—however, the creature seems to have disappeared. We've got a sensor analysis of the proceedings, however. I hesitate to use weapons on what appears to be my own ship."

"I've got the specimen cut from the hull sir," reported O'Brien. "Should I bring it in?"

"Not yet, Chief. I'll want it for analysis . . . but not until I know we can analyze it safely. Give us the coordinates and we'll put a tractor beam on it."

"Yes sir."

"After the analysis, I want a full meeting in the observation deck," said Picard. "Over."

Geordi La Forge looked down at the bloody stretcher carrying away the body of Michaels. "I think we've discovered the problem Beta Epsilon had," he said grimly. "And it looks as though we've brought it along with us."

There had been a few minor injuries when the ship rocked. Apparently the structural integrity field had somehow fouled up the inertial damping, causing a movement trauma. In any event, the only real victims so far, thought Jean-Luc Picard as he confronted his primary crew on the observation deck, were Ensign Michaels and the *Enterprise* itself.

Michaels was unfortunately beyond help.

He dared not think that was the case with the *Enterprise.*

"Good. We're all here. Reports."

Commander Riker spoke first. "I think we've all seen playback."

"Yes. It looked as though the *Enterprise* attacked its own people," said Beverly, unable to get the look of horror out of her eyes. "There was absolutely nothing I could do for Ensign Michaels."

"Dr. Crusher is not far from wrong, sir," Riker said. "This is the reason why this . . . this *whatever* it is . . . was not detected earlier. It *is* the hull . . . or at least a large portion of it. And we have determined how far it's spread."

"I don't understand," said the captain. "Is it some sort of space organism that's attached itself to us?"

Riker answered, "This seems to be some kind of inorganic process or creature that takes inorganic matter and literally *becomes* that matter."

"Imprecise, I'm afraid, Commander Riker," said Data. "With the events that have occurred in mind, I examined the quantity of clay brought aboard from the science station to test."

"We're sure that the two are related?" said Troi.

"It stands to reason," said Riker. "We ejected the clay that we dragged aboard in the shuttle. Looks like it settled somehow on the hull. With the results we've observed."

"Continue, Data," said Picard. "From all signs, this *is* a creature, yet clearly not an organic creature."

"Not exactly, sir. The term 'organic life' comprises living creatures based on the carbon molecule. Carbon is conducive to the development of life because it is so large and can bond in so many different ways. However, other common molecules in nature such as silicon are also large and conducive toward life. And we have encountered silicon-based life before."

"Have we?"

"'Tin Man,' for one," said Troi.

Beverly Crusher nodded. "Lots of others, not so obvious. Silicon-based life might not be oxygen breathers, but they can still consist of stuff analogous to flesh and blood. And then there's the extreme. . . ." She took a breath. "The Crystalline Entity."

Picard nodded. He knew that would come up—the creature that had destroyed the colony on Omnicron Theta IV, and that the *Enterprise* had destroyed years later, before actually being able to contact it or analyze it.

"Similar, perhaps, but not necessarily related," said Data. "However, paths of conjecture concerning the Crystalline Entity are dovetailing in my theories concerning our present dilemma."

"I just want to know how to kill it!" said Riker.

"Please. We don't know if it's intelligent," said Picard.

"It's eating our ship!" said Geordi.

"Again, not precisely, Commander," said Data. "It is *transforming* our ship. The creature clearly maintains the form and function of the matter it utilizes to replicate. It is using the *Enterprise* for a process of replication which proves some interesting theories concerning the beginnings of life on Earth."

"Does this really bear on our problem, Data?"

"Yes, sir. I will make the explanation as brief as possible." Data's fingers played on buttons, and graphics appeared on a screen. DNA and RNA molecules. The building blocks of life. "DNA and RNA, of course, carry the information for replication in humans and life from Earth. Enzymes, amino acids, nucleotides—the chemistry of the genetic code, altered into different organisms and species through mutation and natural selection. In a word, evolution. Scientists assumed that this rose up—at least on Earth—from a kind of chemical soup in the oceans, interacting with lightning. But whither the start of DNA?

"In the twentieth century, Dr. A. G. Cairns-Smith of Great Britain created a controversial theory. He observed that genetic information is the only stuff that actually evolves. Living creatures die. He noted that DNA is a molecule far from natural biochemical patterns. He theorized that there was a scaffolding of sorts that started DNA in the primordial ooze, and noted the natural way that crystals replicate themselves. Indeed, planets make clay all the time . . . Clay is replicating matter. . . ."

"You mean, matter that grows and reproduces itself?" said Beverly. "And this thing is intelligent inorganic matter!"

"Wait a minute," said Riker. "You're saying that this . . . this thing is some sort of ancestor?"

"No. Not at all. Each planet owns a different set of parameters. What I am saying is that, given the proper developmental circumstances, this creature may have developed on Earth instead of the present forms of life . . . But it appears to have developed on Phaedra. Simple clay evolved far past our full understanding."

"A living clay creature," said Beverly, shuddering slightly.

"That doesn't make it intelligent, though," said Troi. "I can't sense any emotions."

"And you also get no readings from me," observed Data. "Intelligent beings need not have emotions. Nor do emotions imply intelligence."

"And your specimen . . . ?"

"The analysis seems to indicate that it is capable of replication as well. However, what appears to be happening is the creation of a neural network of intracommunications between grouping colonies of crystalline cells of the mass of the thing."

"You mean, as it grows, it develops a nervous system," said Geordi. "And a *brain?*"

"Yes and no. There is no central nervous system. In effect, you could say that it *is* one large brain."

"It killed one of my officers," said Picard.

"Only when attacked," said Troi.

"Efforts are being made to communicate with it." Picard stroked his chin. "However, we have evidence other than Ensign Michaels's death that this thing is not from a benign background."

Riker nodded. "The science colony. There was that clay all over. . . . But it didn't attack us. . . . It was just clay."

"Data?" said Picard.

"I am still working on that, sir."

"Then given our current knowledge of the creature, what is its present state and what is its present rate of growth?"

It was Geordi's turn to operate the computer controls. He pulled up a graphic of the *Enterprise.* "Well, sir, the thing comprises about nine hundred and thirty-two square meters of the hull. . . . We're searching for more of the stuff."

"I suggest you check the septic system, too," said Ensign Fredricks. "We sluiced some mud off ourselves and down the drain."

"Good idea."

"Commander Riker," Picard said, "plot a course to the nearest starbase. If we find we have to remove a part of our hull, we're going to have to replace it as well . . . and that large a section can't be dealt with easily out in deep space."

"Yes, sir."

"Data and Geordi . . . continue your work."

"Yes, sir."

Picard swiveled to face Beverly Crusher. "Anything else on Dr. Tillstrom?"

"No, sir. Still in a coma."

"And her son. A recovered memory could go a long way toward helping us."

"We're still working on that."

Data said, "Mikal has returned to his quarters. He is well and trying very hard."

"Fine. I suggest you brief him on this . . . Maybe some of this might jog his memory."

"Yes, sir."

"Any further thoughts?"

Riker spoke immediately. "Captain. Over twenty people were killed on Beta Epsilon. We've lost one person already. I'd strongly suggest that we utilize phasers to destroy that thing on the hull. We can block off that portion of the interior easily. It seems to be like some sort of cancer, sir. I say cut it out, before it metastasizes."

"That's just what I plan to do, Commander, if there is no other alternative," said Picard grimly. "But before then, I need more information. In the meantime, we head for a starbase. From there another ship can take the vaccine to its destination, if we cannot. Is that understood?"

They nodded. Picard's face remained stoic. He didn't want to let them see how worried he was. "Fine. You all know what must be done—find out what exactly this thing is, determine the extent of its penetration. If we can contain it, we shall contain it. If we can communicate with it, then we shall communicate with it." He paused meaningfully. "And if it indeed threatens us further, if the lives of other members of this crew are endangered, then it *must* be destroyed." He stood up. "This meeting is adjourned."

The others filed out, going back to their particular work.

"Data. A moment, if you please."

"Yes, sir." Data hung back.

"You seem to be getting along well with Mikal Tillstrom."

"I am, sir. He apparently respects me."

"Good. I can't help but feel that if we had the information that's locked in his mind—or the mind of his mother—we'd be in a much better position." He nodded, pausing a moment to consider. "Come. We need to have a word with him before you go back to your analysis."

Interlude

It awoke.

The pain was what woke it from its dreaming, and as it came awake, it found itself lashing out at the source of the pain.

At first all was chaos, confusion.

It felt the electronic activity within its body flail and surge, rippling and canceling some of the fields that surrounded it. But then, as it cut off the pain receptors, flowing back into wholeness, it stopped and it re-grouped.

Instinctively it sensed the presence of bad life.

The bad life scuttled and crawled within the confines of the new Vessel of Life that was its home. It knew that the bad life was its enemy, and the bad life would destroy it if it could. The bad life smelled of malevolent intent.

However, the flow and flux of this vessel—it was so complex and puzzling. Even though the majority of the vessel was composed of the Sacred material, there were puzzling forces and energies that pulsed within.

The being sensed that these energies could harm it.

It cataloged its resources. It was not very large yet, only large enough for awareness and consciousness. However, the field lay open for it to grow.

And so it grew. . . .

And as it grew, its crystals breaking the covalent bonds of the molecules of the hull of the Enterprise *and beyond and replicating itself utilizing them, it cataloged itself and its colonies. . . .*

And it cast out mentally for its other parts it sensed within the Vessel of Becoming.

Chapter Fifteen

"I'M SORRY, CAPTAIN. I still don't remember anything."

Picard stared at the young man. Mikal's face was strained, pale even. Clearly he was trying hard, and was every bit as frustrated as Picard. The information that they'd given him about the clay from Phaedra had not jogged his memory at all. It had merely upset him.

"We feel that you must have encountered the like of this entity before," Data said. "Perhaps if I related its composition. You have geological training."

"You know, I feel that way, too. It's like it's on the tip of my tongue . . . but it's also like part of me doesn't *want* to remember."

"Trauma?" said Picard, looking over to Dr. Crusher significantly. "Have you approached unlocking the young man's memory from that point of view?"

"We've tried everything. It's just going to have to come on its own."

"I see. How are you feeling, Mikal?"

"As well as can be expected, sir."

"I mean—your headaches."

"The drugs pretty much wipe them out."

"You realize that it's that engram-circuitry in your head that's causing the headaches, don't you?"

"Yes, sir."

"And you still don't remember why you have it?"

Mikal seemed slightly annoyed. "I told you . . . If I got the slightest memory about *anything* important, I'd tell you."

Picard put his hand on the young man's shoulder. "I know, Mikal. But this business . . . it's a bit of a strain."

"I can well understand that, sir. And I haven't got a single doubt that it's got everything to do with what happened on Beta Epsilon." Mikal Tillstrom stared expressively into Picard's eyes, the image of sincerity. "But I just don't remember!" He looked as though he was on the verge of tears. He grabbed at his head and grimaced. "Well, the headache's back, anyway."

"I apologize," said Picard.

"Perhaps you'd better go, Jean-Luc."

"A word with you privately first, Doctor."

She took him back to her office.

"I have made a decision. I know you, Doctor, and I have a trifling acquaintance with your profession." He paused for a moment. "You're not doing everything you can to extract the memory from that young man, are you?"

She frowned, and shot him a hard look. "There are other more radical . . . more risky methods, sir. RNA de-inhibitors. EM stimulation. The equivalent of shock therapy. Surgery even. The result, though, could leave us with nothing . . . and they could destroy a young man's mind. Would you have that on your hands, Captain? When his mother wakes up, do you want to say, I'm so sorry, your boy's brain-dead?"

"No. You're quite right. Before, we had the leisure

to wait. Now we do not." Picard took a breath. "Continue to do what you can to retrieve young Tillstrom's memory safely."

"Yes, sir," she replied.

"That engram mechanism . . . Can it be removed?"

"Yes. But I'm afraid it will only make matters worse in regard to the boy's memory."

"I see. Can you then tap in to it in some fashion—connect it to a computer to download *its* memory?"

"I could try."

"Only if your other attempts fail. You're a good doctor, Beverly. A good surgeon. I realize you do not care to take these kinds of risks. However, the life of a crew member has already been taken . . . and over twenty lives were lost on that science station. We need facts, Beverly . . . facts buried in that brain, so that no further lives shall be lost. You might ask Mikal Tillstrom how far *he's* willing to go to help us."

Crusher nodded. "Thank you, sir. I'll see what—"

She was interrupted by a communication from Picard's insignia.

"Captain, this is La Forge."

"Yes, Lieutenant."

"Sir, could you get down to Engineering? I want to show you something." There was almost an audible gulp. "We've got problems."

Geordi La Forge tapped the schematic.

"The black stuff, sir."

Picard looked at the three-dimensional representation of the *Enterprise.* He gritted his teeth. He'd been afraid of this, and now here it was. . . .

"We analyzed that section we took off the hull and did an intensive search throughout the *Enterprise* for similar molecular structure. This is what came up."

It was like a fungus, holding his ship in its creeping, crawling grip. There was the large expanse on the hull, of course, black and growing—but there were also spots elsewhere, another large one on the Saucer Module, and smaller ones through the water pipes.

Picard pointed. "This one is—"

Geordi nodded grimly. "That's the biggest problem, sir. Apparently the stuff spread from one of the pipes, directly through the walls. It's touching the engines, sir."

"How is that affecting our progress to the starbase, Geordi?"

"Well, sir, let's just say we don't want to push it. I can still get warp five out of them, but if I take it further, there might be a hazard."

"Warp five it will be, Lieutenant."

Geordi shook his head. "It's like a cancer. Anything more on what exactly it is, sir?"

"We're working around the clock."

Geordi nodded. "I've been thinking about that sir, and that might be another problem."

"Yes? Go on."

"Well, sir, this stuff seems to use inorganic matter to replicate. . . . Are we sure we want Data anywhere near samples of it?"

Picard nodded. "A very good point, Lieutenant. We should speak to him immediately. At the very least, he should take necessary precautions."

"Yes, sir."

Data was running tests.

He was in the geology lab, which had the appropriate equipment, and he was performing the tests on the piece of hull that Chief O'Brien had transported up there for him.

It was all fascinating.

The original specimen of clay retrieved from the shuttle was still in its original form, and seemed innocent enough, albeit with complex layers of crystal structures new to Data's experience. However, the piece of "hull" was an entirely different affair. There were the crystal structures, all right, but they were like sheaths of silicon that had magically reshuffled themselves into something a good deal more sophisticated than an isolinear chip.

And with so much more depth and possibilities. There was not only the equivalent of neurons and nerve pathways—there was the equivalent of muscle and other kinds of cells . . . which was how the stuff had been able to move and react to the intrusion by the EVA team.

He wished he could have predicted this. However, it was still difficult to see the relationship between the mud and this cross section of a living, inorganic being.

Most certainly, though, he should have been working on the matter here and not been at that dance.

However, Data did not waste time with regrets. He continued his work.

No one had been hurt when the ship had rocked. However, it had brought the social occasion to a halt, with people immediately reporting to their duty stations or taking refuge in their quarters. Data supposed that this is what Penelope must have done, though he did not give it much thought.

Other things were consuming his attention.

Nonetheless, a part of his mind thought about the girl and hoped she was well and not too frightened by the experience. She'd not only stayed calm during the crisis, she'd helped with the people who'd suffered injuries.

He was about to perform a chemical experiment on the detached chunk of hull when the captain and Lieutenant La Forge walked into the room.

"Data. Lieutenant La Forge has brought a matter to my attention of immediate relevance," said Picard.

"Yeah. I was just wondering if it's real smart for you

162

to be playing with this stuff. . . ." Geordi motioned with distaste at the specimens in their clear cases.

"You refer to the threat to my own inorganic substances. You do not have to worry. I have taken precautions." He tapped the cases. "Organic plastics. Tests show that the material is incapable of utilizing it for replication. Hence it is not able to grow, thus neutralizing it. Any handling is done utilizing gloves of similar construction. Naturally, I am exercising caution."

"Excellent. Glad to hear it. I can't help but wish we'd exercised caution before in this matter," said Picard.

"Prediction of such an event, given the information we had, was close to impossible, sir. You may congratulate yourself on discovering the creature's activity so soon and taking the proper steps. May I inquire as to what indications you based your decision on?"

"Intuition," said Picard. "The whole thing down on that station bothered me in a way I cannot explain. . . ." He stepped over to the material and looked down at first the mound of clay, and then the transformed section of hull. "Doesn't look particularly impressive, does it?"

"I believe the threat lies in the sum of its parts."

"Well, there's no question that there's a threat here—the question is, if this thing is intelligent, and if the threat is intentional."

"May I inquire as to the attempt in communication?" said Data.

"We beamed a message utilizing the Universal Translator. No response." Picard tapped the table, then turned toward Data. "Anything this beastie doesn't like?"

"I am presently testing a variety of organically based acids and solutions, sir, with no notable result."

"What about removing it the way the Crystalline

Entity was destroyed, with high-frequency vibrations?"

"The problem there, sir, is the extent of the spread. For we would be destroying a substantial portion of the *Enterprise.*"

"Yes," said Picard. "Nonetheless, keep up the good work, Data. We should have realized you'd take care not to get it on yourself—but we just wanted to make sure."

"I appreciate your concern, Captain. And I applaud the wisdom of your decision to reach a starbase. This is a matter best dealt with in dry dock."

Picard nodded. "Please report any further discoveries here immediately, Data."

"Yes, sir."

"Come on, Geordi. We've got work to do."

The two men left, leaving Data alone with the material. He immediately proceeded to continue his testing.

"Captain!" It was Beverly Crusher's voice over the comm. "Hurry."

Captain Jean-Luc Picard sat at his desk in his quarters, poring over screens of information, analyzing, observing, playing with possibility. He'd gone down here for a catnap, but he hadn't been able to relax.

So he'd gotten up and worked.

"Are you in sickbay, Doctor?" he asked.

"Yes."

Generally, when Dr. Crusher had something to report, she did so verbally. The fact that she had summoned him meant that something important had happened with either Dr. Tillstrom or her son.

He hurried to sickbay.

There, he found Beverly sitting at her desk. In a

chair, looking totally relieved of pain and trouble, was Mikal Tillstrom, speaking intently with her.

He turned when he entered, and smiled a troubled smile.

"Captain," said Mikal Tillstrom. "I think I remember." He drew a deep breath and released it. "I think I remember something of what happened on Beta Epsilon."

Chapter Sixteen

HIS EYES WERE HAUNTED.

As Picard looked at him, he could see the change. There was a completeness here, and yet it was not necessarily for the good emotionally. What was that cycle of William Blake poems? Yes, *Songs of Innocence and Experience.* Mikal Tillstrom was singing a song of experience . . . and it hadn't been a good one.

He seemed to be perspiring slightly, and there was the sour smell of fear to him.

"Relax, Mikal," said Jean-Luc Picard, sitting down beside the fellow, trying to look as patient as possible, trying not to make him feel any more tense than he already was. "Don't strain yourself. You're among friends now."

"I know . . . I know . . . It was just so *awful.*"

Picard looked up to Beverly Crusher. The doctor read the unspoken order immediately. "Mikal, I'm just going to give you a mild sedative. You'll feel better, I promise. . . ."

"But I won't forget, will I? I won't forget again?"

Beverly looked up at Picard, then back down at Mikal. "No. And you won't lose consciousness either."

Mikal nodded. The sweat gleamed on his brow. Beverly readied the syringe, touched the edge to his skin. A whooshing, and it was over.

The effect on Mikal was immediate. His eyes steadied and he relaxed visibly.

"Yes. Yes, that's better," he murmured.

"All right, Mikal. You need to tell us. . . . What happened on Phaedra?"

Mikal asked for a glass of water. Beverly got him one, and he drank half of it in quick gulps. He turned and looked at Picard. "The clay . . . it was everywhere. . . ."

"Yes, Mikal," said Picard. "We know that. It's on our ship now. It's taking over the ship . . . It's somehow *becoming* the ship, bonding with the inorganics and replicating its own molecular structure within matter." Picard took a breath. "It's *becoming* the *Enterprise*. Is that what happened on the science station?"

"Yes. Yes, that's what happened. We tried to battle the stuff . . . the mud . . . the awful mud. We achieved partial success. . . ."

"How, Mikal?" said Picard. *"How?"*

"Let me start from the beginning." He took the glass of water back from the side of the bed and took a long swallow of it. He placed it back and then looked at Dr. Crusher and then Captain Picard.

Then he began his story.

When Dr. Adrienne Tillstrom was asked to go to the science station on Phaedra, she'd been thrilled. She had specifically requested the assignment, since the planet was already becoming known in exogeology as a cutting-edge assignment. However, the assignment was for a period of three years, in a segment of time she felt vital to the education of her son—an education the two of them had decided that she would oversee.

"Since we moved around so much, my mother was always my tutor," Mikal explained. It worked out very well because she had such wide knowledge and was such an excellent teacher. She wanted me to attend a good school, but she felt there were things I should have background in first. For my part, there had never been any doubt in my mind that I wanted a career in exogeology, and I saw the assignment as a not-to-be-missed opportunity for field experience as I learned. I figured that I could finish my university education later.

"The problem was that in order to go, I had to fill a scientific function, and I didn't have the necessary knowledge. It was Mom who suggested the engram-circuit, and I agreed. She knew people who cut through the red tape of semilegality, and she knew the people who could supply it and the people who could put it in. It wasn't a long operation. The very next day, I had a whole new vista of knowledge—and I passed the necessary test to fill a technical position on the Phaedran outpost easily."

They packed and left almost immediately thereafter, making sure that Mikal brought along sufficient textbooks to continue his education in his spare hours between work assignments.

"It was a sacrifice. There weren't going to be any people my own age. But my mother had given me such a love for learning that I figured it would be worth it . . . and for the most part, it was. For five months it was hard work and hard learning . . . but I knew even then that the experience would be worth it."

The station studied all aspects of the planet of

Phaedra, mapping the peculiar polar shifts and studying the movement on and below the planet's crust.

"One day we were out, just taking a walk, looking at the auroras. It was a form of exercise and a form of aesthetics, too. . . . The auroras are quite majestic, quite beautiful there. The science station is in a valley, and we were toward the end of that valley, and we noticed that there had been a mud slide off of a ridge . . . a most peculiar kind of clay mud.

"One of the scientists, Dr. Springton, whose specialty was crystals, took a large sample for study, and then we hiked back to the station. A couple of days later, he asked some of the other higher scientists to come and have a look at the stuff, which he'd been subjecting to a lot of tests.

"I remember my mother coming back very excited from a meeting which had involved a number of elaborate tests involving the new kind of clay, and promising to share it with me later.

"The next day, though, there was some trouble. The clay seemed to be growing . . . engulfing . . . changing things around it. Efforts were made to curtail it, but it grew very fast. We had top exogeologists there, too . . . and they attempted to dissolve it using liquids that normally dissolve crystals. . . . Dr. Springton was particularly successful in this. In fact, he came up with a solution that we were all involved in synthesizing. Unfortunately, it didn't dissolve the stuff . . . it just seemed to curtail its growth.

"For a time, we thought that we'd discovered the answer to our problem, we'd contained it, so we didn't think we had to evacuate . . . or signal for help. Dr. Springton expressly told us that we had the problem under control and could proceed with our lives while he continued his experiments.

"But then, the morning of two days hence, all hell broke loose."

Mikal Tillstrom had awoken to cries and the sounds of battle. He'd pulled on his clothes and found a battle from hell raging in the station.

"The clay stuff—it was alive! It was growing and rolling out from its containment—Apparently more of the stuff had come in somehow in the night. . . . And we soon saw why. . . ."

The creature had produced offshoots of itself in humanoid form.

"They were killing us all. They'd cut off the route to the solution we'd developed. It was a massacre.

"I remember fighting one of the things, and it hitting me over the head. . . . The next thing I knew . . . well, I was here . . . on the *Enterprise.*"

Picard nodded. "Incredible."

"He should rest, Captain," said Dr. Crusher.

"One last thing, Mikal . . . Can you tell us what this solution was . . . the solution that halted the growth of the creature?"

"Yes. I recall pretty specifically because I helped mix some of it."

"I think we've got the facilities . . . but we'll just need the listing of components and the instructions, along with the proper procedures."

Mikal Tillstrom closed his eyes. "That's no problem," he said softly.

"Doctor. A recorder if you please . . ." requested Picard.

"Yes." The doctor obliged.

"All right," said Mikal. "Yes. Yes, I think I've got what you need."

He began to reel off the names of chemicals.

"Sir, you called for me?"

"Yes, Number One."

Picard turned away from the report on the screen

he'd been reading and looked up for a moment at Commander Riker.

"The spraying has commenced."

"Yes, with admirable results. Still, it only seems to be slowing the thing down."

"Yes, sir. We should, in my opinion, continue our course to the starbase, where we can seek additional help."

Riker looked profoundly uncomfortable. Something was weighing on him.

"Please sit down, Number One."

"Thank you, sir."

"I thought we should talk."

"Yes."

"I should like your opinions, Commander. We seem to be dealing with a creature the likes of which we have not encountered. The question in my mind is, should we continue our attempts to communicate with it?"

"Of course, sir. That goes without saying."

"Yes. We must continue according to the guidelines outlined by the Federation and Starfleet. And yet . . ."

"Exactly, Captain. And yet . . ." Riker pounded a fist into a palm. "And yet, it's all very well to have a rosy, positive view of life in the universe, but you have to admit that the basic philosophy of many life-forms—those that originated on Earth high on the list—is wanton, selfish survival and expansion at all costs. I'm sorry to say this, sir, but this thing seems to fall into that category."

Picard grunted. "Survival of the fittest."

"Kill or be killed. Exactly."

"That's all very well, but we must first exhaust all other avenues." He tapped the readout. "The spraying that Mikal suggested—it seems to be working."

"It's only *slowing* the growth of the creature, sir."

Riker stood up. He turned to go, then stopped. "Oh. One more thing, Captain."

"Yes, Number One."

"That Mikal Tillstrom fellow—the only conscious survivor—why did he and his mother survive that thing . . . and the others were killed?"

Picard nodded. "Yes, Number One. That is a question that has been weighing on my mind all this time."

When the *Enterprise* came out of warp drive, it took the rest of the distance to the starbase on impeded impulse power and finally docked without incident. A team of analysts, already alerted to the situation, immediately surrounded the ship with a forcefield as soon as the crew was transferred from their home.

Only Data was left on board, because of his inorganic nature.

Although they had concern for Data just as much as their ship, Picard and his crew agreed that this was for the best. Data could thus continue with his work.

However, when Admiral Davies and Dr. Chavez finally communicated their decree—that the *Enterprise* should be towed out to a safe place and destroyed by photon torpedoes—all the built-up hope and optimism seemed to shatter in them all like delicate tapestries of glasswork crushed by sledgehammers.

Perhaps this, Picard thought, was indeed the end of the voyages of the *Enterprise*.

The creature grew.
The creature subsumed.
Its physical growth was minimal, as planned.
Its interior growth was extraordinary.
Inorganic equivalents to synapses and neurons developed complex new pathways. Crystal paths of thought shimmered with purpose.

Grow.

Expand.

It felt the powerful forcefield in which it had been contained, but it was not concerned. There would be other avenues for victory.

As the lattices of its mind interconnected, racial memories keyed by its molecules equivalent to DNA and RNA taught it ploys and methodologies.

First priority: the survival of its race.

Second priority: personal survival of consciousness.

Observing the situation, it saw that there was no reason why it should not be overwhelmingly successful in both.

As it developed, so did the powers of its mind. And although the bits of itself—the clay spores—could not breach the energy field in which it had been enveloped, when it reached out with its mind—there was practically no impedance.

It needed more power, though. The time was not right, so it withdrew.

Soon though. Soon it would quest outward with its tentacles of mental contact.

Soon this vessel of matter and the ships clustering about it would be good life.

Soon the bad life would be extinguished.

Chapter Seventeen

Personal Log, Jean-Luc Picard, Stardate 45230.3:

Even though I have been relieved of my command here at starbase, even though the *Enterprise* is no longer mine and I am a captain with no ship, I feel compelled to continue documentation of the proceedings, if only to bear witness to the last days—no, last hours of the people of the *Enterprise* together as a crew.

These are fine people and will no doubt go on to equally fine careers. I cannot help but feel that our time together on the *Enterprise* was quite extraordinary.

Nonetheless, I am nothing if not a pragmatic man and therefore accept the dictates of my superiors. The people of the *Enterprise* are safe, and that is what matters. Farewells are difficult, but duty is duty.

The cup has passed, and I await my next assignment.

However, I cannot help but wish that Admiral Davies and his scientists paid more heed to the words of Mikal Tillstrom—if only Dr. Tillstrom were conscious and could give a better-documented and authorized version of what happened on Science Station Beta Epsilon. After all, following his suggestions, the growth of the creature has been measurably slowed and perhaps even stopped. True, the threat to the rest of the Federation's fleet is obvious.

However, I cannot help but wish that the patient might be spared, at least for a while.

Nonetheless, I understand, and must accept.

However, I do not think that other members of the crew of the *Enterprise* are quite as accepting as I am.

Personal Log, Lieutenant Commander Geordi La Forge:

When they gave me this recording device, at first I just wanted to toss it right back in their faces. But Counselor Troi suggested that doing a little snarling into it might relieve some of the tension while we sit around in this starbase bureaucratic prison.

It's hard. It's *real* hard just having to sit and wait for a couple of barges to tow your ship out to the middle of nowhere and do the maximum scuttle to her.

At least Data is still there, working away. I guess he's the last hope. I bet, though, if this Admiral Davies dope and his chief scientist Chavez had their druthers, they'd just torpedo the *Enterprise* with Data on her and be done with it. God knows they kicked up a stink about the idea of Data coming off the ship after our report. The funny thing was, they let that Tillstrom kid go off, no problem. Oh, they did a heavy scan of the engram-circuitry in his head first, but still . . . I mean, it's like they were treating Data like he wasn't a person . . . just some machine. . . . Well, at least he's able to work on the problem up to the last moment. Fortunately Captain Picard raised such a stink that they're going to let Data take a clean shuttle out about an hour before they blow the ship up and then stay in quarantine for as long as necessary until they're sure he's no danger. That could be *years*, hell, *decades*, but at least the captain saved Data's life.

I can't help but get the feeling, though, that if they'd let us stay just a little bit longer, we'd have cracked this thing. The information that Mikal Tillstrom gave us worked up that chemical spray that retarded the growth. How the hell it did, I don't know, but at least the crew got back here, with no more casualties.

No more casualties but the *Enterprise,* that is.

You know, I've got a lot of memories on that ship. God, I feel like those engines are as much a part of me as my VISOR.

Captain Picard doesn't seem as upset as the rest of us. Just that usual poker face. I know he cares about the crew. He's always talking about the safety of the crew being his number one priority as a starship captain. But you can't be a starship captain without a starship, and it seems to me that the *Enterprise* is going to be difficult to replace.

Personal Log, Dr. Beverly Crusher:

I find myself beginning over again.

I was not allowed to take my other log with me, nor any of my instruments. I have been given access to the medical equipment here at the starbase hospital to continue the monitoring and treatment of the unconscious Dr. Adrienne Tillstrom. I lack for nothing really, of any importance, and yet not being allowed to bring along my personal effects from the *Enterprise* makes leaving her to the destructive whims of the cold, pragmatic hearts more difficult to take.

I have also asked that I be able to continue to monitor Mikal Tillstrom. Even though he has partially regained his memory, he has begun having his headaches again, and I am not entirely comfortable with his condition, though I'm not sure why. Mikal seems happy enough with being able to stay close to his mother. Now that he remembers more of what happened at the science station, he seems more affected by the trauma of it. Troi reports definite grief and anxiety in the confused mix of his emotions, and I can't blame him for feeling those things.

It's just good that he was able to report his memories when he had them. Actually, he didn't remember everything. Flashes. Sketches of that awful past. The science team apparently had, in fact, been studying the replicating clay when its growth got out of control. Mikal reports that not only were there attacks similar to what the hull crew experienced—but some of the team men were mentally affected and began killing off others. The unaffected were able to develop a chemical spray that hampered growth of the clay—but not before his mother was injured.

He does not recollect what happened to the others, nor the loss of consciousness, but no doubt will soon. His story, awful as it is, seems to check out, particularly in light of his ability to re-create the spray that slowed down the crystal growth.

You'd think that the science team and the admiral here would at least take some time to investigate that spray before they obliterated the *Enterprise*. I know my emotional response is one of pure outrage.

Jean-Luc, however, after considerable thought, concluded that they had no other choice really. While the destruction of a ship like the *Enterprise* is an incredible loss, the risk of the stuff spreading to other inorganics of the starbase, the other ships in port, and through them, to other ships throughout the Federation, was simply too great.

I also pointed out to Jean-Luc that I was a bit upset that they should be so willing to destroy a living being. However, from all signs, he says, the clay crystal thing has the intelligence of the colonies of bacteria that modern medicine regularly destroys in human beings.

I suppose, though, I am mainly upset about losing the *Enterprise* again. I know how much I missed her when I was away on duty at Starfleet Medical. How much more will I miss her when she is simply . . . no more.

It is comforting that I know that the crew and my close friends are safe and will be reassigned. Parted, true, but knowing that they are still well and alive will be a comfort. Nonetheless, being together with them, more than a crew, more like a *family* . . . Yes, the loss of all that will be harder to accept.

Geordi is already on record with the admiral with his objections to quick destruction. "Give us a little more time!"

I, too, wish that were possible . . . but I keep on thinking of Mikal's story . . . and can't help but feel that the admiral, in light of that story as much as the physical evidence of the destructive qualities of the replicating clay's growth, did make the wisest decision.

However, I have the most difficult time convincing my heart of that.

Personal Log, Commander Riker:

These *damned* bureaucrats!

They want to blow up my ship!

Five years plus: we brave the Borg, the Romulans, the Ferengi, and countless threats from all sorts of things the universe has thrown at us. We've been mauled and banged up plenty of times, but what's the force that's finally brought us down? Gravity from a black hole? The raging furnace of a fiery star? A huge berserker radioactive asteroid?

Uh-uh.

Bureaucracy.

Mean-minded little peons who are unfortunately "in charge" of the situation.

When Chavez and Davies advised us that the *Enterprise* was a "total loss," I demanded just a couple of extra days. Okay, I said, so everyone is evacuated. Give us a skeleton crew. Tow us out if you like and then just give us a little more time. Geordi and Data will do their stuff . . .

And hell, if they don't, they can just get beamed off before they (sigh) blow the *Enterprise* to kingdom come.

I'll give the captain this. He supported me. He said, "I, for one, am willing to be on the skeleton crew involved in such an effort."

Didn't work, needless to say.

I guess I'm acting like this because I feel . . . guilty. I was the head of the mission that dragged that replicating silicate junk back onto the *Enterprise*. Well, that could be—but I'm also willing to go down with my ship, if necessary.

I'm just blowing off steam, of course. It's healthy and therapeutic, Deanna says. That's why she encourages us to use these stupid recorders they gave us.

So, anyway, Admiral Davies, needless to say, wouldn't go for it. "It's not just a matter of good judgment that Dr. Chavez and I are exercising here," he says, calm and even-toned as you please. "I'm following the rules. I'm following precedence. You are in my jurisdiction now. The decision is totally out of your hands. I hope that I can expect your full cooperation. If not, I shall be happy to report you, Commander Riker, for insubordination."

Happy. No question, that would make the old bastard happy as a clam.

Soon as the meeting got out, though, I didn't just sit around and wait for orders. I went down to the nearest computer access station and spent about two hours poring over the rules.

That's why I'm railing over the rules. These jackals have got us hamstrung, all right. Theoretically we could go over their heads by demanding intercession by higher-ups in Starfleet via subspace radio, but the procedure there is sufficiently time-consuming as to put the full decision squarely on Davies's shoulders. It's a "time is of the essence" situation, and here the admiral has his finger squarely on the button.

Personal Log, Counselor Deanna Troi:

The doctor should consume her own medicine where appropriate, so I suppose I should use this recorder to express my feelings on this situation. I find it ironic that after all its strange adventures, the *Enterprise* and its crew should come to this peculiar cross-roads.

As a supposed expert on the emotions of others, I have often been quite at a loss about my *own* feelings. However, in this instance, I know exactly how I feel. I do not want to leave the *Enterprise*. I do not wish to break up what we have established. As noble and talented as each individual in the crew is, I cannot help but feel that the synergy created as a team is so much greater than the sum of our parts. And that this magnificent vessel and its mission have somehow not only allowed this but *demanded* it. It is almost as though the *Enterprise* itself is just short of sentience, and we are consigning it now to a fate that is, if not betrayal, then an implicit betrayal of loyalty to something that has supported us, literally, in so many ways.

Projection? Perhaps. Am I anthropomorphizing a collection of metal and bolts? Yes, but that is a long tradition in both Betazed and Earth cultures. I believe in both cases it helped people to establish bonds with the means of their survival. In any case, the underlying emotions that I feel in myself, that I detect in the others, are pure and are not the result of any kind of neuroses.

Should the *Enterprise* be destroyed, we shall all have to endure a period of grief and recovery. A process that will not be mitigated by the presence of the people we have grown to love, our family.

We shall survive. We shall endure. This is our nature. I hope it does not mean the end of our work together, but if it does . . . the universe will still have been a better place for having had the *Enterprise* and its crew in it.

I am not so sanguine, however, about my patient Penelope Winthrop. Wherever she goes, of course, she will go with her parents, and that is good, and will provide her with the security she so desperately needs in this stage of her life. However, we had come so far together. . . . Data has been such a help to her, and the small breakthroughs finally merged into a large breakthrough at that dance. I could see the future opening up for that dear, sweet girl like a blossom—no, an orchard of blossoms—and I longed to see her collect the fruit of it.

I could even see the seeds there of psi powers. They could have been one of the contributing factors in her autism. We talked about them, but the idea frightened her. I didn't push. I just wished to see her get better. Nonetheless, her potential was so great. . . .

However, now it would seem that it was all for nothing.

She's gone again.

Simply withdrawn. The trauma of her worry about Data and Mikal Tillstrom was too much for her, and she simply shut out the world she could not take anymore.

I've visited her and assured her parents that she would come out of it. I know she's still there, I told her parents. I can feel her emotions. She's frightened and confused, but there's no reason to exacerbate that by trying to bring her out too quickly.

I will monitor Penelope, of course, as much as possible. It will be best for her if the *Enterprise* somehow is restored to operation, and I can't help but wonder if that isn't the third and possibly major factor in her withdrawal.

I almost envy her.

It is so difficult to lose home.

The only person amongst us who is taking this well is Captain Picard. It is no astonishment to me that the captain is difficult to read. His emotions hardly come in primary colors. There can be no doubt of his devotion to his crew and his respect for the *Enterprise*.

He is extraordinarily calm and accepting, and his main concern seems to be the smooth transition toward whatever other duties he and his crew may be assigned.

I sense, deep down, he is as frustrated as us all.

Personal Log, Lieutenant Worf:

I do not understand why Counselor Troi has given me this device. I do not like them . . . especially in the current situation!

It is like giving a warrior who yearns for battle a toy to play with while his homeland burns.

Pah! What useless nonsense!

Would that this were a world of Klingons!

At the very least I would be allowed to fight this threat aboard my ship until the very end!

In many ways, although I was raised by humans, I do not understand them. They speak sometimes in such confusing ways. They speak of ideals and yet ultimately they waffle.

And these petty bureaucrats who people the echelons of upper command! They are mindless Yaka worms, feeding upon their own excrement.

Bah. Worse than useless.

I go now to tend to Alexander, my son, who is confused.

"Why do we leave when we can stay and fight for what is ours?"

he says. "Have you not yourself told me how much the *Enterprise* has meant to you? That it is your home, and its people your family? How can we just stand by and do nothing, Father?"

How can I teach him the Klingon ways of honor when the Starfleet Higher Command hamstrings me and my comrades!

Bah!

(crunching sound of recorder being thrown against a bulkhead)

Chapter Eighteen

IT WAS ODD being aboard the *Enterprise* alone.

Data was not lonely in the way humans are lonely. Loneliness is a form of emotion.

And yet, that part of loneliness that is not emotional—that affected the android.

It was an emptiness.

He worked hard at his tasks in the geological chemistry work station.

Emptiness. Yes . . . like the emptiness he had felt in the creature known as Gomtuu, the "Tin Man," that swimmer of the vast seas of the universe, before Tam Elbrun arrived to replace its lost companion.

Data, however, ignored the empty corridors and the hollowness of this *Enterprise* that had once been so full of life, so bustling with energy. He continued his work, trying to perfect the chemical spray that Mikal Tillstrom had suggested.

As soon as the young man had remembered the components of the solution, Captain Picard had ordered it to be created. With the help of the replicator and supplies on hand, the process had been simple enough. The solution consisted merely of a blend of complex hydro-acids and other chemicals that would dissolve crystalline compounds. Utilizing robotic mechanisms, they had "sprayed" the inside and outside of the hull, and though the growing crystalline creature did not dissolve, its rate of growth was curtailed somewhat.

Not enough, however, to satisfy the requirements of the Federation officials who desired to terminate all threat of the material through the unleashing of the energies of matter/antimatter. There could be no question that would work, since the unleashed matter/antimatter would reduce all to their component atomic and subatomic particles.

Theoretically, lasers and controlled explosions would be able to loosen the creature's parts from the *Enterprise*—somewhat like the work of a dentist on the bacteria eating up a tooth. Dr. Chavez's argument, which Admiral Davies had backed up and enforced, was simply that there was too much possibility that the component parts of the crystalline creature's molecules would simply drift away and attach to the starbase or other ships after such an operation.

In theory, Data agreed.

However, he did not agree with the timetable with which they were working. If he could have access to the starbase computers and the help of other scientists, then he felt he could do something about this problem.

The aspect of the situation that baffled him the most, though, right now was how this solution that Mikal Tillstrom had given them had worked at all.

Yes, when he had tested it with small samples of the clay, the clay had dissolved. But when he allowed the clay to resettle at the bottom of the beaker for a few hours, the crystals began to re-form again, in a startlingly coherent fashion.

It was as though they *remembered*.

That was the key, thought Data. The replicating process. It used a different kind of process of re-forming and changing. It was more than simply chemical, and if he could discover the source of that process, then he might be able to use it to neutralize the entire crystalline structure and thus *reorganize* it, not destroy it. Thus the hull and engines and the other parts of the *Enterprise* that had been affected would not have to be destroyed. They would simply reconfigure their chemical structures into their previous formats.

Data wished that Mikal Tillstrom's memory had been less spotty on the matter.

It was a very strange and illogical story the young man had told. Quite inconsistent—due, no doubt, to the erratic nature of memory. They should be happy that he'd remembered anything, Dr. Crusher was quick to remind them. Data did not comment, but he was still somewhat troubled.

He had to focus all of his attention now on the scientific problems immediately at hand.

Data was at work on a variation of the halting solution when the comm unit beside him crackled.

"Data." Commander Riker's voice.

"Yes, sir."

"Just checking in. How's it going out there in quarantine land?"

"I have not made much progress, sir."

"Damn. We just got a report from base sensors. Their sensors show that the stuff is growing again."

"Yes, sir. The solution that Mikal Tillstrom gave us only seems to be partially effective. I am attempting to develop a more efficacious version. So far I have failed."

"Yeah, well, I hope you're still wearing your gloves."

"Indeed, sir."

"Sorry about these guys over here. They're a bit worried you might bring something over. I hope you've got your route to the shuttle all laid out."

"The shuttle is ready to be locked. In preparation I have coated it with an organic gel which should prevent any crystalline "spores" from affecting it."

" 'Spores'?"

"Yes. I have hypothesized the possibility that this creature may create crystal structures, fling them loose, and thus propagate its kind, given the proper circumstances."

"Wonderful news, Data. Damn. I just hate to lose that ship!"

"My neural pathways, too, have grown accustomed to the quotidian sensory experiences encountered here. Although now it seems quite different already."

"You mean you're lonely?"

Pause. "Yes. I do believe I am."

"Well, we'll get you out of this, Data. I promise you that."

"If necessary, I can be quarantined for a very long time with no difficulty. I am confident of success eventually. However, as Admiral Davies says, in the matter of the *Enterprise,* time is of the essence."

"Yeah. But if we could only talk him into giving us a little *more* time."

"Yes. However, it would seem that is impossible at this point. He *is* following rules and thinking in terms of protecting the Federation."

" 'The greatest good for the greatest number,' eh, Data?"

"John Stuart Mill, famous British nineteenth-century economic philosopher."

"That's right, Data." Pause. "Data, you know I've been thinking . . . you've been checking yourself regularly, haven't you?"

"Yes. I have not been affected by the crystallizing agent."

"Yeah, right, stay away from it, certainly. . . . But you know, a part of me wonders—is there a reason why not?"

Data nodded. "Yes. That is a matter that I, too, have considered. Of course, the reason very well could be that the material of which I am composed is not appropriate."

"Yes. Yes . . . could be . . . By the way, all the others wish you well."

"And I would like to express the same toward them. Please tell the captain that I am working very hard to save his ship."

"All I can say is that I'm glad someone is. Well, I'm trying another legal approach involving tossing off some red tape. So I'll be checking back in one hour."

"Yes, sir. Over."

Data went back to work.

Riker had reported before that if Davies had had his choice, the *Enterprise* would already be on its way. However, the towing ships had to be prepared, and their tractor beams had to be refitted.

That would only take a couple of hours, though.

According to Data's figure, there were perhaps seven hours and forty-five minutes remaining to the life of the USS *Enterprise*.

He seemed to be unable to control his memory banks. They continued to flash images and sound bites of his time aboard the *Enterprise,* of his friends there, and of their most marvelous experiences together.

He found himself working faster, although not desperately. After all, he had no emotions in the matter.

None at all.

Chapter Nineteen

IT WASN'T AS THOUGH he heard any voices, nor did he feel like some zombie. To Mikal Tillstrom, it all felt perfectly natural, as though for a time he was missing not just his memory but some other ineffable portion of his makeup.

He was glad to be on the starbase. He felt excited here. The whole universe seemed to be opening up to him, and now he had such an expanded vision of things. Your sense of purpose was heightened when you had a mission.

Seven hours and thirty minutes before the intended destruction of the USS *Enterprise,* Mikal Tillstrom went to kill his mother.

She was in a secluded area of the medical section of the starbase, remanded to the care of Dr. Beverly Crusher. Mikal would need privacy for what he was about to do.

It was a shame that there had been that period of separation between him and his better half, his Other Self. But perhaps it was all for the best. His ignorance had given him the aura of innocence that had made everything possible. Now, as his Other Self grew and developed, gifted also with the blessing of his intellect, it left him just enough time to work with. Just enough . . .

However, should Dr. Tillstrom awake and rattle off the contents of her knowledge, her memory of what had happened on Science Station Beta Epsilon on Phaedra, then the Other Self would be threatened.

And this glorious opportunity missed.

He walked into the silent section of the sickbay, the soft clicks and bleeps of working machines, the faint scent of antiseptic, his only company. Mikal had visited his mother here an hour before. Dr. Crusher had mentioned taking some time off to go for a meal then, and sure enough, she was nowhere around.

He walked into the little cubicle where his mother lay, her long, graying hair spread out on a pillow, her eyes still closed. Monitors and telltales quivered around her. She was unfortunately not attached to any devices that kept her alive. There could, alas, be no malfunctions of machinery.

It was a shame he could not simply strangle her. That would be so much easier. However, it would end the usefulness of this bad life extension of himself that was so important—and that would not contribute to the Greater Good at all.

Instead, Mikal Tillstrom examined the other medical devices. He'd spent enough time with the medkits on Beta Epsilon to be familiar with their workings. He pulled out a hypospray. Yes, so far so good. He pulled open a drawer. No. Another. Yes—it held a full complement of drugs. Quickly he reviewed those that were available, then selected two squibs. He had full knowledge of his mother's medical history, and he knew that she was allergic to certain types of antibiotic. The combination of any two would no doubt be deadly, thus serving his purposes—but just to make certain, he selected two more ampules. A lethal dose of diotoxins.

He thumbed the squibs into place, smiling.

Then he turned and started walking toward his mother.

Why are you doing this?

The question seemed to come from nowhere. A voice that was his, and yet not his, floating up from a part of his mind that was barely within the realm of comprehension.

Why are you killing your own mother?

He stopped. He looked down at the hypospray mechanism. Something in him wanted to drop it, to run away from this place, to turn and run screaming, to hurl himself where he'd be of no harm to anyone anymore. Horrors from the past bubbled up, scenes of destruction and violence, backlit by strobing helplessness.

I killed them. I killed the science team. And they were my family, my friends. . . . I . . . destroyed them, buried them deep in my mass, beyond recovery by their families. . . .

Mikal Tillstrom raised the hypospray, to toss it away from himself. However, suddenly a force that was not him, not him at all, gripped his arm, gripped his whole body.

And suddenly peace and tranquillity flowed through his veins again. He was One again with the truth and the Good cause. He could feel the flow of energy spearing him through his head, spearing him with righteous energy, with the Holiness of Good Life. . . .

He could reach out and touch the glory of himself, growing powerful aboard the Nest.

The Power of Purpose suffused him again.

Yes, he was in control once more.

As he stepped forward toward his mother, so strong was his connection with the Truth and the Way, and his mind snapped back like an elastic band, straight into the energy of his Progenitor.

He could feel it surging through the *Enterprise,* ready for further growth, ready to let pieces of itself drift away, attach to the mass of Nests that this place afforded. He could feel the mounting excitement of realization that it was free of its bonds, that if he could spread through the universe via these ships, then it could grow and grow, its colonies connected by subspace radio much as it connected with the engram-array in the bad life's mind.

Yes. Good life would grow amongst the stars again. Nothing could stop it!

Suffused with this purpose, the creature that was no longer Mikal Tillstrom walked the rest of the way to his mother. He gently, almost reverently, lifted her sleeve, readying the hypospray.

So simple. So *right.*

"Mikal?"

Beverly Crusher's voice hit him like a mallet.

He froze. He was turned away from her, in a way that concealed the hypospray. Quickly and nimbly he pocketed the thing, acknowledging her with a nod, but still looking down at Dr. Adrienne Tillstrom.

"Just checking on her, Dr. Crusher."

"I thought I asked you to check with me before you stayed with her alone."

"She's *my* mother, all right?" he said, turning around. "You weren't here. That wasn't my fault."

For a moment she glared at him, and then gave it up. "I'm sorry."

"That's all right, Doctor. And please accept my apology as well."

Dr. Crusher moved beside him and looked down at Dr. Tillstrom, then over at the telltales. "Hmmm. A slight bit more activity there, I think. A good sign."

The thing that had usurped Mikal Tillstrom considered killing this woman. Killing her quickly, noiselessly. It would be so easy, a twist of that long, elegant neck—

However, that would be senseless. There was no profit in it, and the move could very well cause unnecessary danger. The computers here monitored the colonies of walking cells regularly—there was the possibility that Dr. Crusher's death would be noted immediately.

A chance that it could not take.

The ambulant example of female bad life was spared.

"Yes. Yes, I hope so."

"Any more notions of how she got this way?"

"No. However, you can be sure—"

"I'll be the first to know. Yes, and I appreciate that . . . although in the future, I request that you consult with me before you come in here."

"Yes."

She considered him. "Admiral Davies has, oddly enough, called the main crew of the *Enterprise* together for a small reception. I suppose you might call it a consolation prize for our ship: a wake, if you will."

"Yes, I heard."

"As a guest, you are invited."

"I think, Doctor, that would be in bad taste."

"For heaven's sake, why?"

"If it had not been rescuing my mother and myself, answering that distress signal, your ship might not need to be destroyed."

"We were merely doing our duty, Mikal."

"Still—"

192

She looked at him. "You think I've . . . I mean . . . we have given up, don't you?"

He blinked. "The fate of your ship hardly seems to be in your hands now . . ."

"You don't know the *Enterprise* . . . You don't know our people. . . ." She smiled wryly. "I could tell you stories. . . ."

"But I spoke to your captain. He seems to have accepted it all as fait accompli."

Crusher smiled faintly. "So he says . . . now. . . . Seven hours . . . We've had far less time before. . . ."

"I see . . . but if you can't go back aboard the *Enterprise* . . . if it's restricted . . . quarantined . . ."

"We've got an ace in the hole, Mikal. Don't you see? The others are working on stalling the destruction of the *Enterprise,* yes . . . but in a way, the quarantining of Data is our best hope. If there's anyone that can solve the puzzle of ridding the *Enterprise* of that stuff, it's Data."

"Yes. Yes, of course. How comforting."

It had discounted the simulacrum bad life intelligence. The woman seemed to have a great deal of faith in it, and yet it could still hardly see the threat. Still . . .

"Well, it's a hope, anyway. You've got to hang on to hope. Will you be coming to the festivities, then? It might at the very least be interesting. . . . I suspect a few sparks might fly."

"Might I be permitted to remain here, by my mother's side, during this affair?"

She looked at him in an odd way. "That won't be necessary, Mikal. If you really want to be of help to someone, you might check on how your friend Penelope is doing."

"Of course."

"I'm having another doctor monitor your mother. Should I tell him he can expect a visit from you?"

Why was she being so difficult? Did she suspect something?

"Yes. Perhaps, if I get the time. I forgot about Penelope. . . . There's been so much else going on."

"Fine. I'll give you permission to come then. But you can't blame me for worrying about you . . . being alone with your mother, I mean. . . . It might cause you some trouble. . . . How's your head been? Your headaches, I mean . . ."

"No pain whatsoever. . . . Remembering that stuff must have let off some of the pressure."

"We're going to have to examine you again . . . but not today, if you're feeling all right."

"Yes. At least physically. Emotionally . . ." He gestured over to his mother. "Well, I guess maybe that's one of the reasons I had to come in here and look at her."

"Yes. I understand. Well, the affair I mentioned, such as it is, is going to be held in the main observation deck. Come if you like. And I believe that Penelope Winthrop is with her parents. You might consult Guest Quarters Directory."

"Yes, of course. Thank you, Doctor, as always for your help."

She nodded and turned away to check the monitors again.

For a moment, an atavistic urge came over Mikal Tillstrom.

Kill her. Obliterate, *destroy* her as he destroyed those others.

He stepped toward her.

However, discretion won over impulse once again.

There were other things to attend to. Particularly in light of the information that he had been given.

And he must work quickly.

The thing that was no longer quite Mikal Tillstrom strode away quietly.

Chapter Twenty

JEAN-LUC PICARD thought the entire affair was in questionable taste, and yet it was not without precedent. Other ships of Starfleet had been eulogized before being condemned, dismantled, cannibalized. And why not? Starfleet Medical's Psychology Division claimed that it was a kind of closure for all involved, a way to seal up a portion of one's life neatly and cleanly, and then move on toward the next phase.

Still, when he got the order for the occasion directly from Admiral Davies not long after they'd received the bad news about the fate of the *Enterprise*, his stomach had twisted.

He never liked these sorts of formal occasions, although, like everything else to do with Starfleet business, he excelled in them. And, he well knew, it would be up to him to keep a stiff upper lip in the face of this blow. He'd have to be the backbone for the rest of the crew here, and show them that there was dignity and life after the *Enterprise*. They could get drunk or weepy or upset or whatever, but he would have to stand straight and tall, make a glorious speech about the honor of serving on that superb vessel, and with such an exemplary crew to work with. They would reminisce, they would toast the *Enterprise,* they would say their official good-byes to one another—and then they would go back to guest quarters, where they would wait until they were reassigned.

So cut-and-dried, so clean . . .

Jean-Luc Picard accepted this. It was his duty, and even if he didn't like the rules and the strange structure of hierarchy, they *were* the rules, they *were* the law, and it was his sworn duty to not only obey them, but be gracious and diplomatic in doing so.

That didn't mean he had to *like* them, though.

That didn't mean he wouldn't produce exactly what they wanted, performing his duties well, but not giving one iota more. And if his words occasionally squeaked with irony and if his eyes glinted with anger—well, perhaps that would communicate something to his crew, who were looking up to him to do something to save their ship.

There was simply nothing *to* do now but observe regulations . . . and go on to whatever awaited them in their service to the Federation. Entropy was the ultimate law—and entropy had swallowed the *Enterprise.* His crew was safe, and that was the main thing.

There were still glorious futures ahead of them in separate lives.

And if their old lives haunted them slightly . . . well, that's what most pasts did, didn't they?

With these thoughts and feelings moiling beneath his usual cool facade, Jean-Luc Picard walked into the main observation deck.

"Ah, Jean-Luc," said Admiral Davies, bellying up like some unctuous funeral director, looking every sartorial centimeter a proud admiral, shoes and insignia flashing. He smelled of too much flowery cologne, and it stood out starkly against the smells of the simple foods and drinks that had been prepared for the occasion. "Prompt as usual. Good. I'm afraid I can't say that for most of your primary crew. A sulky bunch, I'm afraid."

Picard raised an eyebrow. "They are the best crew in the Federation. They are losing their ship. I don't expect them to sing and dance."

"No. No, of course not. By the way, Dr. Chavez will be a little late as well. . . . He's seeing to the final details of the scientific observation that will, hopefully, learn more of this condition that has struck the *Enterprise.* Along with the data that you've accumulated, I think this will place us in good standing for any further difficulties with this kind of peculiar inorganic life. The *Enterprise* will not have died for naught."

Picard nodded. "Thank you, Admiral. I appreciate that."

He did not voice any of the misgivings he felt about the admiral's motives, nor recall any of the past with him. On paper and in principle, Davies's moves here were perfectly valid. However, Picard well knew that they'd never gotten along particularly well, and Davies had never commanded a ship quite as fine as the *Enterprise* . . . and he could not help but wonder if maybe the military man might not be getting some kind of subconscious satisfaction from the unfolding events.

If he could not have ever had the *Enterprise* in his illustrious career, then he'd at least be remembered in the history books for *destroying* it . . . and thus possibly be the savior of the fleet.

And there it was, hanging in space in its special removed dock beyond them—the *Enterprise.* Even from here, Picard could see how his ship had been affected. The usually smooth hull looked irregularly corrugated. Around the ship wavered the lines of the forcefield that composed its quarantine bubble, barely visible.

Picard looked away, wishing this damned thing could have been held somewhere else.

"Would you like a drink?" asked Davies.

"Yes, Admiral, thank you. I do believe I can use one."

They walked over to the refreshment bar, where Picard ordered a glass of strong red wine.

He sipped it.

"Ah. Here they are. Not as late as I expected. My apologies for my remarks."

Picard turned and saw Geordi, Beverly Crusher, Deanna Troi, and Worf standing tentatively at the entranceway. They looked as though they were trying to decide whether or not to hazard this party. They all wore copies of their previous uniforms that the admiral had made up for them.

"Captain, perhaps they need further encouragement," suggested Davies.

"Yes." Picard tugged at his own uniform. For some reason it just didn't have the old resiliency of the ones manufactured by the *Enterprise* replicator—or was that just prejudice? Stiffly, feeling extremely uncomfortable, he strode over to his primary crew. "Ah. Glad you could come." He gestured over to others milling about, drinking and eating and talking. Some were looking through the window at the doomed *Enterprise.* Some were concertedly *avoiding* looking that way.

Picard led his people over to the admiral, where they made their greetings and formal thanks for the invitation. The admiral seemed gratified, although he certainly knew they were unhappy with the situation. However, that was the prerogative of rank—you had the power to gloss things over sometimes, even in your own mind.

"Aha!" said Admiral Davies. "Dr. Chavez is here. I suspect he has a report on the status of the operation."

A flicker of hope trembled in Picard. There was always the chance that something could have happened to forestall the destruction of his ship . . . something that would give them the extra time needed.

But there seemed no mercy in the countenance of the physicist, and again Picard had to push back the sense of helplessness before it overwhelmed him.

"Admiral, Captain . . . people," said Chavez curtly, nodding his head. "I have only come down briefly to formally offer my condolences. This is a nasty business. It grieves me to be a part of it. However, what must be done, must be done. I know you are not happy, nor would I be in your situation. The tales of the triumphs of the *Enterprise* arc many. It is a shame to have to destroy it. . . . But then, that is one of the hazards that ships that deal with exploration must face . . . part of the business, I'm afraid."

Picard wanted to believe Dr. Chavez. But he knew too well the ways of some of the bureaucrats in Starfleet. He wondered if any aspect of this expeditious dispatch of the *Enterprise* worked in Dr. Chavez's favor. The fame of having destroyed the great *Enterprise*.

Picard chided himself. No. This was being foolish. His own anger was getting the best of him. These were Starfleet officers, and even if they were bureaucrats, the people of the Federation were simply not that petty. Humans of the twenty-fourth century, generally speaking, had progressed toward a greater nobility of species, and the individuals of the Federation were their finest specimens. . . .

Weren't they?

"Thank you for the comforting platitudes," said Riker. He turned to the admiral. "I for one think I'll forgo a drink. Can we get on with whatever we're supposed to be doing?"

"Yes, of course." Admiral Davies turned and snapped his fingers at a tech-op. The op, stationed at a board in dim light, nodded. His fingers floated over controls. Previously a relaxing subliminal blend of musics had been playing. Now a louder fanfare . . . trumpets . . . announced that ceremonies were about to begin. A little ostentatious, thought Picard. Davies always had been the pompous sort.

"Thank you for your attendance," the admiral said as the music died down. His voice had amplified; Picard could see the tech-op was aiming a directional mike at him. "Today we have the sad duty of bidding farewell to a craft that has put in years of fine service to the Federation. I don't have to tell you what the *Enterprise* has meant to us all. . . . This, not to mince words, is the vessel that stood between the Borg and the Earth, a vessel strong and powerful enough to carry the exemplary crew it held into many astonishing and marvelous adventures. Alas, it has finally met its match, and must be sacrificed to save other ships . . . other lives. I cannot think of a better, or more noble, way of leaving service.

"However, while she is still with us—damaged though she be—let us use this opportunity to toast the *Enterprise* and all that she represents. But first I'd like the captain of that ship to come forward and share a few words with us."

Davies beckoned:

Captain Jean-Luc Picard stepped forward, resisted the impulse to straighten his uniform . . .

And he began to speak.

* * *

Data worked.

The lights burned bright in the geochemical laboratory still. There had been no damage to the interior energy supply, although both the warp and impulse engines had been affected by the spread of the clay.

Data worked on another possibility about this living material. He'd been baffled by the chemical solution that Mikal Tillstrom had prepared. Variants of the solution did not seem effective at all. It was odd that the chemicals had worked to slow the growth of the replicating silicates. Indeed, Data was not at all surprised to see that the growth had continued extensively.

Nonetheless, it was not in his nature to give up, and so he continued working, this time actually examining a computer extrapolation of various crystal growth patterns, in order to hypothesize a de-evolution pattern.

As he worked, the radio frequency he had tuned to aboard the Starbase commenced the proceedings of the final ceremonies to commemorate the demise of the *Enterprise*.

He listened to the music, and then he heard the words spoken by Admiral Davies.

Then Jean-Luc Picard was asked to speak.

Data paid closer attention, but did not drop a beat in his work.

"Thank you, Admiral," said the precise, clear voice of Captain Picard, freighted with gravity. "And thank you all for joining us in this solemn occasion . . . and thank the rest of you who hear my voice elsewhere.

"It is difficult to accept the pronouncement of the fate of our ship. More difficult than *I* can express. I only ask you to believe me when I say that silence and grief have their place, and later I will ask a moment so that we can observe them, along with the acceptance of the decision that is our duty.

"It has been my privilege to serve with many fine individuals. I want to thank them all, from the bottom of my heart, for their contributions. This is indeed a very sad occasion.

"However, let us not forget what our time together with this ship has meant, what we and it have contributed to the welfare of the Federation. Let us not forget the values and goals and achievements we have stood for . . . and let us continue in our quest for excellence, for unity, for the fellowship of intelligent beings throughout the galaxy and beyond."

There was a pause.

"I hesitate, because I find myself at a loss for words. The time we have spent together has much meaning to me. . . . The ship that we spent—"

There was a sudden breakup of transmission. Picard's voice fluttered and sputtered and then simply faded away. Data stepped over to check the comm unit. As he did so, his peripheral vision grazed the telltales on the cross-section schematic of the *Enterprise.*

He stopped in his tracks.

If he had been human, he would have gasped.

The lights representing the growth of the silicate clay had spread markedly. And there was an entirely new swath of the stuff that seemed to have broken off from the main body of the creature . . . and was moving, it would seem, down a hallway.

At that moment, Data heard a creaking sound from outside.

The door was open. His decision took only a nanosecond. He stepped forward to the controls and, not even extending his head to see what was outside, he closed the door and pressed the lock-seal device.

Then he stepped back and grabbed one of the phasers that he'd been given, thumbing the setting to maximum.

Data was puzzled. Thus far, the only thing the silicate-clay creature had done was to grow and merge with the *Enterprise*. Its only actual action could be termed self-defense.

And yet now, here it was. . . .

For all intents and purposes, it seemed to be *coming* for him. Just as it had come for the residents of the science station, according to Mikal Tillstrom.

The creaking grew almost thunderous as the sound of bending alloy filled the room.

Data knew he was in great danger.

The leaves of the door began to bow inward.

Chapter Twenty-one

PICARD PAUSED AGAIN.

He looked out over the listening faces. Admiral Davies and Dr. Chavez seemed patient and bland. Their blank visages indicated that this was just one more cocktail speech, one more duty to perform. Professionally, of course. Then mark the accomplishment off in their log, check out of the office at sixteen hundred hours on the nose, and then see to the important parts of their life, like planning fishing trips or retirement homes.

The faces of his crew, though, were an expressive mélange of emotion.

All the phrases he had used, all the carefully articulated words, seemed so empty now, his rounded enunciations so silly and pointless.

That was their ship out there, and it was dying.

So he paused again, and with every resource of his emotional control, he reined himself in again.

His sense of duty, and his sense of duty *alone,* enabled Jean-Luc Picard to finish the address.

"It is my belief that the *Enterprise* will never be forgotten. However, both the spirit that created her and the spirit that she in turn was shall live on, despite the fact the shell that housed them will be no more. Let us allow that knowledge to comfort us, and let us remember that we have sworn most of all to perform the duties and uphold the laws and principles upon which our Federation is built."

With that, he turned away with an abrupt signal that the speech was over. He stood amidst his crew, looking at the *Enterprise* in its quarantined berth, dry-docked, awaiting its destruction. The crew said nothing, standing awkwardly and uncomfortably, watching the stewards starting to pass around glasses of champagne with which to toast the memory of the *Enterprise*.

Just as Picard received his, Beverly Crusher's comm insignia chimed. It was odd, because it had a different sound to it than it did aboard the *Enterprise*. After all, they'd left their own insignias back aboard the *Enterprise*, and they were awaiting obliteration just like the ship. Moreover, no voice followed the chime.

However, Dr. Crusher seemed to know what it meant.

"It's Dr. Tillstrom," she said, head snapping to Picard, eyes full of hope. "She's awake. We must go to her."

A charge of excitement swept through Picard. "Immediately." He turned to Riker. "You will make our apologies, Number One."

"I'm not going to stay here long," said Riker.

"We shall all stay in contact, however."

They agreed that this should be.

Jean-Luc Picard refused the bubbling glass of champagne offered to him. He took the arm of Dr. Beverly

Crusher, and together they strode purposefully from the room toward the starbase's medical area.

She was only half-conscious.

Dr. Adrienne Tillstrom's eyes were partially open, and the gaze she directed outward was unfocused and glazed.

But she *was* awake, and now there was something that Dr. Crusher could work with.

Jean-Luc Picard's heart quickened with the sight of some kind of awareness in those familiar blue eyes. Adrienne's features may have aged over the years; however, those eyes were still young and vibrant, even behind the haziness.

He walked up to her and grasped her hand, which had been feebly reaching out for something invisible to all but her. "Adrienne. Adrienne. It's Jean-Luc. You're going to be all right."

"Life signs are strengthening. Excellent. All she needs, I think," said Dr. Crusher, "is a bit of stimulation." She went for a hypospray.

"You're on a starbase now, Adrienne," said Picard. "We saved you and your son. You were on my ship, the *Enterprise,* for several days."

The lips moved. "Jean . . . Luc?" She turned her head, and Picard could tell her eyes weren't registering anything. But the way she said his name told him she remembered.

"Yes. *That* Jean-Luc."

"I . . . I . . . was . . . on a science . . . station."

"That's right, Adrienne. Beta Epsilon on Phaedra, to be exact. All of the people you worked with, except your son, were killed. Whatever affected your station seems to be affecting our ship. That's why we're at a starbase—"

"Dead . . . ? Dead?" The eyes blinked and the mind

behind them grappled with the notion, unable to quite understand or accept it.

Slowly, awareness and alertness seeped back into the patient's eyes.

"Jean-Luc," she said, trying to raise up on her arms. "It's not a dream. It *is* you!"

"Stay down, Doctor," said Beverly. "You're going to be a little groggy for a while. There's no need to overexert yourself."

The patient lowered herself, and Beverly Crusher accommodated her by adjusting the bed so that she was in an elevated position. Adrienne Tillstrom's face at first showed relief, then thought—and then grief.

"Dead—my God . . . the team . . . dead . . ."

"How did they die, Adrienne? What happened?" said Picard, gently but emphatically.

"We were performing a series of experiments on a certain extremely complex form of clay that formed whole strata on Phaedra."

"Yes. That would be it," said Picard. "Adrienne, by accident that clay was brought aboard the *Enterprise.* It has replicated utilizing any inorganic material before it. It has subsumed much of the ship, including the engines. It seems to be some form of life. We barely made it to this starbase. The ship is quarantined and will be destroyed unless we can learn how to neutralize or destroy that replicating clay. What experiments were you performing on the material?"

"I don't know. That wasn't my area." She shook her head, then nodded. "It's alive, all right, and it will kill anything organic that opposes it. It can form pseudopods—or detach formed colonies of itself in an ambulatory mode to attack its enemies. It's coming back to me now. . . . I remember. . . . That's how some of the team were killed. We were attacked."

Dr. Crusher said, "But when we were there, there

was no sign of this stuff existing in the form it's attained. What caused it to go back to its . . . well, its clay form?"

Dr. Tillstrom shook her head. "I'm still foggy . . . Mikal would know. Mikal was working with Dr. Springton on that. Thank heavens he's still alive."

"We found Mikal with amnesia, Adrienne," said Picard. "And he's only partially recovered."

"Something about electromagnetic fields! It's a strange planet in that sense. . . . The auroras are stunning!" Adrienne Tillstrom blinked. "Where is Mikal?"

"Somewhere about. He was just here about an hour ago, sitting with you," said Dr. Crusher.

Terror was filling the woman's eyes. "You have to find him."

"You think that the two of you can work out the answer to this puzzle?" asked Picard.

"No, Jean-Luc. You must find him because I think this creature that you've got attached to your ship now . . . Well, not to mince words, but I think that it can control him!"

"The engram-circuitry," Crusher stated. "But it was free of any foreign matter! I examined it myself!"

"It was a special unit. We had it installed so that he could help at the station. I should have sent him to university, but he was having such a hard time . . . I wanted him to feel useful."

"I don't understand. It's just a node of microcircuitry containing data that can be accessed, correct?"

Tillstrom shook her head. "It's a special model. It has a transceiver that accessed separate computer storage."

"So that creature could be in control of him right now," Picard said. He stood up and tapped his insignia comm. "Computer. Location of Mikal Tillstrom."

"Searching," replied the computer.

"I hate to think it, but it makes sense . . . Mikal must have been controlled by something. . . . He wasn't acting like himself," Dr. Tillstrom said in an aggrieved voice.

The computer spoke. "Mikal Tillstrom is presently approaching the Field Generation Control Section of this starbase."

"Why would he be there?" said Beverly.

"If that creature is in control of him and it wants access to other ships . . . it must need to turn off the quarantine force field," said Picard. "He must be stopped." He was about to call for security, but then reconsidered. "I'll go myself. Beverly, call Riker and Worf and tell them what's happened. Do not tell anyone else unless absolutely necessary."

"I understand."

Adrienne Tillstrom looked at him pleadingly. "Please, Jean-Luc. Don't hurt him . . . and be careful."

"I'll do my best," he said, and hurried off.

The door burst open.

Data stepped back.

The stuff poured in like thick, dark molasses clotted with dirt and quartz. Its skin shone in the light.

It poured in, collecting into a pile before Data, smelling of minerals. He adjusted his phaser and aimed.

There were no other exits from this room. He would have to make a stand here.

However, instead of roiling toward him, the clay stopped. Slowly it drew into itself, lifting up from the ground and transforming into a humanoid shape. It looked like an animated statue.

It began to speak, though in a guttural and monotone fashion. "I . . . have . . . pierced your computers. I have a mode of communication now if I like. You are Data. . . ."

"That is correct. And do you have a name?"

"I am good life. I sense that you are partly good life as well. . . ."

"I am principally inorganic in nature, if that is what you mean."

"You seek to destroy me. Why?"

"I seek to neutralize you. You have threatened my ship. However, now that communication has been established, perhaps an understanding can be reached. The Federation I represent has a high regard for life in all its varieties."

"I am free . . . I am . . . unfettered. The universe stands before me and my reflections—ours. Good life shall triumph and grow and nurture the Holiness. Bad life shall be extinguished. This is Truth and Wholeness. Purity shall pervade the Cosmos."

"I do not quite understand what you're saying, but let me explain to you that the Federation recognizes your rights as a living being."

"Rights? I grow. I become. That is my right, and that is my way. I hunger and I devour. This vessel . . . is mine. All these vessels I sense about me . . . The Great Metal Planet. They shall be mine as well. You are good life, too. You will help me destroy the bad life."

"I most certainly will not. They are my friends."

"Friends? I do not understand. You are not as them. They are soft and weak. You are strong and good life. Your being sings with the surge of power. Join with me, and vast parsecs of stars and all their planets will be ours!"

"Can we, perhaps, reach an accommodation?"

"Yes. Tell the bad life to surrender and their lives will be extinguished with a minimum of neural distress."

"I believe that this ship is about to be extinguished, with you on it."

"No. I shall not permit that. I must have your answer, Data . . . good life. You are only an imitation of bad life. Why do you pretend other than that?"

"Perhaps I emulate that which created me in their image," said Data. He wanted to keep the creature talking. He was getting telltale information on his sensor readings that could possibly be of help now—or later, if he managed to survive this confrontation.

"You emulate that which, according to stored information in the computer, is so riddled with faults?"

"Faults imply complexity. Faults can lead to a rebuilding and affirmation of depth and variety of existence. Faults also imply a variegation of levels of life that can progress and grow intellectually and spiritually. Faults are perhaps an important aspect of evolution."

"You would like to confuse me with your sophistry, machine. Yet, according to what I have accessed, you not only seek to emulate them . . . you actually admire and copy their habits and that aspect of their characters they call 'emotions,' when clearly you can have none of your own. Why play this game? Join with true kin. We shall reproduce together and know the pleasures of dominance! That, machine man, is *true* evolution, is it not? Survival of the fittest?"

"Only in the most narrow-minded of terms."

"Why do you seek emotions, machine-called-Data?"

Data considered for a moment, examining the telltales as he did. It was also curious—this creature who had "accessed" the computers and the knowledge contained therein . . . who was not only intelligent but apparently quite capable of learning . . . why had it not taken over the controls of the ship, and broken away from this mooring? If it could have, it most certainly would have.

What prevented it?

"Come. I am curious."

"You are playing with me."

"Perhaps. I should enjoy alliance with you, but I would just as soon destroy you. It makes little difference. I care in neither direction.

"I will tell you, if you tell me of yourself."

"You have a bargain."

"In my intermingling with my comrades here on the *Enterprise,* I have determined that far from being a burden, emotions enrich what are, after all, comparatively short biological lives. Emotions give depth and variety to experience. They create bonds with energies other than purely the physical . . . and bonds that, I believe, may affect, in some way, the spiritual levels—if such exist—in the universe."

"You are a fool!"

"I think not. For true wisdom does not derive from knowledge, but from the proper processing of knowledge. And the human faculties that I would like to emulate are capable of so much more than even I, an extraordinarily advanced machine, can accomplish."

"This silliness must be crushed, and I feel privileged to be instrumental in its destruction. . . ."

"Unlikely. The life you have encountered is tenacious, I warn you. It would be best to simply give up before you fail again."

"You amuse me! You seek to threaten with pure bluff. I presume you emulate these creatures who have created you. Hmm. How interesting . . . But I still do not understand why you work so hard to obtain characteristics that clearly confuse and often cripple them!"

"They are my friends. I . . . I would like to feel for them . . . what they feel for me."

"And you are fool enough to believe they would waste their precious emotions on a machine?"

"I know they do."

"And yet they abandoned you."

Data changed the subject. He did not care to impart to the thing his intended course of escape. "Now it is your turn. You clearly have some sort of recorded racial memory in your DNA analogues. You have a fascinating structure. I haven't begun to properly deduce your origins or actual nature upon the planet of your derivation."

"Alas, Data, that would be more fascinating for you than you deserve. Now join with me . . . or I shall destroy you."

"I am afraid that I have too much loyalty even to pretend to be your ally."

And yet, despite himself, something in him was strongly attracted to this form of life. It was the same with the Crystalline Entity . . . a similar creature, doubtless. He could understand how his brother Lore could have seen his own reflection in that incredible and beautiful creature. But in a creature of silicon, what was the creature and what was the reflection? A philosophical question that could hopefully be analyzed on some other occasion.

"Ah. Then our hello rapidly turns into a farewell, Fool Data."

The humanoid statue thing seemed to fold into itself and *flopped* toward the android.

Data took a step backward, and pressed the trigger of his phaser. The beam of energy connected with it. A piece of the thing was torn off. It crashed back against the wall. . . .

But the lower half hurried forward like some incredibly quick amoeba.

A streamer of it whipped into Data's hand, snapping the phaser away and smashing it against the wall.

The stuff turned into its component sparkling clay and engulfed Data, like a blob of pure hunger swallowing its prey.

Chapter Twenty-two

CAPTAIN JEAN-LUC PICARD approached the Field Generation Control offices warily. There had been no alarms nor any signs of anything wrong as he stepped out of the turbolift, and yet it had always been his experience in these matters to attend to caution as much as to urgency.

As he walked forward, there was a *thwip*ping sound of rushing air. He whipped around and found himself facing Commander Riker and Lieutenant Worf. They were already armed with phasers. Seeing immediately that Picard had no weapons, Worf strode up quickly, pulled a phaser off his belt, and presented it. "You may need this, sir."

"I hope not. Come."

"What about the security here?"

"If it's intact, there is no problem."

They hurried into the rooms.

There *was* a problem.

Two security officers lay unconscious at the door. It looked as though they'd been stunned somehow,

Picard noted. Picard knelt down and felt their pulses. They were strong. Their breathing was regular. "Come on, they'll be all right," said Picard, hurrying forward.

Riker and Worf followed grimly, without comment.

The rooms were built on a larger scale than those of the *Enterprise,* but they had fundamentally the same sort of control PADDs. Everything was dim, and apparently on automatic. The rooms were deserted now, except for one.

They found Mikal Tillstrom hovering over a control board. Two meters away, three operatives lay unconscious.

"Mikal! Stop!" said Picard.

The young man rose, turned, and faced Picard and his companions. His face was quite different from the young, socially adept son of a scientist—it was cold and expressionless. "Captain Picard of the *Enterprise.*"

"Your mother is awake, Mikal. For God's sake . . . fight this thing!" Nonetheless, Picard had his phaser out and ready for anything.

"My . . . mother . . .?" A tiny shiver of change came upon the expression. A little of the true Mikal crept back into the countenance.

Then it disappeared, and the stone-cold expression crept back on. "Ah—Dr. Tillstrom."

"Step away from those controls," said Riker.

Mikal ignored him. "A shame. However, no matter. My goal has been accomplished."

Picard looked over to the graphic that Mikal's eyes were directed toward. It showed the *Enterprise* and the sphere of the red quarantine forcefield around it.

The forcefield was strobing.

"Stand away!" said Worf.

"No!" said Mikal, and he leaned on the controls.

Riker's phaser beam caught him first, and then

Worf's. The alien-controlled young man was thrown off the dais into an opposite wall.

Riker ran up and began punching controls. The forcefield around the *Enterprise* became solid again. "Damn," said Riker. "He got it open for a while!"

"How long?"

"About twenty-five seconds."

"Was that enough for the matter to spread?"

"Without any kind of propulsion, I doubt it."

"We'll have to get Chavez to do an area analysis. Worf—see to Mikal."

The young man's voice spoke from the floor. "That won't be necessary, Captain." He rose up to a seated position, wearing the same lack of expression. "I am done with him. We shall meet again, I know."

Mikal took out a hypospray.

"Mikal! What . . . No!" called Picard, but it was too late.

Mikal Tillstrom jabbed the thing into his arm and there was a hiss of the expulsion of the drugs through his epidermis. He shuddered, his eyes went up, and then he fell over.

"Blast! Get him down to sickbay immediately, Worf! And keep him under restraint there if he survives."

"Yes, sir."

Picard stepped forward. "Riker, get Chavez down here. Immediately."

Picard stepped over to the forcefield controls to see if there was anything he could do in the meantime.

The clay flopped upon Data.

He could feel its force dropping down on him, and he in turn pushed back with his considerable strength.

The thing, though, was too heavy and it pushed him down. It hovered over him for a moment like a wave suspended and frozen. Data thought that it would crush him for certain. What power did this material hold?

However, suddenly the silicate clay trembled. It moved forward a few inches and then it recoiled.

It recoiled and assembled again into a boulderlike shape. The voice, previously clear, was garbled and shaky, though Data made out a few words: ". . . deal . . . destruction . . . later . . ."

Then the silicate clay rolled away and out the door.

Data lay there for a moment, surprised. He ran a quick diagnostic. Nothing had been harmed or broken. However, he was covered with the clay stuff. Quickly he removed his clothing and then washed his body with a wet rag. After thoroughly and speedily removing the stuff, he isolated it for observation.

Then he scanned himself again.

He'd done an amazingly thorough job. Unbelievably thorough, in fact. The clay that had stuck so readily to the hull of the *Enterprise* and anything else inorganic simply sloughed off of him.

Quite simply, previous experience showed that the silicate clay that composed the creature should have stubbornly clung. This was the reason he had not touched the stuff in his experiments. There was too much danger that it would grow on him and subsume his android body.

However, that would seem not to be the case at all.

Something about his body had not only repelled the creature . . . it repelled the substance of it, rendering it inert and inactive, like normal, everyday clay.

Normal, everyday clay—which was exactly what the away team had encountered on Phaedra, covering Science Station Beta Epsilon!

Data accessed the computer information on Phaedra.

And then he began experimenting again with the new supply of silicate clay he had obtained.

"The analysis reveals no sign of spread of the material," said Dr. Chavez after a thorough check.

"I don't know . . . Mikal seemed confident there was," said Picard, looking over to Riker as though for support. Riker nodded. Yes, that was the way it had been.

"We have to rely on our instruments," said Admiral Davies. His nose looked slightly red with drink. He seemed flustered to have been disturbed this way, and yet still, he maintained a demeanor of raw authority.

Picard was used to being in charge in times of crisis and felt frustrated not being able to act immediately. "Look, Admiral. Pardon me if I'm out of line, but I've had experience with that material. It's insidious . . . and from all indications, it's malevolently intelligent. We can't take the chance that it will have affected other ships. . . . Allow my people to go back on the ship. With the help of Dr. Tillstrom—who is awake now—we may very well be able to learn how to neutralize it."

"And save the *Enterprise* in the bargain." Davies considered the notion. "What do you recommend, Chavez?"

"Sir, this frightens me. I'm sure that none of the material escaped the quarantine field, but that doesn't mean it won't in the future." Chavez rubbed his ruddy chin, breathing nervously. "The towing ships have prepared themselves in record time. They're ready to take the *Enterprise* early. I say tow her away and destroy her—and whatever has done this to her— while there is still time."

Admiral Davies nodded. "I'm sorry, Captain. I can't take the risk of infecting my command. I'm going to implement Dr. Chavez's suggestions immediately."

"No! That would be foolish!" said Picard.

"I am in command here, Picard. Need I remind you of that? You are under my jurisdiction." The red-faced man tilted menacingly toward Picard. "I know you've always wanted to get my goat, Jean-Luc Picard. You have always envied me and my placement . . . one step ahead of you!"

"Sir! Nothing of the sort!"

"Don't worry. You'll get another command. But I will not permit you or your ship to ruin my starbase . . . and God knows what else."

Riker stepped in, commendably calm considering the situation. "Pardon me, Admiral, but I wonder if this doesn't go against the Prime Directive. We have reason to believe that the silicate clay lattice creature has developed intelligence—"

"An intelligence that was utilized to attempt to spread to my starbase, Commander," roared Davies, the lion in him coming into full place. "Within Federation law I am fully within my rights to protect property and lives from direct alien aggression!"

"But without an attempt to communicate and/or neutralize?" said Riker. "Are you sure you don't want to go on record as at least attempting?"

"I want to go on record, Commander, as saving the starbase! Now, if you'd like to go back to your quarters, I will see to that right now."

"But Commander Data—" said Picard.

"Your android will be given suitable notice and can plan to evacuate once we have reached sufficient and safe distance from this starbase. . . ."

"If he proves to be uncontaminated, of course," Dr. Chavez added.

Admiral Davies glowered. "I am sure Mr. Data is sufficiently intelligent as to see to that."

"And sufficiently loyal as to not want this silicate clay to spread," said Picard. "Very well."

"Captain!" said Riker.

"The admiral is correct. We are helpless in this matter. He is, as he so eloquently reminds us, in command."

For a moment Riker looked as though he were about to explode. However, he managed to contain himself, heaving a sigh.

He said nothing, merely swiveling and walking away.

Picard followed wordlessly.

"I am sorry, Jean-Luc. I am only doing the wisest thing in this situation," said Admiral Davies.

"Yes, sir," said Picard. "I understand. I'll be in my quarters if there is anything I can do."

"Thank you, Captain Picard. I knew that I could, in the end, count upon your sense of duty and propriety."

Captain Jean-Luc Picard nodded glumly to himself, and helplessly followed Riker.

His darkest day was closing in upon him.

Chapter Twenty-three

"Come in," said Troi.

Picard walked in, his frustration and his burden heavy upon him. He needed to talk to someone, and he couldn't think of a better person than Deanna Troi. He felt he needed to *do* something, but he honestly did not know what he could accomplish now, his hands tied by his superiors.

Deanna looked up from her desk, where she was working on something at a computer console. Her face was full of respect and empathy, and Picard was instantly glad that he'd come here. "Captain . . . how can I help you?"

"I just need . . . to talk," said Picard. He sat down and folded his hands, morosely looking down at them.

"Yes," she said, in her smooth, caring voice. "I've heard the news from Will."

"Yes. What is the news of young Tillstrom?"

"He skirted very close to death, but Beverly saved him. He will be kept unconscious and restrained, in light of what has happened."

Picard nodded. "The engram-circuitry will have to be removed surgically."

"Beverly is enlisting the aid of top surgeons familiar with the procedure."

Picard nodded.

There was a moment of awkward silence.

"I wish I could do something," said Picard. "I have been ordered to just . . . just wait and watch."

"As the Earth poet Milton said, 'They also serve who stand and wait.'"

"I wish that would make me feel better." He sighed. "Well, I suppose I should be happy that the people under my command are well. That is the most important thing."

"Yes. You have always made your crew your number one priority. . . . We all appreciate that."

"Thank you."

"I understand better than anybody how you feel. . . ."

"Maybe better than me."

"Yes, maybe better than you. I think that you should—"

The door was open. An attractive teenaged girl stepped in. "Deanna, could we talk? I—" She stopped as soon as she saw the captain. Her eyes opened wide, and nervousness flickered through them. "Oh, I'm so sorry to disturb you, sir. I'll . . . I'll just come back later."

"No. No, that's all right," said Picard, standing up. "I don't mean to disturb any of Troi's meetings."

"Stay, Penelope," said Troi. "Captain. Do you remember Penelope Winthrop?"

"No—I don't believe so. . . . Oh, just a moment, the daughter of the Winthrop family . . . yes . . . with the rare case of—"

"Autism. Yes, sir," Penelope said. "I'm afraid I just

had a little bit of a regression, but thanks to Troi's help, I'm going to be okay."

"I'm pleased, Penelope. Very pleased. We are, of course, all upset about the *Enterprise* . . . but at least its crew has survived in good health."

"Yes. That's why . . . Frankly, sir, that's why I needed to talk to Troi." She paused, and an aggrieved look marred her pretty face. Then she looked as though she was simply going to check out of the picture entirely. Troi moved to her side and whispered something in her ear. The girl seemed to recover immediately. "I . . . I'm sorry, sir. I have these spells."

"That's all right, Penelope. I understand."

Penelope sighed. "Captain . . . the *Enterprise* . . . Well, it's gotten to be my home. It helped me get better. Troi's helped a lot . . . and my parents, too . . . but there's something *there,* sir. Something great and strong and good."

"Yes," said Picard.

"I don't want to leave it. . . . I don't want this to happen to my home, Captain Picard. None of us does, I guess, but I thought that if I told Troi this—asked her if there was something that I can do . . . absolutely anything . . ." She paused for a moment, and Picard could sense the pure sincerity of her words. "Sir, begging your pardon, but I was alone for years, just tightly bound in myself, frightened of any kind of stimuli or communication. That's autism, sir. And it happens in dysfunctional psychological environments. Sir, the *Enterprise* is a wonderful environment, and you helped make it that way. I just wanted to thank you, to help if I could."

Picard nodded. "Very interesting thoughts. Thank you for sharing them with both of us and for your kind offer."

"Sir . . . I also wished to discover how Mikal Tillstrom is."

"I believe he will recover."

She looked relieved. "Thank you, sir. It was so awful . . . that . . . that thing in his head . . . that creature. . . ."

Picard stood and took a deep breath. "Thank you, Penelope, for your words. I will be in touch later, Counselor. Thank you for your kindness. Good day, Penelope."

The captain marched from the room, knowing exactly where he was going.

"Adrienne," said Jean-Luc Picard. "You have to help us."

He was in Medical again, hovering emphatically over the bed of Dr. Adrienne Tillstrom.

"Yes. Yes, Jean-Luc, of course."

She looked much better and her eyes held more intelligence now, more awareness. She searched herself for a moment, and as she did, Picard looked over to Crusher. "I gave her a slight stimulant, sir," said the doctor. "That should help."

"Phaedra, of course," began Dr. Tillstrom, "is of great geologic interest because things happen faster there. We can study tectonic plate movements and all the aspects of exogeology in short periods of time . . . as well as paleomagnetism. You see, Phaedra has a dense metallic liquid core which creates a dynamo effect. Its about the same size as Earth, but it spins faster. . . . The relevant feature is the pole changes."

"Pole changes?"

"Yes. The planet has a very strong magnetic field. You must have been aware of that when you went there."

"Yes. But what could that have to do with the silicate clay creature?"

225

"Let me finish, Jean-Luc! Can't you see? The poles change! They reverse . . . every few years, and there are time lapses in between those reversals when the magnetism is quite out of kilter. We had not experienced that yet. We were experimenting. I believe that one of the experiments . . . one that I was not involved in . . . consisted of creating the shifting magnetic conditions in a large area to determine effects upon certain strata. We were utilizing the whole area, I think . . . the whole camp in generating a specialized field."

"That affected the silicate clay!" said Crusher. "Causing it to replicate, grow, and become . . ."

"Become what it was during these periods of magnetic free-fall!" said Picard. "A living inorganic composite creature! And once some of the clay was brought into a suitable environment . . ." He looked down at Dr. Tillstrom. "Thank you, Adrienne. That's what we need." He tapped his comm. "Lieutenant Worf. Commander Riker. Meet me in Starbase Transporter Annex."

"Captain, what are you going to do?" said Dr. Crusher.

"What I should have done long ago," said Picard, his face grim with determination.

"Very interesting," said Dr. Chavez, his hands steepled in front of his face.

Admiral Davies sat behind his desk with a pained expression on his face. "But a theory, you say . . . This is only a theory."

"Yes," said Picard. "But it makes sense . . . don't you see . . . ? We have a hope now of saving the *Enterprise.*"

"A hope," murmured Dr. Chavez. "A hope . . . Yes. An interesting theory and quite possible. However, think of the possibility of failure. And then the spread of this alien thing. The risks are too great." He turned to Admiral Davies. "My recommendation stands."

Davies nodded. He scratched his nose, then stood up, hands folded across his girth. He walked for a moment, then spun around, the indecision gone from his face.

"I'm sorry, Captain Picard. There is too much of a risk to other ships, to this starbase—indeed, to all ships, all starbases . . . perhaps all planets as well. The towing will proceed as ordered, at the earliest possibility . . . and the destruction of the *Enterprise* will proceed with all possible speed."

"Sir!"

"Captain! Do not make me cite you for insubordination!" The gruff-voiced man clearly meant the words. "You have a sterling record up to now. Do not sully it."

Picard stood.

"We cannot blame you for trying, Captain," said Dr. Chavez. "It is a difficult decision . . . but I honestly believe that the admiral has made the *correct* decision."

"Good day to both of you," said Picard, and he left.

Riker and Worf were waiting for him in the annex. With them was Geordi La Forge.

"I didn't call for you, Geordi."

"I respectfully request to come along, sir. This thing isn't great"—he touched his VISOR replacement—"but it'll do. Besides, if my VISOR hasn't been affected on the ship, I can use that."

"You are all aware of the danger we face here . . . but more than the danger of this creature . . . we'll have to face the danger of possible court-martial."

Geordi grinned. "I'd rather sit in a courtroom than a lesser ship than the *Enterprise!*"

"My honor is at stake," growled Worf. "Need I say more?"

"I think you can count us all in, Captain. We've faced worse threats," finished Riker.

Picard smiled. "I'll gladly accept your services. Come on. I may be able to bluff my way through the transporter duty man, but if not, we may be in trouble."

Riker grinned broadly. "I don't think there will be any trouble, Captain." He showed them through the nearest doorway, into a large room with the familiar transporter setup.

Standing by the controls was Chief O'Brien.

"Fancy meeting you all here," said the winking Irishman.

"Chief," said Picard. "What are—"

"Let's just say, Captain," said Riker, "that I planned for all eventualities."

"I see. Well, we shall not look a gift transport in the mouth. I believe you know where we're going, Chief."

"Yes, sir, and not a moment too soon. They've got the tugs in position and are about to lock tractor beams out and tow her to the destruction point."

"Hmmm. Well then, we'll at least have until a few minutes before then to notify the admiral of our presence," said Geordi. "They'll just beam us off."

Picard grunted. "Straight into hot water. What's the status of radio contact with the *Enterprise?*"

"That's a little problem, sir. There is none. It went out."

"If you don't hear from us, Chief, we're going to have to rely on you to prevent our destruction with that of the *Enterprise* . . . if indeed that is what happens. . . ."

"Let's hope it doesn't come to that, sir."

"Let's hope indeed, Chief. Can you take us to where Data is?"

"Got the coordinates all logged in, sir. Only I'd advise you to get going. We're cutting it a wee bit fine as it is."

Picard nodded and motioned to the others. "Up we go, gentlemen." They climbed into their positions on the transporter pads. "Chief O'Brien—might I ask how you managed to wrangle duty at this opportune time?"

"Oh, the boys here and I had a little party, and they are not feeling well this morning. Commander Riker and I foresaw this little expedition as a likelihood."

Picard lifted an eyebrow. "I thank you." He looked at Riker, who shrugged boyishly.

"Aye, sir. Good luck," said Chief O'Brien.

"Beam us home, Chief. And buy Fate a round while we're gone."

And they whisked across to the *Enterprise*.

Data was huddled over the work station when they materialized in the chemistry lab.

He registered their arrival without surprise. "Welcome back, Captain."

"Thank you, Mr. Data." Picard looked around. "You seem to have been busy while we were gone."

"I underwent an attack by the creature, sir. It would seem to be extremely hostile toward biological life."

"We've got some possibilities for you, Mr. Data. We think we know what may stop this thing."

"Excellent, sir. I am working on my own solution. However, it will not be achieved without difficulty. I—"

Suddenly the *Enterprise* rocked as the tractor beams of the tugs locked on it.

Chapter Twenty-four

PICARD AND HIS CREW had to steady themselves on the bulkhead. The power dimmed momentarily and then throbbed back to normal.

They were on their path toward destruction.

"Estimation of time, Lieutenant?"

"I make it about an hour and forty minutes before we get to a place where they're going to feel comfortable blowing us to kingdom come," Geordi said.

"Well, no time to mince words. The creature would seem to respond negatively to certain magnetic forces. . . ." said Picard to Data. "It is apparently dormant on Phaedra except for the periods of uncertain polar magnetism, according to Dr. Tillstrom."

"Yes, sir. That would align with my discoveries. When it attacked me, it could not approach my structure.

"Your energy field!" said Riker.

"Wait a minute. There are electromagnetic energy fields all over the *Enterprise*. . . . How—"

"The *Enterprise* indeed has a number of opposing and interacting fields, while I have a coherent electro-magnetic field."

"Rather like alternating current as opposed to direct current?"

"Simplistic, but a good analogy."

Picard nodded. "Excellent. The question is, Mr. Data, by what device can we mimic the fields found on Phaedra when the poles are in place?"

"First, sir, we must analyze the nature of that field," said Data.

"Great," said Geordi. "We're only light-years away from Phaedra."

"We must have taken readings while there," said Riker. "Surely we've got it all recorded somewhere."

"Indeed, Commander. In the computer. However, our adversary also has access to the files. We must hope that it has not been erased. And once we access the information, the creature will doubtless know."

"I don't think we have any choice."

"No, sir. I shall access immediately." He typed in the necessary instructions to the computer.

"Data, you *talked* to this thing?" said Riker.

"Hmmm. Yes, so did I, in a way," said Picard. "It has a very one-dimensional intelligence."

"Well put, sir. I believe it is devious, but it lacks depth. You would think that in reading the computer files, it would be aware of the Federation's respect for alien life. However, it seems bent upon spreading itself. The result of racial memory and compulsion, doubtless."

"Did you receive any notion as to the creature's intentions, Data?" asked Picard.

"Yes. I believe that it is achieving the necessary growth to take over command of the *Enterprise*. It is aware of its imminent destruction. I would not be surprised if it is reorganizing the engines to break free of the tractor beams in order to escape the tow ships, and the starbase area."

"And thus spread itself! This cannot be permitted," growled Worf. "It must be neutralized."

"It is quite sentient, and quite intelligent," Data reminded them.

Geordi nodded. "Yeah. Boy, just because something's sentient doesn't mean it's real smart. And sometimes if something's *too* intelligent, it usually means crossed wiring somewhere."

"Have we got a reading, Mr. Data?" asked Picard.

"Yes, sir." Digital readouts appeared on a screen. Quickly Data transferred the information to a PADD.

Geordi La Forge grabbed it, and nodded.

"Well, Geordi?" said Riker.

"It's a possibility. It's going to take a little time and some significant reconfiguring, but I think with Data's speed, we can do it."

"And what is that, Commander?"

"Sir, I don't see any way around it. We're just going to have to create a strong, specially designed electromagnetic field around and throughout the *Enterprise.*" He stepped forward, tapped a few keys, and nodded. "We've still got the power, sir."

"The matter/antimatter converters?" said Picard.

"Yes, sir. The *Enterprise* has what amounts to a quite complex electrical wiring system through every part of the ship. These power everything from the artificial gravity and the inertial damping field and the structural integrity field, to the lights in the lavatories. We're going to create the necessary electromagnetic fields that will affect the creature. We'll blow some fuses and those lavatory lights for sure. But it's my guess that we'd drum up just the right magnetic field to stop this thing cold."

"And what would happen then?"

"I have hypothesized, sir, that the matter which it has inhabited is sufficiently unaltered in most places to return to normal. However, there may be places in which it simply becomes silicate clay. There may definitely be extensive repairs necessary."

"But the *Enterprise* will be salvageable."

"Eminently, sir."

"I suggest, then, that we make it so."

"We're going to have to get down to Engineering and the power supply conduits, sir. I've got a feeling that we might meet up with that thing along the way."

Picard swept them all with a determined gaze. "We all have phasers and we all know how to use them. And I believe that we know the way to Engineering."

They arrived at the engineering deck without incident.

"Peculiar. I figured it would have detected our presence by now."

"Yes, sir," said Data. "But perhaps it was distracted by the tractor beams."

Picard turned to his chief engineer. Where had La Forge gone? A few seconds ago the man had been standing right behind him—and now he'd disappeared! An awful image of a tendril of that gunk dropping from the ceiling, wrapping around Geordi's neck, and pulling him into a ceiling trap flashed across his mind. "Commander! Where are you?"

"He ducked into his control room," said Riker. "Seemed to have a definite mission."

"Commander La Forge!" called Picard.

The engineer chose that moment to reappear. He was carrying his VISOR, inspecting it as he walked. "Sorry, sir. I think if I'm going to be doing some rewiring, I'll need to be able to see a little better.

Doesn't look as though this has been touched by that clay stuff. Data, there's a tricorder over there. Could you do me a quick analysis?"

"Certainly." Data went and retrieved the device, calibrated it properly, and then aimed it at the VISOR, which Geordi held out.

"In the future, Commander, please advise me of your intended departures."

"Uh—yes, sir."

Multicolored lights on the tricorder blinked and shuddered as Data mused over the results. "There is no evidence of any trace of the silicate clay on your VISOR, Geordi."

"That's good, Data. That's real good!" Grinning, Geordi slipped off the replacement device, stared into nothingness a moment, and then slipped his VISOR on. "Yeah! Now we're talking." He turned and surveyed them all. "Will, I think you've lost some weight!"

"No time for frivolity," said Picard. "I suggest we go to work."

"My sleeves are rolled up," said Geordi.

"You're going to have to advise us all what needs to be done to effect that change of EM fields on the *Enterprise,*" said Picard.

"I've been giving it some thought. It's all a matter of changing some stuff in the energy relays from the matter/antimatter pool. The good news is that most of that can be done right here by switching around some isolinear chips. The bad news is that I'm going to have to do some crawling inside a couple tunnels to change some stuff. No problem, though. You can do the work here while I'm busy in the access tunnels. Now, the first thing on the agenda is those chips."

"I believe that Mr. Data is equipped with the requisite speed. It would be best to allow him to effect those changes while Commander Riker and myself guard against any effort of the creature to stop us." Picard turned back to his science officer. "Which reminds me, Mr. Data. What is the status of the alien?"

Data turned the colored schematic back on again and consulted the results. "Sir. A portion of the silicate clay creature has detached itself from the main body." He looked over to the captain. "It appears to be headed our way."

She didn't know what else to do.

It seemed as though Penelope Winthrop was drawn to the Starbase Medical Section. She was so upset . . . yet for some reason, she did not withdraw again. Penelope presumed that meant that she was recovering, which was certainly good.

Suddenly she wanted to talk to Counselor Troi. No, who she really wanted to see, she realized as she strode through the corridors, was Mikal Tillstrom.

She wanted to maybe just sit with him awhile. Maybe she could help him. What had happened wasn't his fault. Also, being with him might well help heal her.

Dr. Beverly Crusher was sitting behind her desk, poring over a computer screen. She seemed distracted, and Penelope didn't have to be an empath to sense her upset. She hated bothering the doctor in this terrible situation.

"Dr. Crusher."

The doctor looked up, questioning.

"Penelope Winthrop. Counselor Troi's patient?" the girl said.

"Oh. Yes, of course. Hello. What can I do for you?"

"I heard about Mikal Tillstrom. He . . . he's a friend. I was wondering if I could see him. Just to sit by him a bit . . . hold his hand."

Dr. Crusher frowned. "I don't think that would be a

very good idea. The boy almost died . . . and I haven't removed that controlling device from his head. . . . I'm going to have to get a little assistance for that . . . and I'm certainly not going to do anything until I'm certain he's healthy enough."

"Of course, Doctor. I understand. I just thought if I sat with him a little bit . . . well, maybe it might help him . . . help him be more Mikal. And I know that it would help me. . . ."

"He is under considerable restraint, you realize. We don't want a repeat of whatever it was that was wrong."

"I understand."

Dr. Crusher considered. "I don't see how a few minutes could hurt. But I'll just allow a chair a few feet from the bed. And I'm going to expect some kind of notice from you if he wakes up. And I do mean *immediately.*"

"I promise."

Dr. Crusher stood up. She lead Penelope back toward the special room. Outside the room stood a security officer, who gave them a questioning glance.

"She's a friend who'd just like to sit for a while," said the doctor. "I'll authorize it."

"I have to check with my commander," said the man, a tall and bland-faced fellow.

"Unnecessary," said the doctor firmly. "This is *my* jurisdiction."

The security officer looked confused. He reached for his comm insignia—but then seemed to change his mind as he looked at Crusher's stormy eyes and decided it wasn't really worth it.

Beverly took Penelope in and showed her a chair.

Penelope didn't take it immediately. She stood by the edge of the platform bed upon which the unconscious Mikal Tillstrom lay, biomed devices hovering about him like blinking satellites. There were oxygen tubes running up his nose. His head was swathed in bandages, and his arms in other equipment.

Penelope sighed and sat down. "Thank you, Doctor. I think this will help both of us."

"I'll check on you in ten minutes. Please don't touch him or go any closer than you are now."

"I understand. Ten minutes would be fine."

Crusher nodded and left.

Penelope Winthrop sat and just stared at the handsome face of the young man. It was so odd to see him so still, when he was usually so animated, so full of life.

She watched him for a while, trying to reach out with her mind, trying to do whatever she could to help him, to heal him. What must it have been like to have something in your head, making you do absolutely awful things? It must have been far, far worse than merely withdrawing. . . .

Suddenly the patient groaned.

His eyes fluttered.

Mikal Tillstrom was awake.

Captain Jean-Luc Picard's heart seemed to skip a beat. A charge of the adrenaline of fear coursed through him.

"Glad to have the early warning system. Commander Riker, close the bulkhead door."

Riker immediately executed the order. The door slid home with a whoosh.

"As I mentioned, sir," said Data, "the thing easily broke through the geo-science room's door."

"We're a lot stronger down here. Geordi, is there any way that you can work up some sort of energy field that might detain the thing?"

Geordi perused his board. "Well, I can tap in to the auxiliary fusion generators and tamper with the intertial damping field in the area to strengthen the doorway and bulkhead. I can't guarantee how long that will last."

"Make it so," Picard said grimly.

"Meanwhile we make our stand," said Riker. He strode over to the schematic board which Data had abandoned to be about his work. He whistled when he saw what the lights and diagrams displayed. "This thing is *not* wasting any time. Geordi, you'd better get a move on. . . . It's almost here!"

Chapter Twenty-five

CAPTAIN JEAN-LUC PICARD alternated his attention between the closed door and Geordi La Forge. He had to stop himself from shouting out to the Commander, urging him on. The engineer's hands fairly danced over the controls, touching that panel, modulating this vernier. Nonetheless, he seemed very slow. If only, thought Picard, they all had Data's speed. He watched the android's hands fly at his work, and he considered ordering Data to do Geordi's work. However, he stopped himself immediately. Brilliant as Data was, he probably didn't have quite the depth and feeling La Forge had for his instruments. There was a bond there, and Picard would not abuse it. One thing a starship captain learned very quickly was that you had to have faith in the people who worked with you. His faith in Geordi La Forge had always been strong, and he saw no reason now to discontinue it.

However, Commander Riker did not seem quite as sanguine in the matter. "C'mon, Geordi. Get the lead out! That pile of planet dung is almost on top of us!"

Geordi wisely did not take the time to answer. His hands finished up their prestidigitation and then slapped down the final commands in a ragged tattoo.

Whap . . . whap whap!

A humming slapped up into existence within the wall: the field.

"You got it, Geordi!" called Riker. "And the thing is here about—"

Something crashed into the buzzing wall so hard that it shook the room.

"—now!" finished Riker.

But the wall held.

"How long will the field work against the creature?" asked Picard.

Geordi said, "Don't know. Maybe ten minutes if we're lucky. Maybe longer . . . but there's no time to waste." He pointed to Data. "Looks like Data's going to be finished in time. It's my turn to crawl up the Jeffries Tubes and realign those circuits." Geordi stooped down, pulled open a drawer, and pulled out a belt from which dangled an assortment of tools.

"If it gets in, we'll attempt to hold it off with our phasers," said Worf.

"That's about all you can do . . . attempt. Hopefully this won't take long. But just so I don't have to crawl all the way back to implement the result . . ." Geordi beckoned Picard over. "Okay. When I give the go via communications, what you have to do is real simple. Just touch this PADD here. That will cause the relay switch to initiate the first part of the change. What will happen is that all power will first go off. You'll be able to tell that's happening immediately: The lights dim to just the reserve batteries." Geordi took a deep breath. "And then you'll lose gravity. Make sure you're braced here so you don't float off, because then you're going to have to hit this PADD here. . . ." Geordi indicated an adjacent pad, colored a vivid green. "That will put the power back into not just the circuits but through auxiliary paths as well. The result should be a EM field of sufficient gauss to stop that thing."

"And how long should that field be maintained?"

"Not long, I hope. It's going to short out some stuff, I'm sure. Just long enough, I guess, to do the work . . . because I don't think that Mr. Clay's going to be able to reassemble quickly."

"Commander . . . if we lose comm contact. How long before this new alignment will be up?"

"Data's almost there, Captain. Me . . . Give me twelve . . . no, ten minutes from when I go."

"I understand, Lieutenant. You'd better be about your business, immediately."

"Yes, sir."

"And, Geordi . . ."

"Yes, sir?"

"Good work."

"It had better be, sir."

Geordi paused for a moment as the hammering of the creature against the bulkhead continued. Then he turned and hurried off to the Jeffries Tubes to be about his task.

"Mikal!"

The eyes closed again.

"Mikal! Hang on! Stay!" Penelope called out to the supine young man on the biobed.

The eyes fluttered open again.

And this time they stayed open.

"Who . . . What . . ." The eyes struggled to focus.

"Mikal . . . it's me . . . Penelope Winthrop. Do you remember me?"

The young man's head turned and looked at her. He nodded slowly. "Yes. Yes, Penelope . . . I remember. . . . What happened? . . . What's going on?"

"You . . . you were sick, Mikal. Very sick." Best not to load him down with the real truth.

"I still don't feel so well. . . . My head . . . my body . . . It all aches."

"I'll go and get Dr. Crusher."

"No. That's all right. The throbbing is going away. I'll be all right."

"But she told me that I should get her as soon as you woke up!"

"Don't bother her now. Please. Just sit with me a minute. It's so soothing seeing you here. . . . I'm starting to feel better already."

His words were so smooth and so needy that she found herself persuaded. Just for a moment, she told herself. Just until he felt more comfortable, more secure. His eyes were so absolutely charged with fear that she couldn't leave him like this . . . not now. . . . How well she understood that look in those eyes. . . .

"Just for a moment."

"Thanks." He made a movement, reaching out as though to touch her, but was only able to move his hand slightly. Both arms were securely fastened down by his sides. A look of alarm flashed through his eyes. "What . . . Why am I being restrained like this, Penelope? What's going on?"

"You don't remember?"

"No . . . no . . . Damn, and my memory was returning, wasn't it? . . ." His eyes drifted off, returned again, a new fear lighting them. "I've done something awful." He gasped. "It was me back there at the science station, wasn't it? Me who caused the trouble."

"No, Mikal. No. Something controlling you . . . something in your head . . ."

"The engram-circuit. Of course. Why did I let my mother put it in?"

"The creature must have used it to control you.

Mikal, that's why we can't let you go. It might start controlling you again."

Mikal nodded soberly. "Yes . . . yes, I see. I understand now."

"Mikal. Let me go get Dr. Crusher. She'll know what to do."

"No. No, please stay awhile." His face contorted with panic. "If you leave me, I might go mad . . . I might . . ."

Suddenly his face went rigid. His eyes stared off into absolutely nothing, defocusing.

"Mikal! Mikal!" She leaned forward, putting her hand on his chest as if she could draw some of the agony out of him that way. "What's wrong?"

The eyes focused again, and the head slowly turned toward her. Now there was an absolute lack of expression. No pain, or joy, doubt: That face could as easily have been chiseled from stone.

"Release me," demanded something that was most certainly not Mikal Tillstrom.

Geordi La Forge crawled.

Work in the Jeffries Tubes was part of his job, and at less stressful times, he actually enjoyed moving through the squiggly array of wiring, paneling, coils, and blinking lights. However, at times like these he wondered if maybe there shouldn't be some sort of power glide system to get you where you wanted to go quickly when you had to get there.

Hmm . . . He'd have to work on that.

Geordi La Forge crawled quickly.

He was still young and athletic, and he knew every inch of the Jeffries Tubes, so it didn't take him long to get where he was going. The silicate clay creature certainly wasn't going to wait patiently for him to get his work done, and it wasn't just the *Enterprise* at stake now . . . it was his life. But more important, the lives of Captain Picard and Commander Riker and Data.

His friends.

There was also a feeling of anger and outrage that spurred him on toward added effort. That thing was fooling with his ship . . . his engines. . . . It was like a kind of rape.

Starfleet was a good place to serve. They taught you the importance of ideals and duties, and they gave you a wonderful awe and reverence for the mysteries, the sanctities of life.

But when this kind of thing happened, some deep instinct surged up in Geordi, and he could tell his crew mates were exactly the same. They all had the instinct for survival. Emotions and instincts. Some people said that mankind was evolving beyond them, but Geordi La Forge had his doubts. They were the glue that bound. Now, he supposed that the emotional array in man could be fine-tuned and most certainly perfected. But any future society that didn't have emotions was one that Geordi La Forge wasn't particularly interested in belonging to.

The thought spurred him on to further effort, and the result was that he made the crawl to Section Nine Gamma B in record time.

Just as he pulled out his elaborate equivalent of a screwdriver to pry open a casing, however, the lights dimmed.

"Damn!" he said.

They went out.

As the lights in Engineering flickered, Picard looked over to Data. The android was still working at incredible speed; the somewhat strobed effect caught him at improbable changes of position.

However, when the lights went out, the captain saw him not at all.

"That field certainly didn't last long," said Riker. "All I can say is, I hope that that didn't kill the auxiliary."

Abruptly the lights flickered back into a lower grade of normality and alleviated at least that dilemma. Data slammed one last isolinear chip in place and turned to his commander. "I have completed the necessary rearrangement to support a change of electromagnetic polarity."

"Excellent," said Picard. "Commander La Forge. Data is finished. That just leaves it up to you."

"Yes, sir. Thought I was going to have to get my flashlight out. I'm working, though, and it's coming along."

"How long?"

"Five minutes."

There was a screeching and bending of metal and the motors of the doorway squealed with protest as the thing on the other side began to put its full pressure on the entryway.

"Geordi, I'm afraid you're going to have to perform a little faster than that," said Picard.

He pulled up his phaser and aimed it at the doorway.

Chapter Twenty-six

PENELOPE WINTHROP stared at the thing that had once been Mikal Tillstrom in horror. She wanted to move. In fact, she thought immediately, I must run away from here. I must go and get Dr. Crusher.

However, she felt as though she'd been rooted to the spot by some powerful galvanic force that was beaming from those dark, empty eyes directly into her soul.

"You will remove these restraints," said the creature controlling Mikal Tillstrom.

"Who . . . who are you?"

It was a stupid question, but it came out anyway, unbidden. She knew very well who it must be talking to her. And yet she'd never spoken to an alien before, and so the first thing that came into her head rushed out of her mouth.

"You will release me. Immediately."

Curiosity mixed with fear. She wanted to talk to the creature, and she also wanted to run.

However, ultimately fear mixed with prudence won out. "No," she said. She rose to go.

Mikal lunged at her, straining against the restraint field. The veins in his forehead bulged with the effort, and a rictus of determination twisted his face.

It took every bit of her willpower not to allow panic to overtake her. She forced herself to move, and move as quickly as possible. She found her legs taking her out of the room.

"Return!" cried out the creature through Mikal. "Return!"

She put her hands against her ears and somehow managed to put on speed. Soon either she was out of earshot, or the demands ceased.

She found her way to the office Dr. Crusher was using, passing others in the halls with confused and concerned faces.

"Dr. Crusher!" she said breathlessly.

The office was empty.

She checked the other biobed area and found Dr. Crusher standing over Dr. Adrienne Tillstrom, attending to her.

"Penelope? Is something wrong?"

Dr. Tillstrom was awake as well, and she turned a concerned expression toward Penelope.

"It's Mikal! He's . . . he's . . . I guess the word is 'possessed.' Again. He tried to get me to untie him."

"Good," said Beverly Crusher. "I want to talk to this thing!"

"I'll go, too," said Dr. Tillstrom.

"I'm not so sure that's wise," said Dr. Crusher.

"He's my son . . . and it's that damned thing I had put in his head that's caused this problem to begin with. I feel a responsibility."

"I should go back, too," said Penelope.

Beverly looked a little reluctant to allow that but finally agreed. "All right. There's no time to argue anyway."

Together they hurried back to Mikal's room.

It was shrouded in silence.

As soon as Penelope stepped inside, she could tell there was something wrong. Very, very wrong.

"Mikal?" said his mother. "Mikal, are you okay?"

The young man lay back in his bed. His eyes were open, but they stared straight ahead, glazed, at something less than nothingness.

Something deep registered in Penelope, resonating with that look.

It held a dead blankness that she had seen before in early pictures of herself.

Mikal Tillstrom had withdrawn into an autistic trance.

And there was something so incredibly deep about it, Penelope wondered if he would ever be able to successfully emerge from that distant, distant land to which he had departed.

Picard watched as the clay-stuff squeezed through the crack in the door little by little, and then started to pull the leaves, slowly but surely, causing the operating mechanisms to squeal with protest.

Riker and Worf aimed their phasers.

"No, Number One," said Picard. "Wait until it presents itself more fully."

Riker nodded.

The door shuddered all the way open.

What stood before them now was the glittery clay, filled with currents and shudders and ripples, looking like nothing so much as some bizarre computer animation.

It began to slowly creep in.

"Now!" cried Picard.

Twin beams of energy shot out, smashing into the huge moving lump of intelligent silicate clay. The phaser fire ripped whole clumps and divots out of the beast, and for a while it started retreating out the door.

Then it simply stopped and hovered, as though in some sort of holding position.

"Belay your fire."

The phaser energy stopped.

The clay remained where it was.

"It seems to be working. . . . Mr. Data. What is the status of the *Enterprise*'s position?"

"Sir, we are very close to the approximate position in which the photon torpedoes can be fired," answered the android.

"Let's just hope Chief O'Brien has been talking to the higher-ups," said Riker.

Picard hit his comm insignia. "Geordi. What's the status? We're feeling the heat down here."

"Another four minutes. There's some wiring here I forgot about."

"Great!" said Riker.

"Might I be of assistance?" Data asked.

"Sure, Data. If you're finished," Geordi responded.

"I am finished."

"Good. You know which section I'm in. Come on up; I've got the tools."

Data looked over to Picard.

It was the kind of decision that Picard dreaded, but also the kind that he was absolutely the best at. On one hand, if Data stayed here, they'd have a better shot at getting that panel pushed. Data had successful dealings with the creature before, and his strength could possibly be of use. On the other hand, by helping Geordi in the Jeffries Tube, he could cut the time it took to do the rewiring in half.

Picard weighed the odds, and decided.

"Make it quick, Data. And return the moment you're done. You could be of use here."

"Yes, sir," Data said, and sped toward the entrance to the Jeffries Tubes.

"I hope that thing didn't like that phaser fire one bit and decides to stay *out!*" said Riker.

"From what Data tells me of its intelligence and from previous experience, I do not find that a likelihood," said Picard. "However, its response to the last round was, I must say, gratifying."

He checked the power grid on his phaser. Still a hefty power level—and they had stuck a couple of spares in their pockets, just in case.

"Just in case," however, was getting to be more and more of a likelihood.

"I trust you were listening to Geordi's instructions concerning which PADD to press to implement the change of polarity," said Picard. "In case something happens to me, you'll be the one that's going to have to hit it."

"Oh yes. One way or another, that thing's going to be pressed, I promise you, sir."

Picard nodded.

A moment of silence passed between them and they looked at each other. Picard felt a strong surge of comradeship and more with his young second-in-command. He could feel that Riker felt it, too, and was not at all embarrassed to acknowledge it as well.

"I don't think I could have a better partner in a last stand, sir," said Riker.

Picard only nodded.

He hit his comm insignia. "Geordi. I trust that Mr. Data has arrived."

"That's right, sir, and he's already diving in. We're doing well, sir. . . . I think, in fact, that—"

There was a breakup in the message, and then it stopped.

"Geordi!" cried the captain, hitting the insignia again. "Lieutenant Commander! Answer me."

There was no response.

"Captain. I think we've got another onslaught coming." Worf raised his phaser and pointed it toward the door.

Picard spun, training his own phaser in that direction.

What had merely been a formless mass of sparkling clay clogging the bottom of the doorway, chunks and shards removed in the battle to make it resemble some cross section of a moon's surface, was now changing. A polyplike growth was flowering up into existence, first a bump and then flowing out like some metastasizing cancer. It grew limbs and a head.

The humanoid thing grew a mouth.

This, however, was as far as it got toward looking even vaguely human.

Where it should have had eyes, the silicate glittered hard and bright in the light.

It started flowing toward them.

"Halt!" said Picard. "I know you understand."

"That's right," said Riker. "We were firing on 'low' phaser setting last time."

"That is a falsehood, human," said the thing, its voice sounding more like something from an old-fashioned computer than anything human. "Do not attempt prevarication. I have access to your ship's computer."

Time to put on the diplomatic togs, thought Picard. "Have you a name?"

"There is no need of those distinctions in my kind."

"I see. If you have access to our computer, then you know that we are not a warlike race and have great respect for all living beings."

"Why do you attempt to destroy me then?"

"Self-defense. Preservation of our ship and of our base and fleet. You did not seem to be open for negotiation before—indeed, we did not realize that you were intelligent. Retreat into as small an area as will support your neural network, and we will be able to talk. But first open up our communications so that we can speak with the ships towing us out, about to destroy us."

"You have so little understanding. Do you not see? Momentarily I shall be in control of all the systems of this ship. I will break free. And then I shall use this vessel to spread my kind upon the face of space. I shall travel and attach to food and life, and thereby good life shall grow again unto the ends of the universe!"

"Sounds absolutely charming," said Riker.

"Already seeds have been spread . . . thanks to the one of your number whom I control."

"He's referring to Mikal's brief shutting down of the quarantine bubble," said Picard. "The creature must have released bits of itself."

"Indeed."

"Why are you bothering to talk to us now?"

"I am storing data. I am learning. All that I have learned will be filed away into the composite, which will again be re-formed after the destruction of this ship. A conversation with you is a lesson for me. However, I sense that something is under way that I should deal with. Indeed, two of your number are elsewhere."

"You will not even parlay. Perhaps we can offer you something?" Stall! thought Picard. There can't be much time left before Geordi and Data finish their work.

"You can offer me nothing," said the thing. "Save for your lives!"

The human-shaped thing, like the crest of a wave, began to flow their way.

"Fire!" yelled Picard, and again he lifted his phaser and let loose a blast of energy. Worf and Riker's rays joined his and played over the thing.

It halted only a second—

And then it trundled onward toward them.

Data's hands darted one last time into the depths of the circuitry, doing one more amazing display of speedy work. He pulled them out, and La Forge examined the finished work. He reversed one more isolinear chip and grunted.

"That's it. We've got the system ready to go! Let's see if communications is back up yet." He hit his insignia. "This is La Forge to Picard. La Forge to Picard . . . Captain—can you hear me?"

Nothing.

"Damn! Let's hope he gives it a try, and *soon.*"

"I suggest I quickly return and communicate the message," suggested Data.

"Excellent idea, Data. Do it."

Data turned around in the Jeffries Tube and was about to head back when a panel in the ceiling exploded . . .

And a tentacle of clay slipped through, barring his way back.

"Mikal! Mikal, can you hear me!" cried Dr. Tillstrom. She turned to Dr. Crusher and Penelope. "It's like he's not there. As though he were less than a zombie!"

Penelope felt cold shiver through her. She knew that look, all right, and could almost feel the emptiness in Mikal Tillstrom.

"He's just withdrawn," said Dr. Crusher, quickly examining the readings. "There's simply no way I can see of bringing him out of it."

"A kind of autism," said Penelope, in a flat tone. "I was autistic as a child, Doctor. Let me try to speak to him."

She sat down beside him.

She knew what she was going to try.

What was it that Deanna Troi had said to her once? Ah, yes. It had seemed odd then, but now it was making more and more sense to her.

"Could it be possible, I wonder, if autism—at least some cases of it—might not be a child's reaction to too much stimuli because of extra talents? I speak, of course, of telepathy and empathy, abilities of the mind that Betazoids enjoy fully, of which there are only glimmerings in human history. And yet, because there is no social fabric to support and nurture such talent, it would most likely be very frightening to a human child, causing it to retreat. I counseled a young Betazoid once named Tam Elbrun. Tam went on to a wonderful destiny, but he had a tortured life because he was so sensitive to thoughts and emotions of others that he was unable to shut them out. Perhaps some instances of autism could have been explained this way. I sense something of psychic abilities in you, Penelope. We are going to have to explore that possibility."

Yes. She knew what it was to withdraw, and maybe one of the reasons that she'd been so attracted to Mikal Tillstrom was that she'd resonated on some basic similar wavelength as he.

Perhaps she could reach out . . .

Reach out and touch him and bring him out of it.

Tentatively she reached out and placed her hands on his forehead.

"What are you doing?" his mother wanted to know.

"I think . . . I think this might help."

Dr. Tillstrom looked a little dismayed, but Dr. Crusher put a reassuring hand on her shoulder. "Let her try. It certainly won't do any harm."

Mikal's temples were cold against her palms. She closed her eyes and tried to reach out with that something inside of her that had nothing to do with sight, smell, taste, hearing, or touch. For a moment she felt dizzy, but there was a buzz of something ahead of her, an ineffable *quality* that kept her aligned.

Onward, onward she stroked, as though swimming in some depthless pool of liquid mind. It was dark, and the waters felt frigid and tumultuous, but she moved forward toward a distant pinprick of light and warmth.

There it was, a kind of numinous glow of soul in the land of mind she had only felt intimations of before.

She reached out for it, reached out with all her heart, for the effort was the greatest risk that a closeted soul could imagine. . . .

She reached out . . .

. . . and touched it.

Mikal? she said. *Mikal, can you feel me?*

At first there was no answer, but then a soft, timid mind-answer was returned:

Penelope?

Chapter Twenty-seven

HE TRIED TO CRAWL AWAY, but the stuff had dropped onto his boots and he seemed to be sinking in it, like vertical quicksand.

"Get *off* of me, you son of a bitch!" Geordi yelled, pulling with all his might.

Finally he pulled loose.

"This way," said Data. "We must use the other exit."

They started to crawl off, and the mobile clay muck followed with disquieting speed.

"Damn!" said Geordi. He caught himself from saying anything. Who knew what kind of hearing capabilities the thing possessed? What he was *thinking*, though, was immensely upsetting.

If that thing knew where to pull and press, it would ruin everything.

By his calculation, Captain Picard was going to be hitting that control PADD at any moment. But if that clay monster gummed up the works here, they wouldn't have a snowball's chance in a neutron star anyway.

"No. Data! Stop here. Fight it, Data! *Fight it!*"

Geordi pulled out a heavy spanner from his belt and began to pummel the roiling, glittering stuff.

The thing reacted immediately. A pseudopod formed, lashed out like lightning, and curled around his right arm. He grabbed the spanner with his left hand and hacked off the extension of clay.

The stuff rolled his way, and more of it poured out from the broken panel in the ceiling.

Voluminously.

The creature struck Commander Riker first.

Both of their beams were going full blast, but this time for some reason the silicate clay creature was not as affected. Picard watched helplessly as a large lump rolled aggressively up toward Riker and Worf like a breaker toward a beach. Picard kept his phaser beam trained on the stuff as long as he dared. For fear of blasting Riker, he pulled it away.

"Number One! Worf! Get back!"

"Hit the PADD, Captain!" said Riker, defiantly standing his ground under the onslaught. *"Hit the PADD!"*

At even quicker speed, a length of clay, sparkling in the phaser light, reared up and struck. Riker was slapped back against the bulkhead, face-first. Phaser out, head bleeding, he slumped into unconsciousness.

Worf growled a howl of defiance, stepping forward so that the creature would get the full power of his blast. Picard took three steps away from the PADD so that he could fire without striking Worf. His energy beam blasted into the creature in conjunction with the Klingon's, to little effect.

The thing simply thrust the Klingon aside, slamming him against the wall, knocking him out as well.

This was it, then, Picard realized. Either La Forge and Data had finished with the changeover or they hadn't.

Keeping the phaser beam directed on the closest part of the rolling stuff, Picard started walking quickly toward the control panel. It was only yards away. A hop, a skip, and half a jump.

However, before he could reach it, a flow of the clay broke loose and with a speed even greater than it had exhibited before, it flowed between Picard and his destination.

"No!" cried Picard.

He ran and he leaped over the stuff.

Another pseudopod slipped out of the stuff, ramming into the Captain at midjump, slapping the phaser out of his hand.

He fell right into the midst of the clay and he sank to his knees. However, he managed to stay vertical. The control panel was just two yards away. He lifted his foot from the gunk and started for it.

The stuff seized tight around his legs.

And then more of it began to flow over him, enveloping his knees, his thighs, his hips.

He reached, he reached, he strained so hard that he feared for his consciousness.

But he could not reach the PADD he had to push to save himself, his crew . . .

. . . and the *Enterprise.*

In the mind-murk, the spark increased.

Penelope blew on it, fanned it with her hope, and it began to burn hotter.

Mikal! Yes. It's me. Penelope.

I don't understand. Where are we? What's happening?

I'm contacting you with my mind, Mikal. You've withdrawn. You've undergone a terrible trauma . . . a degradation . . . but you're going to be okay. I promise!

Yes. That creature . . . controlling me . . . I remember now. Horrible.

The spark shuddered and tried to withdraw again. But Penelope held fast and would not let it.

No, Mikal. I promise you, you will be all right. It will hurt, but you must feel the pain to get to the other side.

No. No, it's too much. I can't bear it!

There was only one thing that she could do. She had to make him understand that recovery was possible.

Look, Mikal. Experience. This was what it was like for me.

She opened herself to him and let him see.

All the memories flowed to him. The pain and the scars, the successes and the failures, the joy and the fear. It all flickered between them like fireflies, and he *felt* it—she could tell he felt it and he was not only liberated from his retreat by her disclosures, he was astonished at the breadth and depth of the love and caring and concern it revealed.

I . . . I understand. . . .

It will not be easy, she said. *Only time heals properly. But I'll help. I promise. Just don't go away, Mikal. Believe me, it solves nothing.*

Yes. Yes, Penelope. I understand.

Do not hurry it. Do not traumatize yourself too much further—but you must endure the pain of returning. You must risk it as I risked it. Or you will be lost forever.

Thank you. Thank you so much. It is so . . . caring of you to do this for me.

All I ask for, Mikal . . . is another dance. A fast dance this time. Please show me how to dance with heart and soul.

A tinkling of mental laughter.

Yes. Yes, of course.

She was about to leave him. This connection took great energy, and she could almost feel the reserves of her distant body trembling with depletion. But just then, in the quiet of their silent contemplation of each other's interior beings, Penelope sensed something . . . something more than Mikal . . . and yet connected to him somehow.

It wasn't dark or evil, but there was a bulkiness, a dense singularity of purpose, to the thing that could have been interpreted as such. It felt malignant.

The creature on the *Enterprise.*

Mikal. That thing . . . that thing that made you do the things you did . . . it's still in contact with you.

Yes. Yes, I feel it, too, now. But it's preoccupied. It's not controlling me or trying to control me.

And yet . . . I feel almost as though I could reach out . . . touch it.

Not a good idea. Its mind is powerful. I'm really looking forward to getting this thing in my brain ripped out. Now, hurry . . . I want to wake up.

She thought for a moment. *Mikal. There must be a reason it left you. Perhaps it is fighting Captain Picard and the others!*

Perhaps.

Mikal . . . I almost feel that I can touch it, as I touched you.

Stay away from it! No!

*Mikal, if we can make it *feel* the pain and horror it wants to cause, maybe it will stop.*

Mikal was silent. *Yes. Yes, I don't know if it will work, but we can try. I must attempt to undo some of the damage that this body of mine has done. It is only right. But, Penelope—how . . . ?*

She wasn't really sure, but she was confident that it

was something instinctive in her, something that would point its own way as they proceeded.

*Just *be* with me. Concentrate . . . I'll lead the way.*

She felt her strength renew as he flowed into her.

With a shiver of purpose and energy, she reached out again toward the malignant being.

It was a cold thing, cold and vicious and purposeful.

It had but one goal.

She sensed immediately, as she speared them into its moiling morass, that it would not understand emotional pain, for it had no emotions. It only understood force and power.

Maybe, though . . . maybe if she could *communicate,* make it understand . . .

She reached out tentatively into this universe for the thing that she felt there, afraid but determined.

She felt a blow of mind-force, pure energy.

Without realizing what was happening, she could feel the energy of her own mind defending herself . . . and striking back with a force she could not comprehend.

It would all be over soon.

The being sensed the thing of flesh and blood in its grip. It's weapon had been nullified. It was helpless now.

Now the being could crush this foul example of bad life, and feel its plasm squish and spurt like a bag of exploded water.

But just then, something invaded its mind.

A Strange force . . . The being directed its energies against it, to shoo it away. . . .

But like a hot spike of lava, the force dove deep into its center.

In anguish, the being wailed . . .

And, for the moment, forgot all about the carbon-life

261

*protoplasm sack called Captain Jean-Luc Picard it held
in its power.*

Picard could feel the pressure of the clay relax. It
was still there, but there was some play in it now.

Still, the level of the stuff was all the way to the
bottom of his chest, and he could barely move.

Only two feet away was the control board.

If he could just somehow wade through this
thing . . .

That, or pull himself out.

He pushed his hands down in the clay. He could feel
himself coming up just a little, but he had to use
almost all his energy just to work his way out a few
inches.

He collapsed, gasping, his vision blurring.

*He had to get out of here. He had to hit that
PADD. . . .*

It seemed humanly impossible. And yet he knew he
had to try. He thought of his crew and he thought of
his ship. The *Enterprise.* There had been other *Enter-
prises,* and there would be more in the future. But not
this one, not the one that was his and a part of him.

Jean-Luc Picard knew that it was the fate of all life
to eventually succumb to entropy. Dust to dust, ashes
to ashes . . . Even the great and mighty starships
succumbed to that great, inevitable force of nature.

One day he would be a series of punctuated sen-
tences in history books. One day the *Enterprise* would
be gone, and those who served in it together, on their
noble journey through the stars.

One day they would all be dust and dreams in the
snarling jaws of entropy.

"But . . . not . . . now . . . dammit!" Gasping and
groaning with the effort, Picard pushed up with every
bit of his strength.

"Not . . . now!"

Just when he thought he could push no longer, something seemed to give in the clay. Encouraged, he pushed harder yet, scrabbling out on top of the stuff.

Not waiting a single moment to regain his breath, Picard clambered over the top of the clay, and then leaped with all his might.

His hand slapped down on the control PADD.

The result was instantaneous. Lights whirled and skittered.

"Good, Geordi," he said. "Good."

He turned around and faced the solid mass of silicate clay.

"Now get off my ship!"

And then the universe went into free-fall.

When the zero gravity state hit, Data was effectively holding off the wave of silicate clay, and keeping Geordi's head from immersing.

The lack of gravity made it all a little easier.

Geordi had gone unconscious. Data obtained purchase on the side of the Jeffries Tube and was easily able to slip the lieutenant commander from the alien's grasp.

Quickly, with the help of his feet, Data pulled Geordi a few meters away from where the clay was now floating helplessly.

Then, suddenly, the gravity was back, and they bumped back onto the floor.

Data paused and lifted his sensors up and out of himself.

It was hardly necessary. He could almost perceive it buzzing in the air:

The plan had worked.

Captain Jean-Luc Picard did not even wait for the ship's interior gravity to return.

"Computer. Open all radio channels."

"This is Captain Jean-Luc Picard of the Starship *Enterprise!* Cancel destruction. I repeat, cancel destruction. I and my crew are aboard."

The clay was floating as well, wriggling like a mass of eels in agony. He had to drag himself away from it lest it suck him up again.

A voice came over the radio saying the most beautiful words that Jean-Luc Picard had heard in his life. "Acknowledged, Captain Picard. This is the *Albedo*. We will delay destruction until further communication is accomplished with starbase."

"Splendid. I'm sure we'll have a marvelous conversation."

It was then that the gravity returned.

There was a great squelching thud as the stuff dropped onto the floor, Picard falling along with it but managing to avoid falling in it.

He looked toward where the greatest mass of the stuff lay.

It *writhed.*

It writhed and churned and tossed about like a bowl of amoebas attached to electrodes.

And then it simply stopped. The roils and hills subsided into a soft, oozing, still clay and became still and silent as a tomb.

Even the silicate specks in the clay seemed less alive in any sense of the word.

Picard could feel no particular difference in the air or sense any change, but clearly the change in the power system had generated a sufficient field.

The thing had been stopped.

The *Enterprise* had been saved.

He went over to where Riker and Worf had fallen. Both were unconscious and bleeding, but seemed to be breathing normally.

Picard nodded. He stood up and he hit his comm button.

"Lieutenant Commander La Forge. Mr. Data. Are you all right?"

The first reply was a prolonged "Unnnh . . . Yes, sir."

Then Data's voice took up the slack. "Yes, Captain. Commander La Forge has only just recovered consciousness, but is still in good health, I believe. Of course, a checkup by Dr. Crusher is advised."

Picard grinned. "I'm sure she'd be only to happy to oblige. But perhaps Commander Riker and Lieutenant Worf should go first."

"They are well, I hope."

"A little worse for wear, but I think they'll be fine. . . ." He looked down at the mass of clay. "It worked, Data and Geordi. The plan worked. Thank you for helping to save our ship."

"I suspect there will be a great deal more work to do, sir . . . but at least we have rendered the creature into its dormant form."

"Work. That's something, I think, we can deal with."

The computer voice spoke. "Communication from starbase."

The announcement segued immediately into the stern voice of Admiral Davies.

"Captain Picard. What is the meaning of this outrage? You directly disobeyed my orders."

"Yes, sir. And I am happy to take whatever consequences that may mean." He sighed. "However, sir, the *Enterprise* has been saved . . . and we've developed a system whereby the starbase and other ships can be protected from the bits of this stuff that are doubtless drifting nearby now."

There was a moment of silence.

"I see," said the admiral. "We shall have to talk."

"Yes," said Picard. "There will be plenty of time for that, Admiral. In the meantime, I respectfully request that you order your ships to tow us back into dock. There is considerable work to be done on this ship, and I cannot think of a more suitable stardock on which to accomplish it."

"I shall, Captain. And, Captain?"

"Yes, sir."

"Damn your eyes, but a fine job!"

"Thank you, sir, but I was only part of a team." He went over to see to a stirring Commander Riker and a grunting, semiconscious Worf.

"Jean-Luc!"

"Adrienne."

"I'm so glad it's over. And I'm so sorry—"

"Adrienne, don't trouble yourself."

"If only we scientists at the station had been able to defeat the thing . . . all this would never have happened."

" 'If' is a word that I never ponder in the past tense, Adrienne."

"I have. Believe me, Jean-Luc, I have . . . whenever I think about you."

"We made our choices. We've stuck by them. Nonetheless . . . it really is good to see you again, after all this time, Doctor."

"I feel the same, Captain."

"You know, Adrienne . . . the *Enterprise* is going to be in dry dock for at least two weeks. And I'm told that, while you've recovered, Dr. Crusher has recommended that you stay on the starbase for observation for not less than a month."

"Yes . . . that's right, Jean-Luc. . . . Are you leading up to something . . . ?"

"Yes, as a matter of fact, I am. I have never ceased studying, Doctor. And I have never ceased having the damnedest time with higher mathematics. . . . I was just wondering if you'd like to put on your tutor cap and spend a few more sessions with your most grateful student again."

"Only if you show me your marvelous ship, and tell me of some of your star-wanderings, oh, Jean-Luc Picaresque!"

Picard laughed at that. He reached over and took her hand. It was warm and smooth, and the smell of her nearby was surprisingly warm and familiar.

"You have a deal."

Epilogue

THE SUN SHONE and there was the smell of seaside in the air. Laughter drifted in the breeze, and the slap of rubber against hands sounded against the eternal *shoosh*ing of waves.

When you were sitting around, waiting for your ship to be repaired, mused Penelope Winthrop, there were worse things to do than to play volleyball on a holodeck re-creation so real-seeming that it really didn't matter that it wasn't.

Not that she was playing, actually. Oh, she and Mikal had tossed the ball around a bit when it had been a free-for-all, but now that it was an actual game, she didn't really want to hinder a team. She wasn't very good. Nonsense, they'd said, it's not for blood, it's for fun. Still, she'd declined. She wanted to keep at least a *few* neuroses! Mikal was playing, though, and he was doing a fabulous job of it, sporting about and knocking that white globe with hands and palms and knuckles as though he'd been born to play this. He had all his memory back now, and had recovered fully in miraculous time. He gave all the credit to Penelope, but actually it was he himself who had done the work. Or perhaps it was the liberation, knowing that he had undone somewhat the harm that he had participated in. Yet there was more than that, too, and Penelope felt a tingle at the thought: It was because of the closeness that had developed between them. They were actually nurturing each other now, and growing every day.

"Too bad about the competition," said Commander Riker, grinning as he stepped up to the line to serve the ball. "But I'll take out my hunger for conquest right now!"

"Unlikely!" called out a scowling Worf on the other side. "My honor requires vengeance!"

She watched as the ball bounced back and forth, watched and marveled at this wonderful group of people, patiently waiting for their starship to be repaired.

In fact, Data and Geordi were not even here. They were off, working almost round the clock on the project. Everyone was putting in their share of work —what they could do, anyway—but it was generally agreed that some recreation was needed. And as volleyball on the holodeck was all the rage now, why not add a pleasant, sunny beach?

After all, some sort of celebration was called for.

As for her . . . well, she knew that experience had changed her. How exactly, she wasn't sure. Only time would truly be able to tell that. But she knew now that she had a better appreciation of the crew of the ship she lived in. Certainly her parents said now that they did as well. And of course, she had this closeness with Mikal . . . though who knew which way that would go?

She would enjoy it while she had it, enjoy the intimacy and the friendship and allow it to go where it liked, *grow* where it liked. Counselor Troi was certainly pleased. "You're out of your shell now, Penelope," she said. "And it's highly unlikely that once you've seen what's out here, you're going to want to go back in for long."

Penelope could not help but agree with her.

Worf let out a victory cry as his team took the point.

As the players realigned their positions for another onslaught, they suddenly stopped and stared past Penelope.

She turned around to see who they were looking at.

Standing there behind her were Dr. Adrienne Tillstrom and Jean-Luc Picard, both wearing quite flattering beachwear.

As Jean-Luc Picard looked out on the holodeck volleyball activity, he allowed himself to feel good.

He turned to his companion. "Well, here you are, Adrienne. Just as I told you. The beachside volleyball game."

"I can see how it can be diverting, Jean-Luc. It was quite a good idea to come here."

She was remarkably unchanged from their early days together. Picard had found it very easy to be comfortable with Adrienne Tillstrom since she had recovered. He couldn't wait to show her his beloved *Enterprise,* when it was repaired. For now, though . . . they'd been enjoying the starbase.

Yes, he thought. The *Enterprise* . . .

The silicate clay creature had been reverted to its primal form, changed and contained in a special environment resembling that of Phaedra during its normal phase. Indeed, you couldn't even really say that the people of the *Enterprise* had had to destroy it.

Also, the bits of the stuff that had spread from the quarantine shield had been gathered and placed in the same container before they could do any damage.

The hull of the *Enterprise* and the portions of the ship the creature had assimilated had to be replaced, and it wasn't going to be easy. However, the labor was nothing compared to the price of losing a Galaxy-class starship, and so the Federation authorities were pleased at Captain Picard and his crew's accomplishment.

And Admiral Davies and Dr. Chavez?

They'd simply been satisfied with an informal reprimand, apparently quite relieved that their starbase had been spared of this trouble.

Mikal ran up to the new arrivals. "Mom! Captain Picard! You've decided to come down!"

"Yes, we've had our long talk," said Dr. Tillstrom, smiling up at the captain. "And I thought that perhaps a little sunshine might be just the medicine we need."

Captain Picard squared his shoulders. "We were wondering . . . we were wondering, Number One, if there might be places on the teams for us."

Commander Riker grinned. "We'd be glad to have you aboard, Captain."

The captain nodded. "I believe, Number One, that I've been there all along, haven't I?"

"Yes, sir. You have!"

"Well then, let's play!"

The two new arrivals moved out onto the court, the teams easily and good-naturedly assimilating them.

"Okay, Captain," said Will Riker. "Let's start. You serve!"

The ball was tossed to him, and Picard caught it. He moved to the position that Riker indicated, and quickly received his instructions.

"Let's play ball!" said Riker.

"Prepare for defeat . . . sir!" growled Worf from the other side of the net.

Captain Jean-Luc Picard hit the ball, serving it to the opposite team with grace and precision the very first try.

THE BREATHTAKING SEQUEL TO THE CLIFFHANGER THAT ENDED THE SHOW

#2 ALIEN NATION™

DARK HORIZON

THE NEW NOVEL BY K.W. JETER
BASED ON THE SCREENPLAYS 'GREEN EYES' AND
'DARK HORIZON' BY DIANE FROLOV AND ANDREW SCHNEIDER

On July 31, 1991 the final episode of ALIEN NATION™, "Green Eyes" aired, ending the series with a blockbuster finale and an exciting cliffhanger. In "Green Eyes" all of the ALIEN NATION characters were in crisis and George Francisco's family was infected with a deadly, new bacteria --facing nearly certain death. This story was never resolved...until now.

"Dark Horizon" was a two-hour ALIEN NATION script commissioned by Twentieth Century Fox. The story would have resolved the cliffhanger and kicked off ALIEN NATION's second season. With the final cancellation of the series, the script was put away and fans were left with their questions unanswered.

Pocket Books is now proud to present a novelization by critically acclaimed science fiction author K.W. Jeter of the entire action-packed story that began with "Green Eyes" and with "Dark Horizon."

Available in mid-July from Pocket Books

POCKET BOOKS

706

**THE THIRD EXCITING STAR TREK®
THE NEXT GENERATION™
HARDCOVER**

STAR TREK®
THE NEXT GENERATION™
THE DEVIL'S HEART

The Devil's Heart - a legendary object of unsurpassed power whose location has always remained a mystery. But a dying scientist's last words about the location of the Devil's Heart puts the *U.S.S.Enterprise*™ in the middle of a frenzied, galaxy-wide quest for the artifact.

Captain Jean-Luc Picard soon discovers the awful truth behind all the legends and the ages-old secrets: whoever holds the Devil's Heart possesses power beyond all imaging...

POCKET
BOOKS

AVAILABLE FROM POCKET BOOKS

707

ENTER A NEW GALAXY OF ADVENTURE WITH THESE EXCITING

STAR TREK® AND **STAR TREK® THE NEXT GENERATION™**

TRADE PAPERBACKS FROM POCKET BOOKS:

THE STAR TREK COMPENDIUM by Alan Asherman.
The one must-have reference book for all STAR TREK fans, this book includes rare photos, behind the scenes production information, and a show-by-show guide to the original television series.

THE STAR TREK INTERVIEW BOOK by Alan Asherman.
A fascinating collection of interviews with the creators and stars of the original STAR TREK and the STAR TREK films.

MR. SCOTT'S GUIDE TO THE ENTERPRISE by Shane Johnson. An exciting deck-by-deck look at the inside of the incredible U.S.S. *Enterprise*™, this book features dozens of blueprints, sketches and photographs.

THE WORLDS OF THE FEDERATION by Shane Johnson.
A detailed look at the alien worlds seen in the original STAR TREK television series, the STAR TREK films, and STAR TREK: THE NEXT GENERATION — with a full-color insert of STAR TREK's most exotic alien creatures!

STAR TREK: THE NEXT GENERATION TECHNICAL MANUAL by Rick Sternbach and Michael Okuda. The long-awaited book that provides a never before seen look inside the U.S.S. *Enterprise* 1701-D and examines the principles behind STAR TREK: THE NEXT GENERATION's awesome technology — from phasers to warp drive to the holodeck.

THE KLINGON DICTIONARY by Mark Okrand. Finally, a comprehensive sourcebook for Klingon language and syntax—includes a pronunciation guide, grammatical rules, and phrase translations. The only one of its kind!

All Available from Pocket Books

POCKET
B O O K S

555-01